MURDER
at the
PRIORY
HOTEL

Merryn Allingham

Published by Bookouture in 2022

An imprint of Storyfire Ltd.
Carmelite House
50 Victoria Embankment
London EC4Y 0DZ

www.bookouture.com

ISBN: 978-1-80314-513-6
eBook ISBN: 978-1-80314-512-9

1

ABBEYMEAD, SUSSEX, SEPTEMBER 1956

Flora Steele wheeled her much loved bike, Betty, from her wooden shelter and down the red brick path into Greenway Lane, pausing at the cottage's front gate to wipe her forehead, already damp from an unseasonably hot day. She was not looking forward to the sticky ride through Abbeymead or the even stickier afternoon that lay ahead. But Sally Jenner was relying on her friends to make today's reopening of the Priory Hotel a success. The girl had sunk every pound of her savings into its purchase and refurbishment. Once the home of local gentry, the Priory had been transformed the previous year into an elite hotel that had failed to survive. Would this new attempt be any more successful? Flora could only hope. The next few months would be nervous ones for Sally.

Turning out of Greenway Lane, she puffed her way into the village high street, wishing now that she hadn't refused the offer of a lift from Jack Carrington. He was a good friend, a very good friend, and a staunch partner in past investigations, but in keeping with her vow to remain independent, Flora had insisted she'd make her own way to the event. Jack was abandoning a day's crime writing, allowing his novel to languish on the type-

writer in order to help Sally in whatever way he could, and
Flora appreciated his thoughtfulness. Appreciated, too, that
he'd offered to collect young Charlie Teague from Swallow
Lane. The boy would be helping out, too, and the pair of them
must already be at the Priory.

Her route involved cycling the length of the high street and
she was surprised to see how many businesses had lowered their
blinds. It appeared that Abbeymead had decided to shut up
shop – literally – and enjoy the day's celebrations to the full.
Passing her own beloved bookshop, the All's Well, its brick and
flint walls resting quietly in the morning sun, she had to resist
the urge to wheel Betty into the cobbled yard at the rear and
make a final check on her bookshelves. That would be stupid.
The All's Well was fine. She had promised the day to Sally and
the door must remain closed.

On the opposite side of the road, Katie's Nook was clearly
open. Trade had been excellent at the café these past few
weeks, so much so that Kate Mitchell had been forced to hire
another pair of hands – the hapless Ivy – though no longer quite
as hapless as when she'd earned Alice Jenner's censure working
as a kitchen maid. Kate had evidently felt confident enough to
leave her in charge while she joined Sally's Aunt Alice and
Tony, their new sous-chef, at the Priory, in offering afternoon
tea to the whole of Abbeymead.

These last few weeks Alice had been busy with new
recipes, some of them sent by Jessie Bolitho, the same Jessie
who'd looked after Flora and Jack so brilliantly during their stay
in Cornwall. There'd been a tasting session in advance of
today's big event – ladies only, Alice had said, much to Jack's
chagrin. By the end of that evening, the ladies had agreed that
Abbeymead's number one cook had come up trumps. The
syrup and apple dumpling pies were judged mouth-watering
and the mint slices particularly delicious.

At the Priory's ornamented gates, open today in welcome,

Flora dismounted and wheeled Betty slowly up the gravel drive, feeling her neck gritty with heat. She was rounding the last bend in the driveway when Sally came flying towards her, flinging her arms wide.

'Flora, you're here!' she exclaimed. 'You're an angel to come early.' The troubled look in the girl's eyes suggested the day was not running smoothly. 'I'm afraid we're still at sixes and sevens, but I'm crossing my fingers everything will be apple pie by two o'clock. Auntie is doing a sterling job in the kitchen – small cakes already baked, fruit scones, too, and a mountain of individual trifles sitting in the fridge.'

Sally's normally spiky blonde curls lay flat against her head. 'If only it wasn't so hot,' she complained. 'Even the birds have stopped singing.'

'But think how good for business.' Flora shielded her eyes from a sun already high in the sky. 'Anyone who intended to work this Saturday will have waved the idea goodbye. Instead, they'll be making their way to the Priory. How much nicer to laze around to music and eat an amazing tea.'

'Talking of the amazing tea, I've just the job for you.'

Flora waited to hear her fate.

'It's the tables,' Sally said. 'Jack and Charlie have more or less finished in the marquee. They've been carrying in foldaway furniture for what seems like for ever, but the tables are bare and look quite ugly. They could do with some TLC.'

'You're lucky – tender loving care is my speciality. What do you want done exactly?'

'I've stacked tablecloths, cutlery and glasses on a side dresser, napkins, too – though they're paper – and there are flowers as well. The florists from Steyning, Beautiful Bunches, have been so good.' Sally paused for breath. 'I included their advertisement in the hotel brochure for free and, as a thank you, they've sent us a box full of dinky little posies. There should be sufficient for each table.'

'That sounds easy enough. Why don't you leave it to me and go back to the house? You must have plenty to sort out.'

'You *are* an angel. And you're right, I have a mountain of stuff to get through. I must scoot. Dominic is working in the cellar and I want to make sure he's bringing up the right beer.'

Dominic Lister was Sally's new business partner. The village jury was out as to his suitability, but no doubt the 'right' beer would enhance his reputation. With a frantic wave of her hand, Sally turned to run back to the house.

She hadn't had an easy life since losing her father in the war, Flora knew. Her mother had remarried a few years later and Sally had never seen eye to eye with her new stepfather, one of the reasons, Flora judged, that she'd taken a job with the Foreign Office and requested an overseas posting. She sympathised. If it hadn't been for her own dear Aunt Violet, she would have felt equally abandoned.

The beginnings of a heat haze shimmered above the warm stone of the Priory. Avoiding the pillared entrance, Flora walked around the side of the mansion, keeping to whatever shade its ancient walls could provide. A huge marquee had been erected in the grassy expanse at the back of the house, some distance from the building's rear door and the kitchen beyond. Leaving Betty safely parked, she walked towards the enormous canvas structure, calculating how many journeys, how many steps, would be necessary to ferry the food to and fro. It was going to be a tiring afternoon. The marquee itself looked substantial enough and, if the weather should turn, the sun disappear and a normal September resume – more than likely with a heat so oppressively sultry – people could at least find shelter.

Jack emerged from the entrance to the tent as she approached, trailing a smaller figure in his wake.

'I was beginning to wonder where you'd got to.' His face held the hint of a smile.

The familiar fedora had been left behind at Overlay House, a sensible move, but the open-necked shirt Jack wore was already creased from the heat. He wiped a bare forearm across his face, the flop of hair that never sat flat today hanging damply over his forehead. It was good to see him.

'It's only' – she looked at her watch – 'it's only just past ten,' she excused herself.

Jack tutted loudly. '*We* were early birds, weren't we, Charlie?'

The boy had come to stand beside him and was frowning hard. He looked hot and cross, his socks around his ankles and one leg of his shorts sporting a tear that his mother was sure to scold him for.

'We got all the rotten jobs,' he said glumly.

'Heavy jobs,' Jack amended. 'We've had to unpack dozens of trestles and folding chairs from a lorry that's parked round by the stables.'

'*And* carry them all the way here, *and* then fix them up,' Charlie said, still aggrieved.

'But think of the money you've earned.' Jack flicked a finger at the boy's cheek.

Charlie Teague was always eager for paid work, though what he was saving for, no one knew. He still did gardening jobs for Jack at Overlay House – mowing the lawn and trimming hedges – and for the last few months Flora had entrusted him with her Friday deliveries, riding Betty to customers unable to collect orders from the shop.

'And it's not just the money,' Flora added, trying to cheer him up. 'Think of the tea you'll be eating.'

'Yes, indeed. But breakfast comes before tea. For some of us, of course, a second breakfast.' Jack smiled down at the boy, taking him by the arm. 'I know for a fact that Mrs Jenner and Mrs Mitchell have a very large plate of goodies reserved especially for you.'

Charlie looked sceptical.

'Really,' Jack assured him. 'Let's leave Miss Steele to her labours and take a well-earned rest.'

Flora pulled a face. 'Say hello to Alice and Kate for me. And enjoy the goodies!'

Turning back towards the marquee, she was conscious of a solitary cloud emerging from nowhere and, for an instant, blotting the sun from view. Surely, the day's only cloud – today would be the happiest the Priory had known for years.

2

Two hours later, having worked without a break, Flora straightened her aching back and passed a weary hand across her forehead. She'd been forced to clean every table and chair before she could even start on the task Sally had set her and, with every passing minute, the temperature had increased markedly. By now the atmosphere in the marquee was stifling, the heady sweetness of pansies and yellow roses hanging heavy in the air.

'No slacking allowed!' a voice said in her ear. Jack had returned, carrying a column of china in his arms that looked dangerously unsteady. Charlie, similarly laden, was following him.

'I've just finished laying the final table, and I'm exhausted.' She looped unruly waves behind her ears. 'Tell me again, why did we agree to help?'

'You know why.' Jack began winding a path between the rows of tables, delivering white china plates to each, the stack in his arms gradually shrinking to manageable proportions. 'Sally is a friend and this is her big day.'

A very big day. Sally Jenner had shocked them on their

return from Cornwall a few months previously with the news that she had sunk her life savings into a new venture. Both Flora and Jack remained unsure of how wise a move it had been and Alice, too, was uncertain, but seeing Sally so happy – she'd found what she'd always wanted to do, the girl told them – they had tried hard to squash their mutual doubt. Except that Sally hadn't looked too happy, Flora recalled, when she'd met her on the driveway this morning. It was a stressful day, she reasoned – for all of them. They'd worked hard to make the event special and ensure that preparations for the grand opening were exactly as Sally wanted.

'I only hope all this effort pays off,' Flora said, helping Charlie to distribute the last of the plates. 'The event is costing huge amounts of money and that's on top of an expensive refurbishment. Alice says the bill for the food is sky high, not to mention the hire of the marquee and the music group Dominic has booked.'

Jack grinned. 'That's going to be fun. Watching the villagers' faces when Tutti Frutti strike up. Abbeymead's first encounter with rock 'n' roll, perhaps?'

She stood back and surveyed the collection of small tables, each with its starched white tablecloth, glassware, cutlery and plates, and a single dainty vase of flowers. Along one edge of the marquee, a line of long trestle tables covered in white linen stood ready for the food.

'I think we're done,' he said, following her gaze. 'Come outside and cool off. You'll feel a whole lot better.' He shepherded her towards the entrance, holding open the canvas flap.

A breeze had sprung up while Flora had been working in the marquee and she gulped down a deep breath of fresh air. 'You're right. It feels good. My clothes had actually begun to stick.'

The floral tea dress had been a last minute decision, a needlecord skirt abandoned in its favour, but even a cotton frock this light clung uncomfortably to her slender figure. Trying to forget her discomfort, she settled on the view instead. 'It's wonderful to see the Priory looking so good. At last, Jack!'

The grand old building stood ancient and solid, its walls of golden stone basking in the sun. The huge oak door at the rear of the building had been decorated with strings of various shaped balloons, while the leaded windows had been given a colourful new life with looped rows of fairy lights. Stretching into the distance, the rolling green of an immense lawn spoke of hours of labour.

She gave a sigh of pleasure. 'I don't believe I've seen the place look so special since Lord Edward died and that's nearly three years ago. They've even restored the knot garden, did you know?'

Jack look puzzled. 'Remind me, what is a knot garden?'

'I'll show you.' Tugging at his shirtsleeve, she led the way to a sheltered square a few yards distant. The small garden was a mathematical nicety, an intricate pattern of newly clipped box hedges, their lengths and angles measured to precision. In the centre of the square, a wide circular bed overflowed with early autumn flowers – asters, anemones, cyclamens – boasting a riot of colour.

'Isn't it fabulous?' Flora flung her arms wide, as though hoping to embrace the entire knot garden. 'And such a glorious day. Look at that sky – not a cloud in sight now. The village is going to love this afternoon.'

It had been a while since the residents of Abbeymead had been invited to wander the Templeton estate. When Lord Edward had been alive, they'd been free to walk where their feet took them but, since his death and the sale of the Priory, the grounds had been off limits to all but the guests of what had been a short-lived hotel. Now, there was a new Priory, rescued from the ashes of the old, and with a very different owner. Sally had made clear that everyone in the village was invited to today's opening ceremony and was welcome to walk in the grounds any time they wished.

Jack leaned back against the greenery, his changeful grey eyes holding amusement. 'I can see it's special but it doesn't stop me needing to get back to the kitchen.' He bounced himself off the hedge. 'Alice and Kate seem intent on feeding a regiment and I promised that once I'd delivered the china, I'd be back for some of the food.'

Flora angled her wrist to look at her watch. 'It's a bit early, isn't it? We're not eating until after the music and the band isn't due to play for an hour.'

As if on cue, a drum roll and a clash of cymbals announced Tutti Frutti's arrival on a stage that had been set up a few yards from the marquee.

Jack gave a grimace as the musicians began their tuning up. 'Time to go. Alice wanted the non-perishable stuff out as soon as possible, or there'll be too much to do at the last minute. And I think' – he peered around the hedge – 'that we may just have our first visitors. Aren't you down to meet and greet as well as set up tables?'

She gave a small grin. 'I think I must be. Woman of the day, that's me!'

'Of any day, Flora.'

He smiled down at her and she brushed quickly past, slipping out of the square and walking towards the visitors as they turned the last corner of the driveway. Jack Carrington could make her feel awkward. Mostly, they were easy friends, Flora working in her bookshop, Jack hunkered down at Overlay House tapping out his novels, and meeting each other two or three times a week. But every so often he would look at her and smile and she felt herself, even in her mid-twenties, reduced to the foolish young girl she'd once been.

Giving herself a silent scold, she marched purposefully

towards the family party that had just arrived, greeting them with a breezy hello.

'The music begins at two o'clock, after the speeches,' she told them and gestured to the semicircle of seats that had been placed around the stage. 'There'll be food and drink from around three, but if you fancied a walk in the grounds before you take your place, you're very welcome.'

They had only just wandered away when Alice herself came bustling across from the building. 'Where's that Jack?' she asked, her plump figure unusually tense. 'I need him to start carrying the food over.'

'It's OK, Alice. He's on his way back to the kitchen. You must have missed him. You look very hot – do you need a drink?'

'I've a cellar full of drink back there, my love, but no time to drink it, though I could down a river right now. Never known a September day like it, not for years.'

Flora was aware of movement on the stage behind her. The group's drummer had evidently decided his kit wasn't in the right place and was dragging first the bass drum, then the snare, across the wooden boards.

Alice jerked a head of wiry grey hair towards the three young men shuffling positions on the stage. 'They haven't stopped eatin' all day. You wouldn't believe such skinny men could eat so much. In the kitchen, round my feet, somethin' awful.'

'What about Beverly?' Beverly was the singer for Tutti Frutti. 'I haven't seen her today. Is she around?'

'I haven't seen her either. I dunno if she's had anythin' for lunch. It's those men – eatin' everythin' in sight. That Tommy, the one on the left, has had a sandwich in his hand all mornin'. I shouldn't think he'd have the strength to pick up his guitar. Why Sally couldn't have had some nice music – a folk band mebbe, or even strings. But that racket. I heard them practisin' in the stables, the apartment Dominic's let them have. Abbeymead's not ready for this rollin' stuff.'

'Rock 'n' roll.'

'Whatever it is.' She turned, hearing the soft pad of footsteps. 'Katie, love, let me help you with that.' Kate Mitchell swayed towards them, a three-foot wide tray of sandwiches and miniature pies masking her face. 'And be careful of them ropes.'

'I'll get these into the marquee.' Kate's voice was blurred by the giant tray. 'Jack is organising the waiters to bring the rest. There's at least ten trays.'

When Kate emerged from the tent, she was smiling. 'We're nearly there.' Her pale blue eyes held excitement. 'The jellies and ice creams are in the big refrigerator – you are so lucky to have that, Alice.'

Her forehead puckered. 'What should we do about the cakes? Tony thinks we should wait.'

Something in her voice had Flora look across at her friend. Puzzled, she saw Kate's cheeks had turned pink.

Alice nodded wisely. 'We'll let them get into the savouries before we bring the cakes. Jack can help carry 'em, and you, too, Flora?'

'Of course I will. Once everyone is seated, I'll be free. What's Dominic doing?'

'Gettin' in the way, mostly,' Alice said caustically. 'Never known such a man for fuss and bother. He's had the waiters runnin' up and down to the cellars all mornin'. How long does it take to load a stall with beer and lemonade, I ask you? It's Sally that's the calm one. But it's only what I'd expect. She's always been a capable girl.'

'She is, and she'll make this new venture work,' Flora said rousingly, her gaze on the drive for new arrivals. Even at this late hour, it was clear that Alice still had concerns for her niece's grand project.

'I do hope so,' Kate put in, trying to sound positive but not

quite managing to. 'So much money spent. And that Dominic...'
She broke off.

'What's wrong with Dominic?' Flora asked.

Kate looked down at her feet. 'I don't rightly know,' she
mumbled. 'It's just that... just that I don't feel comfortable with
him. He reminds me of Frank Foster. You remember Frank?'
Her audience nodded. Of course they remembered Frank. 'He
seems the same kind of hustling man,' Kate went on. 'Not
someone quiet and dependable – like Jack. Or Tony.'

'I don't know about Tony but Jack Carrington is definitely
not quiet,' Flora protested. 'He never stops scolding.'

The man in question hove into sight at that moment,
carrying yet another tray of sandwiches and sausage rolls, and
followed by a line of waiters similarly burdened. Drawing level
with the stage, Jack came to a halt. The twang of guitars, the
beat of drums, that had formed the background to their conversation, had come to a sudden end and another noise had taken
their place. A young woman with blazing red hair was shouting
angrily at the lead guitarist.

'Keep your nose out of my business,' the small figure was
yelling. 'You've no right to interfere. You're a nothing to me.' It
was Beverly Russo, the group's vocalist.

In response, Tommy May slammed down his guitar and
jumped from the stage, almost landing on his antagonist. 'Is that
what you think?' he sneered. 'That I'm a nothing? Are you sure?
Have you forgotten all those years?'

'Forgotten is exactly what I've done. We're over. You're
over. You don't own me.' Beverly might be small but, in her fury,
she seemed physically to grow, matching her former boyfriend
in strength.

Tommy thrust his face into hers. 'I don't want to own you.
No, thank you! But neither do I want to share the stage with an
out-and-out tart.'

'How dare you!'

Flora saw the woman's lips clenched tight and bloodless. Then her hand came up and smacked her opponent across the face. The thwack as palm met cheek resounded in the eerie silence that had descended.

May appeared unperturbed, grabbing Beverly by the shoulders and shaking her until Flora thought her teeth must loosen and fall out. 'That is exactly what you are,' he said deliberately. 'You couldn't keep your legs crossed when you were with me and now you're doing it to Dom.'

Alice's mouth formed a wide 'O' and Jack started forward as if to stop the dreadful quarrel going further.

The girl tore herself free from May's grasp. 'Double standards, Tommy,' she taunted her adversary. 'What's sauce for the gander is sauce for the goose – ever heard that?'

His fists bunched and it seemed for a moment that he would use them but Jack, having dumped his tray on the ground, had slipped between them, spreading his arms wide to keep them apart.

Beverly Russo, her face contorted with anger, turned her back on the group and stalked towards the rear door of the Priory.

It had been an ugly scene and a collective release of breath followed as the tension dissolved. Flora hadn't realised that Beverly had ever been Tommy May's girlfriend. Over the last few weeks, she'd got to know the girl a little, calling several times at the stables where the group were billeted, sharing the odd cup of tea with her. But in none of their conversations had Beverly mentioned much of her past life.

She was upset for the girl and wondered if she should go in search of her. It was only a few days ago that she'd collected a prescription for Beverly. Dr Randall had handed it to her personally – their long-serving Dr Hanson was on a year's sabbatical – and charged her to make sure Beverly knew it was strong medicine and to be certain she followed the instructions. It would help stabilise her heart rhythms, he'd said.

Tommy May remained still, watching his one-time girl-friend storm a path back to the Priory before he turned to Jack and patted him on the shoulder. 'Don't worry, squire,' he said. 'Beverly's a bitch. She doesn't like to hear the truth. If she wasn't a great singer, I'd have chucked her out of the band months ago.'

He walked away, striding towards the stage. 'C'mon, guys, let's get changed for the big performance.' The drummer and the second guitarist, who so far had said nothing, laid down their instruments and followed him.

'Beverly may not like the truth, but Tommy doesn't like it much either. Doesn't appreciate the competition,' a suave voice said at Flora's shoulder.

She turned quickly. The man who'd appeared behind her was small and slim and, though wearing a sharply tailored wool suit, showed no sign of discomfort despite the heat of the day. He smoothed a hand across hair that was already sleek.

'I'm sorry you had to witness such an unedifying scene, ladies,' he said languidly, his words addressed to Alice and Kate as well as Flora. 'Tommy May, I'm afraid, has always been a sore loser.'

3

'You know Tommy May?' Flora asked.

'I should do.' The man pulled his face into a smirk. 'I've been his agent for the last four years, Miss...'

'Steele.'

'Allow me to introduce myself, Miss Steele. My name is Max Martell.' He fished in the top pocket of his suit and brought out a business card, proffering it with a flourish. 'Agent to the biggest stars, though I say it myself.'

'And Tutti Frutti are big stars?'

She found it difficult to keep surprise from her voice. The reopening of the Priory Hotel might be big news for Abbeymead, but for the wider world it was inconsequential. She'd assumed that Tutti Frutti was little known, a band struggling for recognition.

'On the way to being big,' Martell answered smoothly, 'and destined to be even bigger once...' He trailed off. 'This afternoon is small fry. The band is simply doing a favour. I warned them against it – no kudos in performing in a small village – but musicians, you know, you can't tame 'em.'

Flora felt indignant at this dismissal of her village and what was a very special event for Abbeymead. The band should be glad to have the chance to play here. Max Martell was a little too glib for her liking. Jack, she saw, was glaring at him and both Alice and Kate had shrunk back as though not wishing to come too close.

'It's a beautiful venue,' she said, a challenge in her voice, 'and I'm sure the audience will be appreciative.'

The man sucked in his lips. 'Sure, but it's not the kind of audience the band needs. Not the kind they deserve. But Tommy has a mind of his own. "I owe Dominic," he said, "and I'm gonna repay him." Quite a repayment! They've been off the road for three weeks and not earning a cent.'

'So what's the favour they're repaying?'

If a mystery lay behind the band's appearance at the Priory, Flora wanted to know, but Max wasn't about to enlighten her. 'Really not my business, Miss Steele. You'll have to ask the lord and master. And here he comes.'

Dominic Lister was walking across the lawn towards them, Sally almost running to catch him up. Flora blinked. Were they leather trousers he was wearing? Surely not. The small beads of sweat trickling down his cheek suggested they were and, in this weather, extremely uncomfortable. He must think he's one of the band, was her first thought.

Slightly out of breath, Dominic roused himself to sound enthusiastic. 'Our visitors will be arriving soon. Are we ready to greet them?'

'You're a little late.' Flora pointed to the family she'd spoken to earlier. 'Some are here and have already taken their seats.'

For a moment he looked confused, then took in the small party in the front row. 'Good, good,' he muttered. 'And, by the look of it, there are more on their way.' Several groups of villagers had appeared around the side of the building, having crunched a path up the front driveway, a slow business in the overpowering heat.

'Sal' – he turned to his co-owner – 'has the newspaper wallah arrived yet, do you know? Important he's here for the speeches.'

'There'll be speeches?' Jack's tone was laconic.

'Short speeches,' Sally reassured him. 'And the man from the *Worthing Echo* is setting up his camera right now. Why don't you go and speak to him, Dom? I'll walk across and welcome our new guests.'

'Hello there,' she greeted the recent arrivals, smiling broadly and handing them a programme from the stack she was carrying. 'How good of you to come, and on such a hot day.'

Sally was naturally charming, Flora thought, and she had the looks to match. She was dressed today in a polka dot shirt-waister and, since Flora last saw her on the driveway, the spiky blonde curls had been brushed anew and shone in the sunlight. What she liked in Dominic, and she obviously liked something, was beyond Flora.

Over the next hour, the seats around the stage gradually filled and Jack, with one or two of the waiters, was forced to make several return trips to the Priory in search of more chairs. The village, it seemed, had turned out en masse. Curiosity over the Priory's refurbishment was paramount, but there was also a great deal of goodwill that this time the ancient seat of the Templetons might prosper. The estate had meant a great deal to the village over very many years and people had been sad to see its slow deterioration while a new owner had been sought.

Sally had been right about the speeches once proceedings had begun – they were mercifully short – the vicar, the Reverend Hopkirk, officially opening the ceremonies, followed by Dominic's effusive welcome. Guests were free to stroll around the hotel at their leisure, he told them, but he hoped that before they did, they would enjoy the wonderful spread awaiting them in the marquee. First, though, there was music!

He gestured to the empty stage, where two guitars had been left propped against the drums.

For most of the mainly middle-aged audience, there was attraction enough in Alice Jenner's food, followed by an exploration of the hotel, where notice could be taken of new carpets and curtains, of the size of the bedrooms, the fittings in the kitchen, the changes wrought since Lord Edward's time. Sitting through the music would be pure concession. Within the younger ranks of the audience, though, there had been bright eyes and a decided wriggling in their seats at the sight of a drum kit and guitars. For once they might get to hear the music they enjoyed.

'And here they are,' Dominic finished grandly. 'The amazing, the brilliant, Tutti Frutti!'

'It looks like all is well,' Flora murmured, as the three men appeared to one side of her and strode past the audience. Tommy May had been the one to form the band, she'd learned, and it was his prerogative to be first on stage.

'Until the next bust-up.' Jack pulled a face. 'Beware the artistic temperament!'

Tommy was dressed in a scarlet shirt slashed to the waist and the tightest trousers Flora had ever seen. There was an audible intake of breath as he leapt on to the stage, scooping up his guitar and aiming it towards the audience as though a threatening weapon.

'Not the best idea in those trousers,' Jack murmured.

Shane Carter, the rhythm guitarist, was similarly dressed, but with a collection of heavy silver jewellery filling the naked V of the shirt's neckline. It was Jarvis Redmond, the drummer, who presented an entirely different picture. He wore a pair of blue jeans and a check shirt, the sleeves rolled to the elbows. A black peaked cap sat squarely on his head, long blond streaks of hair falling down his face on either side.

'Is he the local lumberjack?' Her companion was laughing.

'Be quiet. He's the drummer, as you're well aware. They dress that way.'

'And you know because...'

Flora's response was lost in the amazed hubbub that rose from the audience. Beverly Russo had somehow materialised in the midst of the band and every eye was on her. If Tommy and his men had surprised the villagers, Beverly's appearance shocked them. She wore a scarlet dress, presumably in line with her male fellows, but glittering with sequins and so short they could almost see her knickers. It clung to every curve, plunging at the neckline to breasts that looked as though they might jump out and walk away at any moment. On her head, not that anyone was looking at her head, Flora reflected, was a bright pink jewelled headband that fought with the singer's deep red hair.

Jack gave a low whistle and Flora glared at him. He held up his hands in mock apology. 'You've got to give it to her. The girl knows how to make an entrance.'

Tommy struck a chord, Shane following him, and Jarvis caught the beat on his drums. Beverly sashayed across the stage, her hips gyrating, her breasts with a mind of their own. The sun caught a large jewel on her fourth finger – a ruby – sending sparks of scarlet skywards to match her dress. She grabbed the microphone, bringing it close to her lips, and opened her mouth.

But no sound emerged. Instead, her body appeared to judder, shaking from head to toe like a column that had lost its foundations, while all the time she desperately clutched hold of the microphone as though it would save her from collapse.

Jack was the first to realise what was happening and the first to react. He rushed towards the stage, yelling, 'Switch the mic off!'

Shane leapt up, flinging his guitar to one side and rushed to the side of the stage to disconnect the microphone. Jarvis and Tommy appeared utterly dazed but, as Beverly's trembling limbs finally crumpled, it was Tommy who caught her and lowered her to the ground. By this time, the audience were on their feet, mothers sheltering their children against their chests, daughters shepherding their elderly parents from the scene. Max Martell ran past them, jumping onto the stage and leaning over the singer, his fingers pressed to the side of her neck.

'I can't believe it,' Flora heard him say, though his voice was barely above a whisper. 'The girl is dead.'

4

'Fetch the doctor!' Martell's voice was stronger now. 'We need a doctor – urgently.'

'I'll have to go, Flora,' Jack muttered in her ear, and set off running towards the Priory, calling over his shoulder to anyone listening, 'I've a car parked at the front of the house.'

Flora watched him go in stupefied silence, then swivelled around, as though by fixing the scene in her mind, she could make sense of what had just happened. Dominic, she saw, had remained rooted to the spot, unable to move an inch, it seemed, but Sally, having cast a swift glance in his direction, had climbed the steps to the stage. She took care, Flora noticed, to walk as far away from the dead woman as possible.

'Ladies and gentlemen.' Sally's voice was shaking and barely audible. 'I am so very sorry for the distress this has caused. We are fetching a doctor and will do everything we can for Miss Russo. But please salvage something from your visit. There is food and drink in the marquee and my aunt and Mrs Mitchell are ready to serve you.'

She looked desperately towards Alice and Kate, standing

like statues in front of the stage, seemingly as mesmerised as Dominic.

Her niece's voice appeared to penetrate Alice's torpor and, clasping Kate by the hand, she shuffled them both towards the marquee. Thinking they might need extra help, Flora followed. Very few of the villagers, however, made an appearance at the tables she'd so carefully dressed, most of the audience choosing to return home, drifting down the driveway, their heads together in feverish discussion of the latest calamity to hit the Priory. *It don't seem right...* went the mutters. *One piece of bad luck after another... Ever since Lord Edward died...*

The small number who'd refused to let death get in the way of a good spread were soon served. Alice and Kate, still stunned by events, insisted they would stay to clear the tables and Flora, with little to do, emerged into the fresh air and set herself to wait for Jack's return. Max Martell, she saw, had remained on the stage along with the band, the four men forming a kind of ceremonial guard. An uneasy silence filled the vacuum left by the departing villagers.

Where *had* Jack got to? Flora wondered, as the minutes ticked by. Dr Randall shouldn't be this difficult to find.

'Where's that dratted doctor?' Alice asked trenchantly, echoing Flora's thoughts as she joined her outside the tent. 'And what on earth are we goin' to do with all this food? Kate's tryin' to encourage 'em to take some of it home' – she jerked her head back towards the marquee – 'but even so it won't be more than a gnat's bite.'

It seemed an age before Flora spotted Jack's rangy figure in the distance, appearing around the side of the Priory with Dr Randall at his side.

The doctor was soon on the stage and, bending over the dead woman, began his examination.

'I couldn't find him,' Jack said to her quietly. 'He wasn't at the surgery, nor at his house – he *is* renting Dr Hanson's place, isn't he?'

She nodded.

'I banged on the door for a good five minutes and I'd given up and was on my way back when I spotted him outside the Priory gates.'

'What was he doing there?'

Jack spread his hands. 'Who knows?'

'Well, thank goodness you saw him when you did.'

Flora's inner voice was not quite so quiescent. Not at the surgery, not at his house, so where had the doctor been? She had an uneasy suspicion she knew the answer. Several days ago, when she'd collected Beverly's prescription, she had witnessed something she shouldn't have seen. As she'd opened the waiting room door – empty at that time of day – the doctor, a married man with two small children – was quick to break away from what looked suspiciously like an embrace with his receptionist, an attractive young Scot called Maggie Unwin. It was more than likely that Randall had been involved in some kind of secret assignation today, or why had he been so far from his usual haunts?

'I'm afraid there's nothing I can do for her,' Flora heard the doctor say from the stage, 'but she's a young woman and her death is unexplained – you'll have to call the police.' Randall stood up, the sheen on his face glinting in a sun that was now directly overhead. Seemingly irresolute, he stood bag in hand, making no effort to leave. At length, he said, 'I imagine they'll need a pathologist's report.'

The words galvanised Tommy May who jumped down from the stage and strode towards Dominic. 'Can we take her up to one of the bedrooms?' He nodded towards the Priory. 'Until the police come. I don't want her left here.'

'Yes, yes.' Dominic appeared a broken man, his voice cracking, his face a mask of disbelief, as Tommy and Jarvis lifted

Beverly's lifeless body between them and carried her down from the stage.

'I'll go ahead. Open a room.' Dominic was making a monumental effort to kick himself into life. 'Then I'll telephone. The police... the undertaker... Sally.' He swung round, for the first time seeming to notice his business partner. 'Can you sit with her? I don't like to think of her on her own up there and it needs to be a woman.'

Sally shook her head. 'No, I can't. You'll have to find someone else.' It was a very definite refusal.

'I'll sit with her,' Flora offered. 'Just tell me where.'

It was several minutes before Dominic returned. 'They've put her in room 102,' he said, hardly able to get the words out. 'On the first floor – and thank you, Flora.'

Left alone in one of the hotel's premier suites, she gazed around. Sally had good taste, she thought, taking in the pale blue carpet and curtains, the light oak furniture, the Sussex watercolours hanging on cream-coloured walls. Then chided herself. A woman had just died, soft furnishings could wait. She jerked her attention back to Beverly. It must have been the poor girl's heart – there was evidently a medical problem or she would never have consulted Dr Randall. Perhaps she hadn't taken the medicine he'd prescribed for her. Perhaps the excitement of the moment had been too much.

But hadn't there been something wrong with the microphone, too? It had been when Beverly had begun to sing that tragedy had happened. Whatever the cause, it was heartbreaking – Beverly Russo was so very young. Flora gazed down at the pallid face. In death, the dead woman looked no more than a child, all creases and lines erased. She felt a sudden lump constrict her throat. She'd had nothing in common with Beverly but she hadn't disliked her. Thought her a little brash, maybe, a little too concerned with herself. But that was simply the girl being an artiste, Flora supposed.

She looked again at the soft smoothness of the girl's arms. Beverly should be out there right now, stalking the stage, microphone in hand, working her audience. Flora had heard her sing for the first time last week. It was when she'd delivered the new medicine to the stables and she'd been entranced. Beverly's powerful, deep-throated voice was perfect for the music she sang.

She looked back at the woman's body and frowned. The ring. Beverly had been wearing a large ruby on her left hand – Flora had seen it spark scarlet in the sunlight – but it was no longer there. Where had the ring gone? Had someone removed it from the dead woman's finger? And, if so, why?

It was nearly an hour later that Jack put his head around the bedroom door. By then, Flora had sunk into a mild depression. Keeping company with the dead, a young woman who only yesterday had been so full of life, had had its effect.

'You're excused duty,' Jack said. 'The undertakers have arrived – they're taking Miss Russo to the mortuary.'

Flora rose stiffly from her chair. 'I'll be glad to go,' she said, collecting her handbag from the window sill. 'Beverly will be looked after now.'

Jack had turned to walk out the door when she caught hold of his arm. 'Jack, you haven't seen a ruby ring on your travels, by any chance?' The missing jewellery was still bothering her.

He looked mystified.

'Beverly was wearing one and now she's not,' Flora explained. 'I wondered if it might have fallen off her finger when they carried her across from the stage.'

He glanced at the body lying on top of the counterpane. 'If it did, we'll be lucky to find it again. There's a fair stretch of garden between the stage and the Priory door. But I doubt a ring would have slipped off.'

'If it didn't, it means someone stole it,' she said gloomily. 'I don't want to think we're in grave-robbing territory.'

'It's not likely, is it? There must be another explanation.'

'Did you notice anyone in the hotel when you walked through? Anyone you didn't recognise?'

'The only person I saw was Sally. She was in the foyer, speaking on the phone to guests due to arrive tomorrow. Trying, as far as she could, I think, to soften what's happened, though how they'll respond is anyone's guess. She seems braced for cancellations once the news seeps out.'

'Let's hope that won't happen or, if it does, that Dominic has a plan. Where have you been for the last hour anyway?'

'I took Dr Randall back to the village. He was pretty agitated and needed to get home.'

'Agitated because of a dead body? That seems unlikely. Did he say why he wasn't at the surgery when you called earlier?'

'He made some excuse about feeling unwell at work and needing to go home, but he wasn't at the house either when I called.'

Flora wondered if she should share her suspicions, but decided it was tittle-tattle that had no real bearing on what had happened to Beverly. A noise in the corridor spared her from comment and heralded two men dressed in white who, between them, shuffled a stretcher through the open door.

Jack held out his hand to her. 'We should get going. I've promised to give Alice and Kate a lift and, if you're very good, I might offer you the front seat! I've asked Charlie to ride Betty back to the cottage.'

'You think of everything, kind sir.' She bobbed a small curtsy and followed him into the corridor, then walked beside him down the stairs to the hotel's foyer, for centuries the baronial hall of the Templetons. There was no sign of Sally, and Flora could only hope her friend had managed to persuade the Priory's first guests to continue with their booking.

'Do you know what's happening to all the food?' she asked. 'Very little of it was eaten.'

'Alice may be very upset for her niece, but she's still super organised. Kate has snaffled the sausage rolls and Scotch eggs to sell in the Nook and together they've crammed what other perishables they could into that fancy American refrigerator Sally ordered. The waiters have been given plates of scones and cake and bowls of jellies to take home, and what's left has been packed into a hamper and Dominic instructed to drive it to St Luke's so the hospital can use it in their catering.'

'Phew! I know Alice was in a dither about the food, but that's some organisation. How sad, though, that all our plans for a glorious party have ended like this.'

He didn't respond to her immediately, walking in silence through the Priory's rear door and making for the marquee, but halfway across the lawn, he stopped, saying diffidently, 'You might get interviewed by the police, Flora, so be prepared.'

'Why me?' She frowned. 'You saw what happened as much as I did. Kate and Alice, too, and that horrible agent, Martell, not to mention people sitting in the front row of the audience. *And* the musicians who were actually on stage with Beverly.'

There was another silence and, when Jack spoke again, his tone was cautious. 'I'm not sure it's today's events they'll want to talk to you about – if, in fact, they do. It was something that Randall said in the car on the way back to the village that made me think you might get a visit from Alan Ridley or his sergeant. The doctor told me that Beverly Russo was on medication for a mild problem with her heart and you were the one to collect her medicine from the surgery.'

Flora looked fixedly at him, her hazel eyes perturbed. 'There's a problem with the medicine?'

'Not necessarily, but it's something the police are bound to check. Randall seemed nervous about it. The girl was extremely young to die of heart failure.'

Flora walked on a few paces before saying, 'There's something here that doesn't add up. She must have had a problem with her heart or she wouldn't have consulted Dr Randall in the first place. But if it was only a mild abnormality, as he told you, why did he tell *me* to warn her the medicine was very strong?'

Jack's eyebrows rose. 'He said that?'

'He did. Beverly was to take only the recommended dose, otherwise the liquid could be dangerous.'

'That *is* strange. The police will have to get to grips with it, but in any case it's likely to be only a small part of their investigation. They'll want to look at the microphone. There was definitely a problem with that.'

'It didn't really register with me at the time. Everything happened so quickly. I remember you yelling for someone to switch off the electrics.'

Jack passed a hand through his hair, then smoothed down the chunk that was forever seeking to escape. 'She looked as though she was being electrocuted,' he confessed. 'But what do I know? Maybe someone suffering a severe heart attack has similar reactions. All I could think of was that it was important to switch off the current.'

'I suppose Beverly could have died from a heart attack that was brought on by an electric shock,' Flora hazarded.

'Whatever the cause, it's a pretty dreadful thing to have happened.'

They were almost at the marquee now and Jack gestured towards Alice and Kate standing by the entrance, a collection of bags at their feet. 'Best not to say too much about it. Alice already has a face somewhere around her ankles.'

'I won't,' she said quietly, 'but if it turns out there's a fault with the electrics, the Priory will be blamed and its reputation ruined. Perhaps even worse, Sally will blame herself.'

Jack shook his head. 'She shouldn't. Dominic is equally responsible. In some ways, more so. He was the one who booked

Tutti Frutti and oversaw the setting up of the stage, including the electrics.'

Flora gave a subdued snort. 'He'll slide out of any problem, I can tell you that now. Sally will be the one to shoulder the worries.'

5

Flora was poaching an egg for breakfast the next morning when she was surprised by a tap on the kitchen window. Turning from the cooker, she saw Alice waving at her through the glass. She glanced quickly at the clock. Surely her friend should be at St Saviour's? – Alice never missed the Sunday morning service. It could only mean trouble. More trouble. Opening the back door, she took one look at Alice's unhappy face and her heart sank further.

'I had to come.' Her friend puffed into the kitchen and collapsed onto a wooden chair, her weary figure seeming to sink into itself. For a moment she sat silent, then clasped her head in her hands, fingers digging deep into the grey curls.

'Whatever's happened?' Flora was alarmed.

'It's Sally,' the older woman muttered to the kitchen table, unable it seemed to raise her eyes to Flora.

'Sally is unwell? Alice, tell me! You're worrying me.'

'Sally's OK.' She looked up at last. 'More than OK.' There was an unfamiliar bitterness in her voice.

'I'll make tea,' Flora said decidedly.

Putting the kettle to boil, she rescued her poached egg,

sliding it on to the slice of toast she'd made earlier. This was one egg that wouldn't be eaten, she guessed. Once the teapot was filled, she sat down opposite Alice and settled herself to listen.

'We had a row,' her friend announced dramatically. Then, to Flora's horror, tears began to furrow their way down a pair of cheeks that had lost their usual ruddiness.

'When was this, and where?' she asked.

'I went up there first thing...'

'You went up to the Priory this morning?' Flora prompted.

'I couldn't sleep, worryin' about the girl and what would happen to the hotel now.'

'And...'

For several moments, Alice couldn't speak, then seeming to gather strength, she said forcefully, 'I told her – that Dominic is a no-good. He's taken your money and what have you got out of it 'cept a pile of trouble?'

It was very much what Flora thought herself, but it wouldn't do to agree. Alice was overwrought, sick with worry over the hotel's future and desperately upset at the quarrel with her niece. It was reassurance she needed.

'The hotel might not suffer as badly as you think. There'll be people who won't want to come, I know, but not everyone will cancel and this whole Russo business could soon be forgotten. A temporary blip.'

'Temporary! It'll go on for months. Can't you see, Flora, it's the same as what happened to you at the All's Well? The gossip starts, you lose your reputation and things just spiral downhill. The hotel will have to close, you'll see, and with debts galore. That girl has sunk every penny into it that my brother left her, and given up a secure job with prospects to do it. It couldn't be worse.'

'You said all this to Sally?'

Alice looked crestfallen. 'I know I shouldn't have but I'm so upset I don't know which way to turn.'

There was a long silence, their cups of tea standing untouched, until Alice said, 'Would you go and see her? Try to patch things up, mebbe. Give the girl some support.'

Flora leaned across the table and grasped her friend's hand. 'Of course I'll go. If there's any way I can help Sally, I will.'

As soon as Alice had left, Flora tipped her uneaten breakfast into the rubbish bin and washed the teacups. Donning a light jacket, she locked the cottage door and hurried along the path to the garden gate, deciding she would walk to the Priory. Behind her, the old red brick and flint walls dozed in sunshine once more, but thankfully yesterday's extreme heat had disappeared. Once on the lane that ran past her cottage, she stepped up her pace and, within twenty minutes, had reached the iron gates.

The estate this morning looked even more beautiful than yesterday, and Flora felt a real sadness that Sally's dream could be about to tumble to the ground. From the front drive, neither the marquee nor the stage were visible and she wondered when they would be dismantled, or indeed if they had been already. But Sunday was a day of rest, and it was unlikely.

She was halfway along the winding driveway when she saw a man's figure coming towards her. The black peaked cap was a clue to his identity – Jarvis, the drummer. His head was bent as he walked, his eyes fixed on the ground, and she was within touching distance of him before he looked up.

'Good morning,' she said brightly.

'Is it?'

She'd never actually spoken to Jarvis Redmond before. When she'd called on Beverly at the stables apartment, she'd occasionally noticed him lurking in the background, but he'd always been the band member who was silent. Now she was glad she hadn't tried to make conversation. He appeared a surly individual, but one who stood blocking her path.

'On your way to the village?' she asked, trying to sound as though she was interested.

'Nothing much else to do, is there?'

'I suppose not, though I thought you'd be busy packing up to leave.'

'I thought so, too. We all did. But some plod came round this morning – Trimble, Trundle?'

'Constable Tring,' she corrected him.

'Him then. Told us we weren't to leave, strict instructions from some inspector or other. We can't leave until he tells us, and that won't be till they've done a post-mortem on Bev and investigated why she died.'

'That sounds reasonable,' Flora said, 'and it shouldn't detain you long. In any case, you can't perform without Beverly, can you?'

'We'll get another singer. They're ten a penny.'

'But surely not with a voice like Beverly's.'

He scowled. 'Too much of a voice, if you ask me.'

Flora didn't respond and, veering around him, walked quickly on. She was shocked. She didn't expect members of the band to love each other – it was clear from Tommy May's outburst yesterday that they didn't – but Redmond had shown not the slightest regret for the death of a young woman who, for months, had performed alongside him.

After such an acrid exchange, the tranquillity of the Priory came as a balm. Generations had passed beneath its beautiful honey-coloured stone, the building a witness to tragedy and triumph alike. Its very stability through all those long years was a promise to cling to.

Leaving the front drive, Flora rounded the side of the mansion and immediately saw the truth of Jarvis Redmond's words. In the distance, a team of blue-jacketed policemen were scouring the stage and its surrounds, while a second group were in and out of the tent. Alan Ridley meant business, it seemed. Or perhaps he just didn't like rock 'n' roll, she thought wryly.

Sally was standing at the rear door of the Priory watching the distant figures as they bobbed and weaved their way between stage and marquee.

'How are you?' Flora asked, as she approached the girl. 'Or is that a silly question?'

'I couldn't feel much worse, but I'm glad to see you. Unless, of course, you've come to scold me, too.'

'Alice came by the cottage this morning,' Flora admitted, 'and told me you'd had words. She's feeling very bad about it.'

'And so she should. Talking to me as though I were a child who needed dressing down. And how dare she say those things about Dominic? She hardly knows him.'

'And you do?' she asked gently.

Sally tightened her lips. 'A good deal better than anyone else. This ghastly business isn't his fault and he's been hit as hard as me.'

'He must be concerned,' Flora agreed, 'but I'm hoping for both your sakes that it won't be as bad as you fear.'

'It will, and it's already begun. I've had five cancellations this morning and I've no doubt the telephone will be ringing most of the day. Now we have the police all over us, it can only make the situation worse.'

The police presence had been puzzling Flora. They would naturally want to examine where the death had occurred, but the number of men involved seemed excessive.

'There has to be a post-mortem,' she said, 'and I can understand why the police might stop Tutti Frutti from leaving until they're sure how Beverly died, but there seems to be a massive search going on. Do you know why?'

'Not really. The inspector has said nothing. He came for an hour, then disappeared and left his sergeant to question the waiters. One of them was stupid enough to mention the row

Beverly had with Tommy May. That might have propelled them into this pointless investigation.'

'An hour after the quarrel, Beverly was dead,' she remarked, thinking that maybe the investigation wasn't so pointless.

'That was just coincidence. The police are being ridiculously suspicious.'

'Why do *you* think she died?'

'Heart attack, wasn't it? Brought on by drink, I expect. Or worse, drugs.'

For the second time that day, Flora was shocked. Did Beverly have no supporters?

'I never saw Beverly drink and she had a heart condition,' she said neutrally. 'Dr Randall prescribed for it.'

Sally shrugged. 'Frankly, I don't give a damn how she died. All I want is for the police to go and leave me to get this place back on its feet, if it's at all possible.'

'With Dominic's help, presumably? He'll want to shoulder his share of the problem.'

'What makes you think he won't?' Sally snapped.

'Good morning, Flora.' Dominic had slipped through the open doorway and was walking towards them. 'Come to view our brilliant constabulary at work?' he asked.

'The more brilliant the police, the quicker you'll be free of them,' she responded, his attempt at irony falling flat.

'Some hope. Why the blighters have descended on us, the Lord only knows. We've enough to do without their interference, haven't we, Sal?'

He put his arm around Sally's shoulder and gave the girl a hug. Sally looked up at him and smiled. Flora stared. The girl's face was radiant, her eyes glowing. Sally was in love! Dominic Lister wasn't just a business partner then – it was exactly what Alice had feared when Sally had first told them her plans. *You're buyin' the place to put it back on its feet, young lady,* she'd warned her niece. *Not for any other reason.*

It seemed there *had* been another reason. But Dominic? How did he feel? For no apparent reason, the image of the ruby ring swam into Flora's mind. She would have liked to ask them both if they knew anything of the missing jewellery, but something held her back. She was unsure what exactly was going on between these two, unsure what had really happened between Tommy May and Beverly. Did the ring have anything to do with any of them and, if so, how?

6

She hadn't stayed long at the Priory – it was clear that Sally's mood was unforgiving. Having said what she could to smooth her friend's anger, Flora walked slowly back to her cottage in low spirits. At her garden gate, she paused, her hand on the latch, gripped by the impulse to walk on to Overlay House and share this morning's upset with Jack. But she knew she shouldn't. That would be admitting she couldn't cope with difficulties alone. She had done all she could to heal the breach between Alice and Sally, Jack could do no more, and she must simply get on with her own life.

Two days later, having heard no more of the dispute, she locked the bookshop door and, packing Betty's tray with several parcels of books, set off for the post office. In her own way, Aunt Violet had been a pioneer, establishing a collection of valuable second-hand books as soon as she'd opened the shop and, afterwards, setting up a delivery service for customers living at a distance, including those on the other side of the world. Her aunt had built up the All's Well stock over years, concentrating mainly on out-of-print books as well as the occasional rare volume: first editions, signed copies, those with special jackets. Violet Steele had loved her afternoons at local auctions, or at the sales that occasionally took place when an old house in the district was sold and the new owners wished to create an entirely new library, or no library at all. And loved finding the very book on her shelves for which a customer had spent months searching.

When she'd inherited the All's Well nearly two years ago, Flora had followed in Violet's footsteps, even though continuing the service brought in little money. But customers were the lifeblood of the business – that had been Violet's mantra – and now it was hers. Owning a bookshop was the best feeling in the world and every morning she opened the All's Well's white-painted door, she was filled with joy and a sense of wonder.

Over the last month, she had been saving up parcels to spare herself too many lengthy visits to the post office. Dilys, the postmistress, was Abbeymead's most fervent gossip and Flora knew she would be lucky to escape her clutches within half an hour. But lunchtime was a sensible choice, since Dilys liked her food almost as much as she liked gossip.

Flora rode into the small square outside the post office and slid Betty into the bicycle stand, collecting the goods from her wicker tray. She was turning round, her arms full, when a figure dashed past, almost knocking her off her feet and sending the parcels skittering across the cobbles.

'Sorry.' The man slewed round, his breath coming in spurts, and repeated, 'So sorry.'

It was Dr Randall. How extraordinary! What could have prompted him to behave so recklessly?

An older woman emerged from the shop at that moment, looking harassed and glancing nervously at her watch – Dilys had obviously been on top form. The woman shook her head at Flora as she passed and glared at the disappearing figure of the locum. 'These young men! Good job when old Hanson gets back,' she said.

'Dr Randall seems a little upset,' Flora said mildly, when she finally made it to the counter.

'Him?' Dilys's ample bosom quivered slightly. 'Can't make the chap out. He called in for forms to renew his driving licence, leastways that's what he said, then when it took me a bit of time to find them – you should see the stuff I've got under this counter, Flora – he started huffing and puffing, and when Mrs Crabtree walked in to look at birthday cards – she didn't buy one, typical of her – he said, don't bother I'll come back later and ran out of the door. Can you imagine?'

There was something decidedly odd about Dr Randall, Flora decided, apart from his unprofessional relationship with his staff. It wasn't just a question of where he'd been when he was needed at the Priory, but also a mystery over the medicine he'd prescribed for Beverly Russo. Questions that wouldn't go away.

The postmistress turned back the cuffs of her hand-knitted jumper, bubblegum pink today, Flora noticed – Dilys's taste rarely favoured the subtle – and weighed the parcels.

'These'll cost you a packet. Not worth your while sending 'em, if you ask me. I know your aunt was always keen on serving the whole world, but it doesn't mean you have to be.' She accorded Flora a sage nod, then rolling down the shutter, walked around the counter and turned the shop notice to Closed.

'I don't want another person through that door,' she said. 'Not until I've had a decent lunch. I'm that tired today, you wouldn't believe.' In passing, she patted a pile of magazines into shape. 'Messy and demanding, that's what folks are. And me desperate for a break.'

'Can't the Post Office find help?'

'They did. Some temporary woman. And I was looking

forward to it like nobody's business, but now... all this trouble...'

'Trouble? You mean at the Priory?'

Dilys planted herself across the aisle, her arms folded and looking indignant. 'Irene, she's my sister, was coming down from Devon. She'd planned to spend a few days in Abbeymead and then go on to Eastbourne. Not any longer, though. Now she's going straight there to stay with friends, so not much point me taking time off, is it?'

'But why isn't she staying?'

'It's obvious. Rene doesn't feel safe here.'

'I'm sure your sister would be fine in Abbeymead. It was a heart attack Miss Russo suffered, nothing more sinister.' Privately, Flora thought that Irene must be an exceptionally timid female.

'That young woman,' Dilys snorted. 'That Miss Russo. I didn't hold with her myself, all fur and no knickers, you know the kind, but she shouldn't have had a heart attack, not at her age. I did hear as the doctor' – she nodded meaningfully towards the door – 'prescribed medicine for her and it does make you wonder.'

Flora's eyes widened. It may have made *her* wonder but she was naturally suspicious. She was surprised the village was already speculating.

'"What if I got sick?" Rene asked me. "Would I want to go to this doctor? Would you, Dyl?" When I thought about it, I reckoned I wouldn't. Thank the Lord that Hanson is back next year, is all I can say.'

'Thank the Lord,' Flora agreed faintly.

Collecting Betty from the stand, she rode on to the Nook, hoping to get to the bottom of Dr Randall's strange behaviour. Kate Mitchell had quite recently consulted the locum – an unknown quantity to Abbeymead when he first arrived – and she wondered what her friend had made of him.

Kate was carrying steaming bowls of soup to a table when

Flora put her head round the café door. Alice, pad in hand, stood by a second table waiting for a couple to order. Until the hotel reopened, it seemed, she was continuing to help Kate.

'Good morning, Miss Steele.' The man who'd called out to Flora shot back the cuff of a sharply tailored suit and consulted his watch. 'In fact, good afternoon.'

Max Martell laid aside the newspaper he'd been reading and gestured to the spare seat at his table. 'Have you come for lunch?'

'No,' Flora said. 'I was hoping to have a word with Mrs Mitchell.'

'Your friends are a trifle busy right now. Do sit down while you wait.'

Unwillingly, Flora slipped into the seat opposite, aware of Martell's eyes on her. His scrutiny felt uncomfortable and she was about to bob up again with the excuse that she needed to be back at the All's Well, when he said, 'I wonder, have you news of how the police investigation is going?'

She stared at him. 'Why would I?'

'I understand that you and your... friend – Mr Carrington, isn't it? – know the inspector well. A little bird whispered to me that you've solved a few crimes together.'

Flora felt her face freeze. Max Martell had been busy, it appeared, picking up the village gossip, hoping no doubt to use it to his benefit. 'The little bird was mistaken,' she said stonily. 'I hardly know Inspector Ridley and Jack's— Mr Carrington's relationship with him is purely professional.'

'Ah yes, the chap is a crime writer, I believe. He might be just the man to tell us why Beverly died so inconveniently.'

'I imagine you'll know the cause soon enough – there's to be a post-mortem, isn't there?' She kept her voice prim in an attempt to mask the dislike she felt for the man, but on second thoughts decided to use this enforced intimacy to good purpose. 'I believe Beverly had a heart problem.'

'So I understand,' he said lazily. 'Though I can't say I ever noticed it and I certainly wasn't told. Perhaps as her agent I should have been.'

'Do you know everything about your clients?'

His smile verged on the smug. 'I wouldn't say everything, but their health, Miss Steele, is obviously a concern. Tommy May, for instance, suffered a hernia last year when he moved equipment he shouldn't have and I have to ensure that in future he's never involved in heavy lifting. Insurance, you see. Shane's immune system isn't all it should be – prison can do that to people – and Jarvis. Well, Jarvis has rather too much partiality for the bottle.'

Flora gaped at these revelations, but pounced on the mention of prison. 'Shane has been in prison?'

'Minor trouble. And prison isn't strictly true. It was a young offenders' institution. It happens, boys get led along the wrong path and before you know it, the police are involved. But Shane has turned his life around so one must be generous. Tommy, as well.'

'He was in this institution, too?'

'He was, which if you look at it in a certain way was serendipitous. Foolish youngsters, both of them, from one of the poorest areas of Portsmouth. Tommy Meyerhoff, in particular, has done brilliantly in overcoming a bad start.'

'Meyerhoff? Not May then? It's a German name, isn't it?'

'Regrettably so. A liaison with an enemy alien who left his mother to fend for herself and her child as best she could. Hardly surprising the boy went off the rails. But we should look at the bright side.' The smugness had grown. 'Meeting as young offenders has made the two of them the greatest of friends. Camaraderie – it's what you need in a band.'

'And Beverly? Did she enjoy the same camaraderie?'

'Ah, Beverly.' He sighed. 'What a voice! Now, she was the real deal.'

'And Tutti Frutti isn't?'

'They're good enough but unlikely to progress much further. Beverly's voice, though, was sublime. She was made for the biggest stages in the world.'

'Flora?'

It was Kate who had come quietly up to their table. 'Can I get you something?'

'Nothing to eat, thanks. I just wanted a word.' Flustered, she got to her feet.

'Before you go again, Mrs Mitchell, may I have my bill?' Max smiled. A smile so insincere, Flora decided, you could peel it from his face.

'The bill's here.' Alice bustled up and handed Max a white slip of paper.

In response, he slapped a ten shilling note down on the table. 'Do keep the change. It was a delightful meal.'

'He's that slimy,' Alice said, watching through the window as Martell raised his umbrella against a sudden gust of rain. 'I wouldn't trust him further'n my big toe and that's sayin' somethin'.'

He was slimy, Flora agreed silently, but also a valuable source of information. Information that he'd passed on freely. Had that been a deliberate ploy?

'Kate, I came to ask you about the doctor and got caught by Max Martell, if that's his name, which somehow I doubt.'

'Dr Randall?' Kate sounded puzzled.

'You went to see him recently.'

'Oh, the back pain.' She began to clear the table, piling empty dishes onto a large wooden tray. 'He said there wasn't much he could do for me. I should take care not to lift anything and have as much rest as I could, which isn't easy in the café. And swallow an aspirin if it got really bad.'

'Not much help then.'

'I only went because Alice insisted.'

'You should have seen her, bent double, she was,' Alice protested, her arms nursing her ample stomach. 'Course I insisted. Why do you want to know about Dr Randall anyway?'

'His behaviour seems a little odd, that's all. He seems terrified of speaking to anyone.'

'There's a rumour goin' round,' Alice confided. 'Likely, that's the problem.'

'What kind of rumour?'

Alice moved closer. 'Someone, I dunno who, told Mr Houseman when she was buyin' her veg – then he told me – that the singer who died was seein' the doctor and he'd given her stuff to take. It could have been one of the band who told this woman. That Jarvis is always around the village. Anyways, Beverly takes Randall's medicine and then what happens? She dies.'

'And the rumour says the medicine was to blame?'

'Somethin' like that. All rubbish, but I'm not keen on him myself. I'll be glad when Hanson gets back, even if all he gives you is a pat on the shoulder and tells you that you'll be as right as ninepence in a few days. By the way, Flora love, thank you for talking to Sally.'

'Things are back to normal?' she asked hopefully.

Alice looked unsure. 'Better, I s'pose you'd say.'

Balancing the tray on her hip, Kate was making ready to retreat to the kitchen when Flora put a hand on her arm. 'We haven't seen each other properly for ages, Katie. Those bus trips we had in the summer – they were good fun. If your back's up to travelling, why don't we have a last fling before winter closes in? Sunday perhaps?'

'I can't, I'm sorry.' Kate was blushing furiously. 'I've agreed...'

Alice waggled her eyebrows at Flora and mouthed, 'Tony Farraday.'

7

Jack hadn't seen Flora since the disastrous opening of the Priory nearly a week ago. Since then, he'd been locked in his study, spending every daylight hour trying to pummel his ideas into a coherent whole. His agent had been patient – the first draft of the novel was already late – but having promised Arthur he would get something to him by the end of the month, Jack had barely had time to feed himself, let alone go visiting.

Returning from Cornwall earlier this year, he'd been unsure whether he would ever write again. Write fiction, at least. The words simply wouldn't come, the plot, if it was there at all, was all over the place, and his characters bored him. He'd had several difficult weeks when he'd flip-flopped this way and that, the question of his future wide open and dominating his every waking minute. Should he go back to journalism as the only trade he knew, or attempt to bulldoze his way through his current impasse? Maybe he should try something entirely different and become a full-time sleuth!

The idea of setting up a detective agency was stupid. He'd suggested it to Flora as a joke and why it was still in his mind, he had no idea. As for journalism, deep down he knew it would be a retrograde step. Six years ago he'd begun to make a happier life for himself, had believed wholeheartedly that he'd found where he belonged. But when failure came knocking at his door, his certainty as a novelist fizzled, and the struggle to regain a lost confidence had been painful.

It was only gradually that he'd summoned up the belief to begin again. Or at least to try. It hadn't been easy and it still wasn't – what he'd managed amounted to no more than a synopsis. But he considered it a victory that he now had several pages to post to Arthur Bellamy, and should be able to relax a little. Should, but couldn't. Not quite. Saturday's dreadful events had never been far from his mind the whole time he'd been working on his proposal. An unease over Beverly Russo's death had taken hold of him. It was shocking that such a young woman had died in full view of the public, that went without saying, but it was the way that she'd died that bothered him most.

He'd known for a while about Beverly's heart problems – Flora had collected medicine for the girl – but he'd been stunned that her illness might have been severe enough to kill her. Certainly severe enough for the doctor to prescribe medicine. Except there were questions, weren't there, over what precisely Dr Randall had prescribed? He'd insisted to Flora that the medicine was very strong, dangerous even, if not taken correctly, yet Beverly had told Flora that she'd only recently begun to suffer uncomfortable jumps in her heart rhythm, suggesting that such strong medicine was unnecessary. So what was the truth? Had she been seriously ill or merely suffering a mild abnormality? And if it was mild, how could she have died so suddenly?

Jack felt irritated with himself that he was unable to settle and, after he'd walked to the nearest post box and sent the brown foolscap envelope on its journey to Arthur, he donned his oldest clothes and collected a spade from the garden shed. He would dig his way out of annoyance.

In a couple of hours he'd harvested two long rows of potatoes and, following Charlie's guide, put them to dry in the
greenhouse. Once dry, they'd be packed into hessian sacks and
squirrelled away in the dark – another of his young mentor's
instructions. Feeling pleased with his progress, he walked back
to the house and quickly washed and changed. It was time he
caught up with Flora, the girl he'd been missing this last week.
He'd wear his new jacket, the one he'd bought in Derry & Toms
the last time he'd been in London.

Walking into the village once more, this time making for the
All's Well, he hoped the jacket didn't look as if he'd made too
much of an effort. Today, at least, he had a ready excuse for calling. Conscious of how wary Flora was of too warm a friendship,
he liked to have a definite reason for his visits. It was almost a
year since they'd met and, from the outset, she'd been careful to
keep a distance between them, ready to withdraw into herself if
she sensed him getting too close. But his pretext today was cast
iron. He'd collected together a small pile of books that he no
longer needed, destined for the village market next weekend.
There was a regular Saturday gathering on the green, unless
inclement weather prevailed, but the following week would see
a very special sale, all proceeds going to St Saviour's, the parish
church.

Jack offered her the bag of books as soon as he walked into
the shop. 'I know you'll have your own collection for the market
– I thought I'd bring the Austin round to the All's Well early
that morning. Deliver all of them together.'

Flora gave a faint smile. 'Good idea,' she murmured. Her
mind, it seemed, was elsewhere.

She was wearing her usual shop uniform of cotton skirt and
blouse, today a navy-and-white-stripe affair. Nothing too smart,
but she looked fresh and neat. She also looked very pretty, but
he wasn't going to notice that.

'What have you brought?' She tipped the books out of his

bag and shuffled through them. '*Poisons of the Levant.* That should go down a storm. Have you decided against poisoning your victims in future?'

'I'm sure I can manage a drop of arsenic here and there, but the poisons in that particular book are so rarefied that no ordinary person in this country would ever get hold of them. And I don't want to cheat.'

'How would it be cheating?'

'You have to give readers a chance to solve the puzzle. Make your clues fair. If it's a poison no one has ever heard of, that's cheating in my view.'

'I suppose.' She gave a long sigh.

'What is it?' There was a pause before he asked, 'Are you still thinking about the Priory?'

'Aren't you?' She looked up at him. 'You know your hair has gone quite mad today.' He smelt jasmine as she reached up and smoothed down the recalcitrant flop of hair. He wished she wouldn't do that and gave himself a mental shake.

'I'm not happy about what's happened at the hotel,' he said. 'How could I be? But I can see it's worse for you. You've known the Priory since childhood, all those years when Lord Edward was still alive, and you're desperate for it to do well.'

'It's gone from bad to worse ever since he died,' she said drearily. 'I'm coming to believe there's a jinx on the place. Perhaps Lord Edward cast a spell from beyond the grave – that the Priory should stay in the Templeton family or trouble would follow.'

'According to Dominic Lister, it *has* stayed. Isn't he supposed to be some kind of relation?'

'Some kind! If you believe that... now, if Aunt Violet were here, she'd know for sure. Family trees were imprinted on her brain.'

'Sally believes it's true.' He settled himself on the window seat.

'Sally is in love.'

'With Lister? She told you that?'

'She didn't have to. I only had to look at her. It was obvious.'

Would there be a day when he looked at Flora and saw the same? Somehow, he doubted it. 'You sound disapproving,' was all he said.

'Sally is too good for him,' she declared. 'If anything, he's more of a liability than an asset.'

Twisting his head, Jack looked through the bookshop's latticed window at the high street beyond. Mr Preece, the butcher, appeared busy, but otherwise the street was largely empty. It was that time of day, he thought. Most people were still at work and those that weren't had already done their marketing. As for the children, any moment now the school bell would be sounding to signal their release. He glanced at the Victorian station clock that hung on the opposite wall, one of Violet Steele's jumble sale finds, Flora had told him, and decided he'd better get back to Overlay House or Charlie Teague would beat him to it. Charlie had promised to give the lawn one last mow before autumn set in for real.

'Don't get too down in the dumps,' he said, getting up to go. 'Sally is a big girl. She'll make her own decisions, whatever you or Alice or Kate advise.' He bent his head and squinted through the window again. 'The village is very quiet. Why don't you drop in at the Nook and treat yourself to tea and a bun?'

'The village is very quiet because everyone is at home gossiping about the Priory.'

'You think so?'

'I know so. I've been in the same position, remember? But a sticky bun sounds good.'

She slipped from behind the desk and collected her handbag from what Jack called a cupboard but what Aunt Violet had insisted was a kitchenette.

'By the way, I posted my synopsis today.'

She bobbed her head round the door. 'That's wonderful, Jack! You're on your way again!'

'Right now, chickens are not being counted, but maybe. Are you coming?'

He had reached the All's Well's wide white-painted door but before he could grasp its large brass handle, Sally Jenner almost fell into the shop, her cardigan half off her shoulders and a pair of scuffed shoes on her feet. She had evidently dressed in a hurry.

'Sally! Whatever's happened?' Flora asked.

'The police,' the girl began, her voice so tight the words hardly sounded.

Jack put his hand on her arm and steered her towards the stool at Flora's desk. 'What about the police?' he asked quietly, depositing her on the seat.

'They're not happy,' she managed to say. 'I think... I think they don't believe Beverly's death was natural.' Her eyes filled with tears and she rummaged in her pocket for a handkerchief.

An intense silence filled the shop, broken only by Sally's violent blowing of her nose.

'What is it that's making them doubtful?' Flora asked at last.

She hadn't seemed surprised at Sally's words, Jack noticed. Hadn't dismissed the idea that, once they'd examined the scene, the police would have concerns. It was as though she'd known it was inevitable that questions would be raised and, thinking about it now, he'd known it, too. It was why he'd been feeling so uneasy.

'They're looking at the amplifier.' Sally wiped her eyes. 'They think it might have been tampered with and they're going to question the team who set it up. Maybe call in independent experts as well.'

'It could all be a fuss over nothing,' he said soothingly. 'The post-mortem is sure to show Miss Russo died of a heart attack.' Sally needed something positive to hang on to, though in truth he suspected the post-mortem might show something very different.

He'd always been uncertain that a heart attack alone could have caused the young woman's fierce juddering. Beverly had just unhooked the microphone when it happened, and it had been a reflex action on his part to yell for the electrics to be switched off. Instinctively, he must have fixed on the microphone as the culprit and only later toyed with the idea of a medical problem. Beverly's heart was likely to be a distraction and now it seemed the police, in examining the amplifier, were following the same line of thought.

Sally jumped off the stool and faced them directly. 'I need your help,' she said baldly. 'The two of you.'

He felt Flora's gaze rest on him and looked across at her. It seemed they were both unsure of what Sally wanted from them.

'You've solved other crimes, Flora, other mysteries. You and Jack,' Sally said a little desperately. 'You can solve this one.'

'But that was when the police had no interest in the crime,' Flora argued. 'We got involved when they didn't think it worthwhile to investigate, but that's not the case here. This time they *are* interested. They're interviewing the men who set up the system, they're calling in experts. Inspector Ridley and his team will get to the bottom of what happened.'

Sally bounced towards her, reaching out her hand. 'I wouldn't ask you, if I thought I could leave it to them, but I can't. These so-called experts will take an age to come. Even the team who set up the electrics on Saturday have moved on to another job – in Newcastle. The inspector will have to contact his counterpart in Northumberland and ask the police force up there to interview them. They'll be toing and froing for weeks. You'll be tons quicker. And it's speed I need.'

'What exactly do you want us to do?'

'Poke around. Investigate. Find clues as to what really

happened. You could report anything you found to the police and maybe work with them.'

'Inspector Ridley and I don't often see eye to eye,' Flora said ruefully.

'The inspector likes Jack, though.' Sally's voice was pleading. She turned to him. 'He helps you with your novels, doesn't he?'

'I check policing details with him occasionally,' he admitted.

'Then the two of you have a good relationship. Please help, Jack. My future could depend on it.'

He looked into a pair of troubled brown eyes and felt himself soften. It wasn't what he wanted to do, but he couldn't leave Sally Jenner in such a mess. He hadn't known her long but he'd come to like her and admire her energy and tenacity. There was a small voice, too, whispering that it would be another reason to see Flora. He was surprised she hadn't sounded enthusiastic. Ordinarily, she would have jumped at the chance of what she called an adventure. More often than not, she would jump before she was asked.

'We'll help in whatever way we can,' he heard himself say, turning to the slim figure by his side. 'Won't we, Flora?'

8

Flora held back, refusing to be bounced into the investigation. Ignoring Jack's question, she flashed a smile at Sally and hoped her reluctance wouldn't mean an end to their friendship.

Jack, she saw, had a crease between his eyebrows. 'We'll be in touch,' was all he said and guided their visitor to the shop's front door. Pausing for a moment, he offered his hand. 'Try not to worry too much, Sally. The hotel will survive, I'm sure.'

As soon as the door clicked shut, he turned to Flora. 'Why were you so hesitant? It's hardly your style.'

It wasn't, and she was unsure what had made her dig in her heels. Perhaps the knowledge that at last the All's Well had been returned to profit, a small profit but far better than the penury that had haunted her for the last year. Involving herself in an investigation would disrupt the smooth running of the shop she loved. Maybe, too, after the last few adventures she craved quiet, time spent promoting her business, time enjoying the rhythms of village life. More likely, though – and she was trying to be honest with herself – it was the fear that another enquiry would inevitably lead to Jack becoming a bigger part of her life again, throwing them too closely together, something she had always to fight against.

He hadn't moved, his tall figure filling the doorway. He was looking fixedly at her and it was clear he expected an answer before he left.

'I don't see that we need to be involved,' she said at last. 'Inspector Ridley is unhappy. He's suspicious about Beverly's death and is asking questions, which means the police will get to the bottom of whatever wickedness went on – if any did. Sally needs to be patient and let them do their job.'

Jack's gaze was unwavering. 'You've never championed the police before. I'm not sure I believe you.'

His scepticism was well-founded, she knew, and in response she resorted to attack. 'Tell me why *you're* so keen? It's hardly your style. Normally you're the one to insist I leave any problems we uncover to the police.'

Jack allowed himself a faint grin. 'It looks as though we've swapped roles, doesn't it? I just wanted to help Sally. I didn't like to see her so upset.'

'Neither did I but, unlike you, I don't fancy playing knight errant. Maybe you're too intent on rescuing the damsel?'

'If you like. But I genuinely believe that something odd did go on that afternoon. Tutti Frutti aren't exactly an amiable group, are they? There was evident hostility between at least two of them, and I'm pretty sure Beverly's sudden exit had a lot to do with that.'

Max Martell's words floated into Flora's mind. Jack was unlikely to know anything of the band's background, yet he'd already homed in on the group as a source of trouble. Should she mention what Martell had been so keen to tell her in the café? She thought not. At least, not for the moment. It might give Jack ammunition to argue for an investigation she'd no wish to join.

'I'd best be off,' he said, glancing at the clock again. 'By now

Charlie will be hammering my front door down, but you've still time to make it to Katie's Nook.'

'I think perhaps I'll give it a miss. I've still work to do.' Flora's appetite for a sticky bun had vanished.

The next evening she was finishing a tasty meal of steak pie, part of a batch that Alice had cooked for the café, when there was a knock at her front door. Tipping the empty plate into the washing bowl, she went to see who was calling at this late hour. Late, at least, for Abbeymead.

Alice herself stood on the threshold. 'Sorry to knock at this time, and after you've had such a busy Saturday.'

'It's always good to see you. Come on in.' Flora led the way back into the kitchen, her mind busy with what could have brought Alice from home at this hour. 'Can I get you some tea? That steak pie was delicious, by the way.'

Her friend smiled a trifle wanly. 'Good to hear, my love. I hope you did some nice mash with it.'

'I did. Some of Jack's potatoes. I'm quite jealous of him, his vegetables have done so much better than mine and he hasn't a clue what he's doing—' She broke off. 'Is everything all right?'

Alice had slumped against the kitchen counter, her hands thrust deep in her jacket pockets. 'It wasn't a heart attack,' she muttered, staring at the opposite wall.

Flora forgot tea making and walked over to her friend to give her a big hug. 'How do you know it wasn't?' she asked gently, her brain beginning to whirr.

'The post-mortem. That Beverly. Sally got the details this afternoon. It wasn't a heart attack like we thought. Leastways, that wasn't what killed her.'

'What did?'

'She was electrocuted.'

Flora gave a gasp, her hand to her mouth. 'Are you sure?'

But of course Alice was sure. People didn't go round talking of electrocution unless it was true. And a problem with the amplifier had already been mentioned by the police.

Her friend gave a subdued sob. 'I don't know what to do. Sally's frantic. Ever since that sergeant called, I can't get her to calm down.'

'It's terrible news, but Sally – why do you think she's taken it so badly?'

Alice took her gaze from the wall and looked at Flora. Her eyes were red-rimmed and tired. 'The police mentioned to her before that somethin' might have been wrong with the equipment, but Sally wouldn't believe it. Not really. Mebbe she didn't want to believe it, just hoped the girl died of natural causes. She thought Beverly was sickly – we all did. I said to Sal that buildin' up for that performance had been too much for the girl if she had a weak heart, and mebbe it was. But now they're pretty sure it was a problem with the electrics and it's them that actually caused her death.'

Flora put the kettle to boil, then pushed her friend gently into a kitchen chair and sat down opposite. How was she to comfort Alice?

'Maybe Beverly's death wasn't natural,' she tried, 'but it could still be an accident. Faulty electrics occur all the time, not often with such unfortunate results, I grant you, but if that's what's happened, Sally can't be to blame. Whoever set up the system is responsible.'

'It doesn't much matter who's to blame,' Alice said miserably. 'The hotel can't open while the police enquiry's goin' on.' For a while, she relapsed into silence, then leaning forward, clasped Flora's hand. 'D'you know,' her voice trembled slightly, 'the bank has already been on the phone – Sal took the call. Somehow, they've got wind of the problems. Warned her that the first loan repayment is due at the end of the month.'

'And where is Dominic in all this? He was the one who negotiated the loan.'

'Where d'you think? The chap's a waste of space, like we always warned. He's only gone and locked himself in his bedroom and says he's not well enough to deal with anythin' right now and Sally will have to do the best she can. Poor lass. How can she do the best? She's not a clue where to start.'

Flora jumped up and, filling the teapot, brought it to the table. 'Have the police definitely stopped the hotel from opening?'

'The sergeant said they could open as soon as Inspector Ridley was happy, but when's that goin' to be? And who's goin' to come even if it is open? The newspaper man that Dominic asked to attend the openin' wrote about it in the *Echo*. Now other papers have got hold of it. It's even in the nationals. Who's goin' to book a stay at the Priory after readin' that?'

Flora thought there might be quite a few guests who'd enjoy the notoriety of staying close to the scene of such a tragic incident, but it wasn't what Alice wanted to hear. She poured a cup of tea for them both and nudged the sugar bowl towards her friend. Hot, sweet tea could work wonders.

'Once the inspector has given the go-ahead,' she said, 'and that could be quite soon, you must persuade Sally to reopen. If she keeps it low key, brings in a skeleton staff to begin with, she can see how business goes. It might surprise you both.'

Alice shook her head. 'It won't go anywhere, not till we get the truth. Not till people know for sure what happened.' She looked at Flora over the rim of her teacup. 'I know Sally came to you, but she said you didn't want to help.'

'It's not that I didn't want to.' Flora was reduced to a murmur.

'Then what was it? I thought you could have helped a little seein' as you've helped others.'

'I believed it was best left to the police,' she said helplessly.

'Inspector Ridley is on the case. Jack considers him a very good policeman and I'm sure he'll wrap up the enquiry as soon as he can.'

Alice shook her head again. 'He's gone. Seems he's been sent up to Suffolk, sortin' out some other problem. His sergeant's been left in charge and I dunno how much *he'll* bother. Looks like he's frazzled already with all the work he's had dumped on him.'

Flora didn't know either. Without Alan Ridley in charge, the investigation might well stagnate.

'And what happens,' Alice went on, 'if it turns out that it wasn't an accident?'

She looked across at her friend, surprised. Alice's view of life was generally benign and wouldn't normally have leapt to considering murder. 'You think Beverly might have been killed deliberately?'

'Why not? The business that set up the equipment have a good reputation, and they'll have done hundreds of similar events, so why would they have made a mistake this time?' She paused. 'Then you've got that strange bunch at the stables. The band,' she added, seeing the question in Flora's eyes. 'They're enough to give you the creeps.'

Flora was inclined to agree, but said as cheerfully as she could, 'We're probably worrying unnecessarily.'

She didn't truly believe her own words and neither, she thought, did Alice. Looking at her friend's doleful face, she made a decision. 'I'll speak to Jack,' she promised.

The following day was Sunday and Jack was bound to be at home when she called at Overlay House. She would have to eat humble pie, she accepted, now she was about to suggest they look into Beverly's death, but that didn't matter. Sally was more important and humble pie or not, Flora would do it in style.

Squaring her shoulders for the climbdown ahead, she shrugged herself into her favourite pink jacket, pulled on a pair of shiny black boots – though it really wasn't cold enough – tugged her hair into a swinging ponytail and, halfway through the morning, set off to see Jack.

She found him working in the vegetable patch he'd established on one side of the path that bisected his large back garden. He was lifting potatoes while Charlie Teague was in the greenhouse, shovelling those that had dried into hessian sacks.

Jack straightened up as he heard her approach, leaning on his spade and wiping his forehead. It was still warmer than it should be for late September.

'Come for more of my wondrous Maris Pipers?' he asked slyly. 'Pity yours aren't doing so well.'

'Mine are doing fine,' she said crossly. It was always a sore point that she had not inherited Aunt Violet's green fingers. 'I've plenty in the store cupboard – enough to last me.'

'But think how many more delicious roasts you could enjoy with these.' His hand traced a wide arc across the rows of potatoes he still had to harvest.

'Your cabbages don't look too healthy,' she said sniffily.

'Don't they?' He sounded worried. 'What should they look like?'

Flora smiled. 'Relax. I'm only teasing. They look brilliant and it's extremely annoying.'

'I can cut you one for supper,' he suggested as a peace offering. 'Charlie's taking two back for his mother.'

'Hello, Miss Steele.' Charlie waved from the open door of the greenhouse. 'Mr Carrington's done well, han't he?'

'Or you have,' she said shrewdly.

'Definitely Charlie,' Jack confessed. 'Do you fancy a decent cup of coffee? Arthur has sent me a precious packet from his den in Bloomsbury. Special delivery.'

'It sounds good, but I don't want to stop the hard work.'

'We'll have that drink and you can talk,' he said decidedly. 'You haven't come here to watch me dig potatoes. I'll make some lemonade for Charlie while the coffee brews.'

After the boy had collected his glass and returned to the greenhouse, they sat down on opposite sides of the kitchen table.

'Alice came to see me last night,' she began.

'Really? A bit late for her, wasn't it?' Jack poured coffee from the percolator and reached over for the milk jug and sugar bowl.

'She's very worried about Sally. The girl has got herself into a terrible state over Beverly's death.'

Jack was silent, his expression bland.

'I know, you're longing to say I told you so.'

He held up a hand as though to protest. 'Not at all. But I did.'

Flora sipped her coffee and thought how best to proceed.

'Go on,' Jack urged. 'What did Alice want with you? I'm presuming she did want something, calling so late.'

'You know what she wanted.'

Jack sipped his coffee. 'Your help?'

Flora nodded.

'And are you likely to give it now?'

She didn't answer directly. Instead, she took a deep breath and said what she still didn't want to believe. 'Beverly was electrocuted.'

He didn't seem surprised. 'So no heart attack,' he said.

'She suffered a cardiac arrest but that was the result of electrocution rather than any problems with her heart. So... it was either a dreadful fault in the electrics or...'

'Deliberate,' he finished for her. 'A murder.'

'And reading between the lines, I imagine fear of murder is what's lurking deep in Sally's mind. If Beverly's death is proved to be an accident, it's certainly tragic, but after a few weeks of interest the subject will die. Not in Abbeymead, of course, but in the wider world which is who Sally is concerned about. If the equipment has been deliberately tampered with, though, it becomes a big problem for the hotel.'

'It's the All's Well all over again.'

'It seems so. Although, personally, I think she'll still get bookings. Some people are plain gruesome.'

'But Sally doesn't see it that way?'

'No, and the bank are on her tail, threatening that if she doesn't make the repayments she's agreed, she'll be in trouble. There's no help from her so-called partner either. Dominic is holed up in his bedroom – he's divorced himself from the whole dreadful mess – and Alan Ridley has been seconded to Suffolk on another case, leaving an inexperienced sergeant with very few staff to carry on any investigation he thinks necessary.'

Jack gave a quiet whistle. 'No wonder you're here.'

'What do you think?'

'What I thought two days ago. We have to help. If we don't, it sounds as though Sally could go mad before she goes bankrupt.'

Flora leaned back in her chair and took up her cup again. 'So where do we begin?'

'At the Priory, I should think. That seems the most obvious. It's more *when* we begin. I can park the writing for a day but the shop is a different matter.'

'How about Wednesday – half-day closing?'

'That should work.' He reached for the percolator and held it aloft. 'Tell me, what do you think of the coffee?'

'Delicious,' she said, offering her cup for a refill. 'You must ask Arthur to send another packet.'

9

It was several days before Flora was free to make good her promise to Alice. She was disappointed at the delay but, after a difficult year financially, she couldn't afford to shut on a whim. On Wednesday, as soon as the station clock struck one, she locked the All's Well's door and turned the notice to Closed. When Jack knocked minutes later, she was finishing a hasty lunchtime sandwich.

'I'm ready – well, almost,' she said, opening the door to him and brushing her skirt free of crumbs.

'Here's hoping there aren't too many people around when we get to the Priory.' He steadied the door notice he'd sent swinging. 'I've left the car at home. I thought it best we walk – the Austin might be too conspicuous.'

Flora retrieved her handbag from the kitchenette. 'Are you thinking that if there *is* a villain, they'll be watching?' she asked, unhooking her jacket from the peg.

'Possibly, but more likely it will be the police we need to evade. They could be poking around the estate – I don't imagine the stage has been dismantled yet and they might still be working on it.'

'According to Alice, the stage is still there, cordoned off apparently, though the marquee has gone. But you're right. It's definitely the place to start.'

'It's the only place if it was faulty equipment that did for the poor girl.'

'There's a question over whether it was faulty or not.' Flora darted back into the kitchenette to check she'd switched off the gas. 'You would think,' she said from behind the door, 'that the police would get their team of experts on it straight away. Then they'd know whether or not Beverly's death was an accident.'

'They've probably been waiting for the post-mortem, hoping it was natural causes after all.'

'In other words, they've let it slide,' Flora accused, 'though I can see why, if they're short-staffed and the inspector is busy elsewhere.'

'So... it looks as if it's up to us.' Jack's expression was wry. 'It should be fun.'

The day was sunless, the sky overcast, a light grey blanket pressing down on them, but it was still mild, exceptionally so for late September. Walking along the high street towards Fern Hill, Flora noticed how lightly dressed most people were. The longer this gentle weather continued, the better – the villagers had suffered one of the worst winters on record last year and were already dreading the weeks of snow and ice ahead.

She glanced across at the Nook as they passed and saw it was doing a brisk lunchtime trade. 'It's lucky for Kate that she has Alice's help,' she remarked.

'Though frustrating for Alice that she's still not in charge of the Priory kitchen.'

Flora gave a quiet sigh. 'I know. She's been longing to work in the hotel again, and so excited about the equipment Sally has installed!'

'I saw some of it on opening day. It looked terrifying.'

'But not to Alice.'

'Not to Alice,' he agreed. 'She deserves a break. Her niece, too. Let's hope we can do something to help them.'

The long pull up Fern Hill put a temporary stop to their conversation and they were still breathing heavily as they approached the Priory's tall gates. The sound of a distant mowing machine floated towards them. At least the gardeners were at work and, once the inspector gave the word, Flora was hopeful the hotel could burst into life again.

'We'll have to hope the grass cutting keeps the gardeners busy.' Jack nodded in the direction of the humming. 'It could be difficult to explain why we're here.'

Hydrangeas on either side of the gravelled drive were still in bloom, their flowers tinged a rusty pink, forming a guard of honour on their walk to the house. The Priory, as they rounded the final bend, stood serene and tranquil. Even in the muted light, its stonework glowed. Flora wondered whether she should go in search of Sally, tell her they were here to look for any clues that might help solve the mystery, but then decided it might raise the girl's hopes unnecessarily. If they found nothing, it was better that Sally didn't know they had tried.

Walking around the side of the house to the open space beyond, it was immediately clear where the marquee had once stood – a huge rectangle of bleached grass marked the spot. To the right of it, the stage looked unchanged from the afternoon they had witnessed Beverly's dreadful death. The tumbled microphone remained on the floor, its steel column, surrounded by a cluster of snaking cables, sprawled lengthwise across the wooden boards.

Ignoring the mic, Jack said, 'We should look at the amplifier first. It's what's given the police pause. You'll have to duck, though.' He held up the rope cordoning the area. 'We best not disturb anything.'

It was easy enough to do and they soon located the equipment that had powered the band's electrics, tucked to one side of the stage behind a hinged door at its base.

'Padlocked,' he said, disgusted. 'Though it's something we should have expected. The police won't want any random passer-by taking a look.'

'Can't we break the lock open?'

'What do you suggest? Borrow a hammer from the gardeners?'

She looked at him to see if he was serious. It had been her first thought.

Jack shook his head at her. 'We need to be subtle, Flora. We don't want the police alerted to our interest. Ridley might be happy for us to muck in, but in this case we're dealing with a new sergeant, and he definitely won't want us stepping on his toes. And, if there is anything untoward going on, we don't want to forewarn the guilty person either. Hammering a padlock open might not be the greatest idea.'

'OK, clever one. What is a great idea?'

Jack stood for some minutes looking down at the ground, seemingly deep in thought.

'Let's assume for the time being that it was murder – how would the killer ensure that it was Beverly who was attacked and that she definitely died?'

'Search me. I haven't the foggiest clue about electrics. What about you?'

'Only a little from army days. She would have to be pummelled by an enormous electrical charge, and the only way that could happen is through the microphone.' He waved his hand at the abandoned mic, lying unplugged and innocent.

'She grabbed it to begin singing,' he went on, 'and that's when it happened. The current flew through the microphone into her body and caused her to spasm. Then the muscles in her hand probably contracted and made her grip the mic even harder.'

He began to pace along the front of the stage and then back again. 'If the amplifier had been tampered with and the circuit adjusted, it would mean prolonged exposure to a dangerous level of current. Add in a heart condition, even a mild one, and you have certain death.'

Flora shuddered. 'What a fearful way to die. So go on then, explain to me how the killer ensured it happened to her and not any of the other band members.'

'The guitars are acoustic – they wouldn't be directly connected to the supply. The mic is the only piece of equipment that would, which means that police suspicions over the amplifier being tampered with are probably correct.'

'So the murderer breaks into the amplifier and flicks a switch?'

Jack shook his head. 'No switch. That wouldn't be a safe set-up. A switch could be triggered by accident. What it would need is two separate wires to be connected – one coming into the amplifier from the Priory, the main electrical source, and the other exporting power to the microphone at a much lower level.'

'So how did the wires get mixed up? Presumably that's what happened.'

'There'd have to be another cable. One that connected the two wires, so that the mic received the highest level of current.'

'And this other cable...'

'Could still be here?' He glanced at the wide expanse of grass surrounding them. 'Let's think back to that day. Our villain would only have a small window of opportunity to creep to the side of the stage, open up the amplifier and connect a new cable. He or she wouldn't dare do it much before the performance or the wrong person might have died. It would have to be done at the last moment, just before the band arrived on stage. And the killer would have to pray it was Beverly who took hold of the mic and not one of the others. That's not such a long shot, though. She was the singer, after all.'

'We can't discount the possibility that one of them was the target and not Beverly. Tommy May, for instance, and he just got lucky.'

'True, but my money's still on Beverly.'

Flora folded her arms. 'OK. Our murderer sets up this extra cable just before the band leaps on stage. Beverly dies as he or she planned. Then what?'

'They'd have to dispose of the evidence,' Jack said with certainty. 'Or it would be spotted. The police would have found the rogue cable as soon as they took the back off the amplifier.'

'How much time would this person have had?'

'Very little. The killer has to have been someone close to the action, someone who was on the stage or standing close to it. Not anyone in the audience – they were all seated.'

'If it was one of the band, they couldn't have hidden a thing in those costumes, no matter how small.' Flora couldn't prevent a giggle.

'It would be difficult to hide in any costume. There was a kerfuffle getting Beverly off the stage and up to the house, and maybe in the general mayhem that was when the murderer got rid of the cable. It would have to be quick, but it's possible.'

Flora's ponytail had loosened and, impatiently, she pushed back a long strand of reddish-brown hair. 'What was everyone doing at that moment? Do you remember, Jack? The afternoon has become a complete blur to me.'

'Shane disconnected the mic,' he said slowly, 'as soon as I yelled. When Dominic came out of his trance, he raced to the house to get a bedroom organised. I ran to the car to drive to the village and fetch the doctor. Tommy and Jarvis carried the girl into the house.'

'Max Martell?'

'He was close behind the group, following them into the Priory. Kate and Alice stayed beside you, but where was Sally?'

'I don't know. I don't think I saw her.'

'Whoever rigged the microphone had virtually no time to get rid of the evidence, that's clear. It would have had to be a hasty dump, a knee-jerk reaction almost. Now what would I do in that situation?'

'Throw it away?'

'Yes, throw it away. Into the meadow over there?'

'Don't tell me we'll need to search through knee-deep grass,' she said dolefully.

'It looks very much like it, but think how chuffed you'll be if we find something.'

It took a good half hour of wading through long and uncomfortably damp grass for them to find anything, and then it was nothing more interesting than a spanner.

'A spanner could be evidence, I suppose,' Flora muttered disappointedly. 'Here, take my handkerchief in case there are fingerprints.'

Jack tucked the offending spanner into his coat pocket. 'There'll be fingerprints, but probably only the gardeners'. Let's keep going.'

Reluctantly, Flora began the search again, her eyes fixed on the ground, walking back and forth across what was left of the area Jack had suggested they cover. After another fruitless half hour, she was ready to give up. Jack had wandered some distance away into a swathe of grass which, judging by its length, had never seen a mower since the day it was first laid.

'Nothing here,' he called to her, straightening up. 'And my trouser legs are soaking.'

'We'll call it a day, shall we, and go up to the house? I've just remembered I've still a missing ring to find.'

'Fine by me. I'll be glad—' he started to say, but Flora never heard why he'd be glad because he had bent down and scooped an object into his hand. Holding it high between two fingers, he sang out, 'Just look what I've got!'

She walked towards him, stopping at the point where the

grass ran entirely wild, and squinted at his raised hand. 'It looks like a piece of cable.'

'It is a piece of cable,' he said triumphantly. 'And not just cable, but two plastic clips, one at either end. That's how it was done, Flora.'

He bounded forward, his face alight with discovery. 'See.' He was at her side now, pushing the cable towards her. 'One clip went on the mains outlet and the other on the microphone lead.'

When Flora looked uncertain, he said, 'It's as I said. This small piece of cable redirected the mains current into the mic which got the full charge. No wonder it was "goodbye, Beverly".'

'That's another huge chance the killer took. Not properly hiding what's turned out to be the murder weapon.'

Jack slipped the cable into a second pocket. 'Throwing it into long grass that never gets cut was as good a solution as any, I guess.'

'It still risked the police finding it.' It seemed to Flora too much of a dangerous gamble. 'Would the murderer really have taken that risk?'

'It was probably his or her only chance. And if you think about it, would the police search that area? Would they even be looking for a cable? They've called in experts and when these chaps examine the amplifier, they'll agree with the police, I'm sure, that it's been meddled with – the back taken off and possibly replaced awkwardly – but then scratch their heads over what might have happened. There'll be nothing to show what was done. The normal cables will be where they should be, and perfectly safe. They're unlikely to don gumboots and scour the estate. They'll put it down to an unexplained accident.'

'But why hasn't the murderer returned to look for this piece of cable? It's incriminating evidence. There's been time –

Beverly died nearly two weeks ago.' Flora still felt doubtful that someone would actually take such a huge risk.

'They might well have done. We can't know. But look where I found it.' He pointed back to the wide arc of long, wet vegetation in which he'd been walking. 'The grass is way beyond my knees and it was pure luck I saw it. The killer will have thrown it away in a panic without any clear idea of where it fell. Since then, the place has been swarming with police and they'll have had little opportunity to search – it's quite likely they're still looking.'

Flora slipped her arm in his. 'So what now?'

He looked down at her and smiled. 'What else? We take it to the police. But first we should tell Sally what we've found. She deserves to know.'

10

They were making their way to the rear door of the Priory, hoping to find Sally, when Jack came to a sudden stop, a detaining hand on Flora's arm.

'Listen!' he said. Somewhere to the right of them a noisy argument had broken out. Her eyes widened at the sound.

'Shall we?'

He nodded agreement and, ignoring the large oak door of the Priory, rounded the corner of the house with Flora close behind. To one side of them, a stone archway led to a courtyard with low-level buildings lining three sides of its cobbled square. These were the Priory's former stables, although it was many years since they'd housed any horses.

The hotel's previous owner had converted what had become ramshackle buildings into luxury accommodation, hoping to add more guest rooms to the Priory's tally, but until Dominic offered the stables to Tutti Frutti, none of them had ever been used. The plan, Sally told them, had been for the band to have a short holiday prior to their appearance at the Priory's big reopening, spreading themselves across the available bedrooms and using the large central space as a communal lounge and practice venue. Today, the room's windows had been thrown wide open and loud voices filled the air.

Jack slid quietly into the courtyard, taking shelter behind a thickly leaved magnolia and pulling Flora in beside him. From here, they would be able to see and hear the group without being noticed.

'Max Martell is there, too,' Flora whispered in his ear.

Jack could see him clearly. Martell was in the centre of the room, looking as suave as ever – the continued mild weather had not persuaded him to relax his dress code: silk tie, dazzling white shirt and a beautifully cut light grey suit. Towering over his slender figure was Tommy May. Jack hadn't realised before just how large a man the lead guitarist was. Tommy, in patched jeans, a vest-like top and a chin that sported several days' stubble, could not have provided a greater contrast to his agent.

'Tommy May looks mean and sweaty.' Flora had bunched herself by his side.

'Sssh!' he counselled. 'They mustn't know we're here. Can you read his tattoo?'

Flora gave an irritated pff but peered ahead. 'Something about his mother? I'm too short to see properly. Don't you have your tortoiseshells with you?'

She meant his reading glasses, an object of joy for Flora. Almost as much joy as when she'd discovered his true name was Jolyon. The fact that his glasses were black-framed and had been nowhere near a tortoise didn't spoil the fun.

'Look, Tommy,' Martell was saying, laying a placatory hand on the younger man's arm. 'You need to calm down. We all do. Whatever Beverly did or didn't do, the girl is no longer with us. We have to plan for the future – but a different one.'

'And what future were the two of you planning?' Tommy leered. 'Or was the keenness all on her side? Bev's insatiable appetite, eh?'

Martell stared at him. 'I have no idea what you're talking

about.' His voice had acquired a sharper edge. 'Please, do
enlighten me.'

'I'll do more than enlighten you,' he threatened, pushing up
against the smaller man. 'I know what I saw and it wasn't a
pretty sight. On the landing, your hand up her jumper.'

Jack felt Flora recoil against him.

'You're badly mistaken, Tommy,' Max said smoothly,
'though your upset is perfectly understandable. Beverly's death
has knocked you sideways. Why wouldn't it? You were
her... friend... for years and I know how much she meant to you.'

'She meant nothing to me.' Tommy May spat out the words.
'Beverly Russo was the perfect tart who'd go with anyone if it
meant a bigger billing.'

'What, even Max?' That was Jarvis. He'd been leaning
against the back wall, hardly visible in deep shadow but now, as
he walked forward, Jack saw an unpleasant grin on his face.
'You'd have to be desperate.'

Martell held up his hands, as though to ward off an attack,
and cleared his throat. 'Beverly made advances to me, I don't
deny, but that was all. And it's hardly my fault if the lady
favoured a sophisticated man. Really, we shouldn't be talking of
the dead in this fashion.'

'What a sanctimonious creep you are, Martell.' Jarvis
lurched forward again, a half-full bottle of whisky held high in
the air.

'Sober up, J. Max is right.' Shane, wrapped in a droopy
cardigan, had joined the trio in the centre of the room. 'We
gotta move on. We're short of a singer and we've at least
another four dates to play. We gotta decide how we'll
manage it.'

Max looked grateful for his intervention. 'I've been making
calls, letting people know the band needs a singer. We may be
lucky but, at such short notice, I suspect we'll need to go ahead
without one. Tommy, you and Shane will have to split the

vocals. Not ideal, but you've done it before and in the circumstances, it's the best we can do.'

'Not going to happen.' Tommy turned and walked away, slouching down into the brocade-covered sofa. 'I'm not singing. Neither is Shane. Get another Beverly or we quit. Only this time, sign one that's not desperate to suck us dry.'

Max tightened his lips. 'Beverly was committed to Tutti Frutti,' he said repressively.

'You gotta be joking! We were never enough for her, right from the start. It was always more, more, and more.'

'She was a tart, that's for sure.' It was Shane again. 'I hated the way she treated you, Tom, hated the way she lorded it over all of us. Never mind that I was the singer before she appeared, never mind that I wrote the band's bestselling song. But she's gone now and we're still a band without her. We gotta do what we can for the next few weeks.'

'He's evidently the peacemaker,' Jack murmured. 'But what a crew!'

'Shane has the right idea,' Martell was quick to say. 'Once we get the plods off our backs – any day now – we'll be on our way. The group needs to be ready, which means practice, and plenty of it. Jarvis, I'm looking at you. No more drinking and—'

'We're not gonna leave,' Tommy interrupted him. 'Let's get that straight. Bev died from electrocution – you've just recited the post-mortem. Electrocution doesn't just happen. Someone tampered with the mic and the police won't let us go until they find out who did. And guess who they're going to land on first? Her ex-lover – naturally – who happened to have a row with her just an hour before she snuffed it.'

Max sat down, taking care to wipe the brocaded chair with his linen handkerchief. 'You're wrong, Tommy. The fault with the mic doesn't have to have been deliberate. Beverly's death was almost certainly an accident, in which case the police will have no reason to detain us. The firm who built the stage and set up the electrical system – it's them the police need to investigate. They're the ones responsible. I'll be having words with Dominic. He booked them and I'll want to know why.'

'What good will that do?' Jarvis had slumped down beside Tommy. 'Useless kinda bloke, anyway,' he jeered.

'I'd agree with him there,' Flora muttered.

'Quiet,' Jack warned. 'And keep still. We're in shadow but if you keep bobbing around they'll spot you. I want to hear the end of this conversation.'

'Dominic's done all right by us,' Tommy said defensively. 'He's given us the run of this place for weeks, hasn't he?'

'Yeah, so that we'd play for free.'

'Not free, Jarvis,' Max countered. 'My invoice is on his desk and it mentions a very respectable fee. Though,' he added acidly, 'you've probably drunk most of it already.'

'I dunno why we ever came,' Jarvis grumbled, his words slurring slightly. 'Why we're cooped up here. We should be on the road right now.'

When Max answered, there was a sneer in his voice. 'You can blame Tommy for that. We came because he wanted to repay a favour.'

Tommy leapt up from the sofa so swiftly that Flora bounced back, treading heavily on Jack's toes. He had to clamp his lips together to stop himself from calling out.

'You wouldn't know what repaying a favour is, would you?' Tommy clutched the agent by the lapels and dragged him close against his chest. 'Dom was good to us when no one else was interested. The bloke let us play sessions in his club when we sounded half of what we are today. He believed in Tutti Frutti. And as for you, you giant scumbag, if you think you're going to carry on as our agent after this...'

Jack saw the surprise on his companions' faces.

'Don't be too hasty, Tommy,' Shane warned.

'No, don't be too hasty.' Max's lips made a thin line. 'Tutti

Frutti may be good, but not that good. You'd find it difficult to get an agent half as interested in you as I am.'

Jarvis staggered up from the sofa, his head shaking from side to side, and picked up a couple of drumsticks. He began beating out a noisy tattoo on the polished table, putting an end to any further talk.

Clutching hold of Flora's arm, Jack pulled her back through the stone arch and headed for the driveway. It wasn't until they were a safe distance from the Priory that he spoke.

'There are enough snakes in that particular basket to keep us busy for weeks,' he muttered.

'They're certainly a mixed bunch. It's clear that Jarvis has a problem with drink and I never told you, but two of them – Tommy and Shane – were in trouble as youngsters.'

'How...?' he demanded.

'Martell told me when I saw him one lunchtime at Katie's Nook.'

Jack felt annoyed and, if he was honest, hurt. 'You didn't think to tell me. Why not? We're supposed to be partners.'

Flora shrugged awkwardly. 'He spoke to me when I was still unsure about getting involved. At the time, I wanted to keep the whole horrible business at a distance.'

'And now?'

'Not any longer. I'm with you. Completely!'

He felt relieved. For a moment, he'd wondered what else Flora might be keeping from him. 'Listening to that clash of egos just now,' he mused, 'makes me think it would be a good idea to dig a little – maybe start with our friends, Tommy and Shane.'

'We still have the cable as evidence,' she reminded him, 'though finding out more on the band might be useful.'

'The only problem is *how*. I know nothing about these men.'

'Their home town is Portsmouth, so Martell said.'

'Portsmouth is a big city. It will be difficult to find anyone who knew them or their families.'

'Maybe not as difficult as you think. There can't be too many Meyerhoffs. That's Tommy's real name,' she said, as they came in sight of the Priory's decorative gates. 'His father was German.'

'Hey, that could be helpful. How about I drive down to Portsmouth at the end of the week? The Austin could do with a longer run.'

'What about petrol? Will you have enough?'

Fuel had been in short supply since the commandeering of the Suez Canal several months previously, and ominous mutters had already surfaced that rationing would shortly be reintroduced.

'I struck lucky and managed to fill the tank yesterday. It will easily get me to Portsmouth and back.' He smiled slightly. 'I might try to find Tommy's mother. She of the glorious tattoo.'

'If you can... any idea how you'll track her down?'

'Call at a police station, perhaps. Ask if they have a list of German internees from the war. If Meyerhoff was living with Tommy's mother when war broke out, he would have been interned and there should be an address for him. Before I go, though, I'll pass the cable and spanner onto the police and hope the sergeant in charge shows some interest in our finds.'

'You could telephone Alan Ridley as well. Tell him what's been happening.'

'No, I couldn't,' Jack said firmly. He was always circumspect when it came to involving the inspector. As a writer of crime, he'd no wish to pester a man he'd found to be a useful contact.

'And Sally?'

'I'll leave you to find the right time to talk to her. You'll do it so well!'

11

The following day, Flora was too busy to think much more of Jack's plan. Two separate deliveries from the warehouse arrived early, filling what little empty space the shop possessed and needing to be unpacked as soon as possible. Scissoring open the first box, she breathed in the bookishness of its contents. This was a moment she always savoured: the touch of smooth covers, the smell of print, the solidity of pages beneath her hand.

By the time she had collapsed both boxes, she had upwards of forty brand new books to display and, despite the lack of space, decided to add an extra showcase with *Peyton Place* in prime position. The novel might shock the more conservative villagers, but it would most definitely sell. It proved a shrewd calculation. The whisper that new stock had arrived at the All's Well spread through Abbeymead in a matter of minutes and the afternoon was punctuated by the clang of the doorbell. When Flora cashed up that evening, there was a satisfying sum in the till.

Jack had said he intended to go to Portsmouth before the weekend and, since Flora had no wish to be left behind, she decided to speak to Sally as soon as she could. Closing the All's

Well a little earlier the next day – yesterday's rush had abated and Friday afternoon was usually a quiet time – she wheeled Betty from her shelter in the yard and cycled along the high street and up the long climb of Fern Hill. At the top and just after the road bent right, she reached the Priory gates only slightly out of breath. The weather had definitely cooled. Riding Betty made her visit more conspicuous, she supposed – that was Jack's word – but today it seemed unimportant. She wasn't looking for clues this time. She already had one.

From the gates, she wheeled her bicycle along the driveway. It was an old habit, her aunt's voice still echoing in her ear. *You don't ride in the Priory grounds, Flora. It's disrespectful.* She was rounding the second bend of the drive when she had quickly to pull to one side. The figure of a woman, head bent, eyes fixed on the ground, was racing towards her.

'Miss Unwin?' she asked, as the girl came abreast.

Maggie Unwin jerked her head upwards and looked wildly at Flora.

'Good afternoon, Miss Steele.' She was struggling to speak. 'I'm sorry, but I can't stop right now. I have to get back to the surgery.'

In a blink, the girl was gone, and Flora left in something of a daze. Why had Maggie been scurrying down the drive in that frantic fashion? And why was she visiting the Priory in the first place? Was someone sick? But Maggie was the receptionist at the surgery, not the doctor. Hopefully Sally, when she found her, would know what was going on.

Sally's office was a small room off the foyer. It was the office Polly Dakers had once occupied. Occupied rather than worked in. Flora smiled to herself, remembering the pile of unpaid invoices and the desk drawers filled with dead make-up and packets of chewing gum.

The magnificent wood-panelled room, once the centre of aristocratic family life, glowed bright in the afternoon sun, a huge improvement from the last time Flora had visited – for a wake she'd had no wish to attend. The high gloss of its beautiful oak floor once more dazzled, the valuable Chinese vases brought to England as trophies by past Templetons had been lovingly washed, and the portraits of those very Templetons looked down on the scene – this time, if not with pleasure, at least with resignation.

Sally wasn't in her office and Flora walked along the corridor to the library, thinking her friend might have retreated to this peaceful space to work. Its double doors were open and the series of tall, arched windows at the far end flooded the room with light: white plaster walls, shelves of polished mahogany, and the lustrous green and cream patterned ceiling that Flora loved. There was no sign of Sally, though, and Flora left the room to rest in the gentle sunlight.

She would have liked to scurry past the small office that had once been part of the library – it held such bad memories for her – but steeled herself to peer through the doorway. It looked to be Dominic's working space and no longer quite as sparse as the room she'd walked into a year ago. A wide oak desk now commanded the space and it was a desk she remembered. It had been Lord Edward's favourite and, as a young child, she'd been fascinated by it.

A double row of small drawers rose from the desk top and it had been Lord Edward's habit to keep a variety of treats in them. Every time she visited, she would have to guess in which small drawer she'd find her present. For some reason, she almost always chose the middle drawer on the top row and almost always she was wrong. Not that it mattered. Lord Edward always allowed her to guess again.

Feeling nostalgic, she walked over to the desk and opened the self-same drawer, expecting it to be empty – she couldn't imagine Dominic would ever make use of such a tiny space. She was wrong. As wrong now as she had been as a child. In the centre of the drawer lay a ruby ring. Beverly's ring. The ring the girl had been wearing when she died, and hadn't been wearing when Flora had watched over her body in a bedroom on the floor above.

She heard herself give a loud gasp, a flush of adrenaline tingling through her body. When she reached out to touch, her fingers were trembling. What could Dominic be doing with the ring? Had he taken it from the dead woman's finger? The thought made her shudder and she snatched back her hand as though burnt by flames.

She was closing the drawer, wanting to shut away the ring's red sparkle, when Dominic's voice sounded from behind her. 'What exactly are you doing here, Flora?' He came to stand so close that she could feel his breath on her neck.

When she turned to answer, she found herself barricaded against the desk. She held out the flat of her hand, encouraging him to move back, but he stayed exactly where he was.

'You haven't answered my question,' he said, his face stone-like. 'This is a private room. A private bureau. I think you have some explaining to do.'

'I was simply saying hello to an old friend.' She gestured towards the desk. 'It holds happy memories for me. And I think if we're justifying ourselves, you have some explaining to do, too.'

This time her hands made contact with his chest, pushing him out of her way and allowing herself to walk free.

'Don't go!' His voice was urgent.

She stopped at the door. 'I should stay for you to threaten me again?'

'I didn't threaten.' He pulled roughly at his hair and Flora became conscious of how unlike his usual self he looked. As so often, he was dressed in a dark suit but his trousers were badly creased and there was a visible stain on his jacket.

'I'm sorry if it seemed that way,' he went on. 'I'd no intention of upsetting you. It was just... you caught me by surprise.'

'I was caught by surprise as well. Finding Beverly's ring. Why do you have it?' she asked boldly.

'I didn't steal it, if that's what you think.'

'I don't know what to think, Dominic. Perhaps you can tell me.'

'I didn't steal it,' he repeated. He looked down at a pair of unpolished shoes. 'The ring belongs to me.'

Flora's brows rose sharply. 'Yours? You mean you gave it to Beverly?'

'It's what she wanted. What she kept banging on about.'

She frowned, trying to make sense of his words. 'Are you saying you were engaged to her?'

'I was pushed into it,' he said aggressively. 'It wasn't something I wanted.'

Flora's silence while she tried to absorb this unexpected turn of events prompted him into further denial. 'She nagged and nagged me until I agreed. My life became unbearable. Jarvis called her a leech and he was right.'

'Why would she want to marry you – I presume that's what she planned – if you were so unwilling?'

'I wasn't unwilling at first,' he confessed. 'When I first saw her singing at my club, I thought I'd met the girl of my dreams. Some dreams!' He sounded sour. 'She was glamorous, charismatic. I admired the way she'd left a difficult background behind and made a better life for herself.'

'You fell in love with her?'

He pulled at his hair again. 'It wasn't love,' he said fiercely. 'More like infatuation. She turned out not to be the person I thought she was. Then, when she got her hooks into me, she wouldn't let go. Shane said she would eventually, once she found a better bet. It was the way she operated, he said. Give her time.'

'But Beverly wasn't given time,' Flora observed trenchantly. There was a long silence before she asked, 'Did Sally know of your engagement?'

Sally was in love with this wretched man and Flora wondered how her friend would take yet another blow.

'She didn't. She mustn't,' he said desperately. 'I really like Sally but I had to get rid—' He broke off. Sally had appeared in the doorway.

'Flora, you're here! One of the maids saw you in the foyer and told me you'd come. I wondered where you'd got to.'

'You've found me now!' Flora said brightly, casting a severe glance at Dominic.

He was shaking his head very slightly, his eyes boring into her, willing her, she knew, to keep her counsel. And she would – for the moment.

But this altered things, didn't it? Dominic had been engaged to Beverly but desperate to break it off. He'd met Sally and his preference was obvious. It was certainly a motive for murder. And Tommy May – he'd mentioned Dominic as Beverly's latest craze, but had he known of an actual engagement? And, if he had, had he felt sufficient jealousy to kill his one-time lover? He'd seemed indifferent to her love affairs, even ready to defend Dominic's claim on her, but how did Tommy really feel? His bitter words an hour before Beverly's appalling death suggested a dangerous passion that was still alive. Two motives, two men, who were either on the stage or close by when Beverly Russo was killed.

'You must come and have tea in my sitting room,' Sally told her. 'I've bagged one of the smaller rooms upstairs and made it into my retreat.'

The bedroom Sally had appropriated was on the first floor of the hotel, at the rear of the building. It enjoyed a narrow Juliet balcony with tall windows that overlooked smooth green parkland and, in the distance, a thick copse of trees, still heavy with late summer leaves. Sally had made it cosy, with two squashy chintz-covered sofas, cushions and curtains to match, and a delicate maplewood table.

As soon as one of the maids had delivered their tray of tea, Sally looked enquiringly at her. 'Dominic seemed a little odd just now. Any idea what was wrong?'

'I'm not really sure,' Flora prevaricated. 'It was probably my fault. I shouldn't have been in his office and I think it put him out rather. But something stranger than that,' she rushed on. 'I met Maggie Unwin on my way up the drive. She seemed to have every one of the Furies pursuing her.'

Sally leaned forward. 'Really? She *was* strange. She turned up here after lunch, asking to collect Beverly's medicine, of all things. When I asked her why she wanted it, she got herself in a frightful muddle. What it seemed to boil down to was that Dr Randall didn't want the medicine hanging around. Presumably because it could cause harm. It seemed pretty odd to me but she was in such a flap that I took her over to the stables to find the darn stuff. Of course, the way those musicians live, you can't find a thing. It's chaos there.'

'Did she get the medicine?'

'No. She left empty-handed. To be honest, I didn't do much of a search. I really don't want to be touching Beverly Russo's belongings.' Sally gave an extravagant shudder.

To Flora, her friend's reaction felt exaggerated. Sally had disliked Beverly, it was clear, and, equally clear, her dislike had been based on jealousy. And with good reason, as it turned out, though Sally had known nothing of the engagement. Dominic had promised to marry the singer and then spent weeks trying to squirm from his commitment. The question was, had he eventually given up persuading and resorted to more direct means?

Then there was Dr Randall. There was definitely something peculiar about him. The man appeared scared and now so did his receptionist. What were they frightened of? The *rumour* spreading its tentacles through the village hinted at Beverly's medicine being to blame for her death. But she hadn't died from poisoning and, as far as Flora knew, there'd been no mention in the post-mortem of any noxious substance being found. Why, then, all the fuss about Beverly's prescription? And it was a fuss – Flora had never heard before of any doctor demanding their medicine back. A call at the surgery seemed an important next step.

'I could look for you, if you like,' she said, emerging from her daydreaming. 'It would save you being bothered again.'

'You're very welcome. Call at the stables any time you like, though I warn you the place has become a complete tip. Anyway, did you have a reason for coming today? Not that you need one – it's lovely to chat.'

Flora felt a heaviness in her stomach at the thought of what she must tell her friend. 'There was a particular reason I came today and I'm afraid you're not going to like it. After you asked us to help, Jack and I decided to take a look at the stage. We came to the Priory a few days ago.'

'I didn't see you.' Sally wrinkled her forehead.

'We came looking for you once we'd finished, but you'd disappeared.' She decided to say nothing of the quarrel they'd witnessed at the stables. 'The stage itself turned out to be hopeless – the amplifier has been padlocked by the police and there was no way we could see if anything was amiss, so instead we made a search of the surrounding area. We did find something there.'

'You did?' Sally bounced forward. 'That's wonderful,' she said excitedly. 'If it's a vital clue and the police can follow it up, we may soon be able to reopen. Needless to say I've heard nothing from the sergeant who's supposed to be leading the investigation. But why do you say I won't like it?'

'We found a piece of cable with two clips.'

It was evident that meant nothing to Sally but, after Flora had related what she remembered of Jack's explanation, her friend was no longer excited. 'The post-mortem was right, then? Beverly was definitely electrocuted?' she asked, her voice low.

Flora nodded sympathetically.

'And deliberately?'

'That's still to be decided, but it's beginning to look like it.'

'It will be,' Sally said drearily. 'I kept hoping the pathologist had made a mistake, that someone would come and tell us it was all a misunderstanding and Beverly Russo had died from a problem with her heart.'

'I'm afraid not.'

'Electrocuted, though.' Sally chewed at her lip. 'Who on earth would do such a terrible thing?'

'At the moment, we haven't a clue. Do you have any thoughts?'

Sally looked startled, her figure stiffly upright. Her gaze slid downwards, her eyes fixed on the embroidered moccasins she wore.

'None at all,' she said.

12

It took Jack nearly two hours to cover the fifty miles to Portsmouth. Much of the journey was open road, but winding his way through the narrow streets of Arundel and Chichester proved a slow affair and he was relieved when he saw the sign-post for Portsea Island emerge from the low cloud that had begun to settle over Hampshire.

Driving towards the coast, he was struck at how battered the outskirts of the city appeared. Presumably the centre must have suffered even worse damage. Portsmouth had been bombed extensively during the war, he knew, particularly the port area, a major embarkation point for the D-Day landings. Thousands of people and houses must have been lost to the Luftwaffe and, though the wreckage had been cleared, rebuilding was not complete. Clusters of prefab houses, constructed to provide temporary accommodation, were still clearly occupied.

Jack had no idea where to begin his search. He had a vague idea that in a city this large there would be a number of police stations, but where they were situated and which of them would prove the most useful was a void. Having crossed onto Portsea

Island, he reached what appeared to be the main shopping area. London Road, with its jumble of small, individual shops – True Form, Suzanne and Carol, he noted – was a typical English high street. There were few cars, but cyclists zigzagged in and out of a crocodile of double decker buses and pavements were thronged with shoppers. Steering the Austin through the morass of traffic, Jack got his first taste of life in Portsmouth: billboards advertising a variety show at the Theatre Royal, hoardings plastered with posters for the Marilyn Monroe competition held that summer on the South Parade pier. It looked to be a lively place.

It was pure luck that impelled him to continue driving south and onto Fratton Road where he spotted his first police station, rubbing shoulders with one of Portsmouth's many public houses.

With difficulty, he unwrapped himself from the car and spent several minutes stretching cramped limbs. He hated to admit it but his legs were too long for the Austin, and he invariably ended any lengthy journey with muscles so tight he felt they might snap if he took too sudden a movement. Once he could walk easily, he crossed the road to the impressive building opposite – a fire as well as a police station – and walked through the ornamented pillared doorway. The reception area smelled of beeswax and sported a bold notice hanging from the ceiling that told him the building was home to Portsmouth City Police. Creaking across the polished floorboards, Jack presented himself at the front desk.

The sergeant in charge finished his telephone conversation and offered him a professional smile. 'Good morning, sir,' he said briskly. 'How can I be of help?'

'I'm not sure you can, officer, though I'm hoping you might.'

The sergeant waited patiently.

'I'm looking for someone with a name which I hope might ring bells,' Jack went on. 'He was a German, living in

Portsmouth during the war years.' He'd decided it would be best to ask for Tommy May's father, since the police might look askance at a request to search for a woman that he'd never met.

'An enemy alien? He'd have been interned.'

'Were they all?'

'Eventually. I daresay some of them made it back to Germany before they were rounded up.'

'Did the police keep any kind of register?' Jack crossed his fingers.

The sergeant screwed up his face in thought. 'We'd have had a list of local men, that's for sure. It must still be around somewheres. What's the name you want?' He bent down and started rooting through shelves fitted beneath the desk top.

'Meyerhoff.'

'Christian name?'

'Tomas,' he said in a moment of inspiration.

The sergeant's grunts and the sound of ledgers being heaved to the floor and back again filled the otherwise silent atmosphere. 'Here's the chappie I was looking for.' He brought up an enormous leather file from below and slammed it down on the desk.

'Now let's see. There were a fair number of 'em locally. Quite a few Ms – Madler, Marz, Mergens – Meyerhoff! There's your man. Tomas Meyerhoff. Twenty-two Frogmore Road, that's where he lived. Doesn't look like he was interned, but I doubt he's in Frogmore Road these days. Must have gone back to the Fatherland.' His tone was wry.

Jack hadn't expected it to be so easy and, taken aback, he stood for a second thinking exactly what he'd say when he got to Frogmore Road.

The sergeant was beginning to look peeved, his face still red from his efforts.

'Thank you so much for the information,' Jack was quick to

say, smoothing whatever feathers he'd ruffled. 'It's a tremendous help. Is Frogmore Road walkable from here?'

'Depends if you like walking.' The man wrinkled his nose. 'I'd say, if you've got transport, use it – no more'n ten minutes by car, and simple enough to find. Keep following the road you came on till you hit a roundabout' – he pointed through the open station door – 'take a left turn, then carry on for about two miles, I'd say, before you turn left again. That'll be Frogmore Road.'

Jack bowed himself out with more prolific thanks and walked thoughtfully back to the car. Would Frau Meyerhoff, or Mrs May, as she might call herself if Tommy's father had indeed trotted back to Germany, still be living in Frogmore Road? And if she was, what was he going to say to her?

He drove slowly, looking first for the roundabout, then for the left turn that was Frogmore Road. As his informant had promised, it was an easy find. The road had to be a fair distance from the docks, he reckoned, yet evidence of bomb damage was everywhere and relatively few attempts had been made to rebuild the crumbling terraces. He squinted through the passenger window, looking for the magic number, but none of the houses appeared to be twenty-two. Before he knew it, he'd reached the end of the road and was forced to an abrupt halt. A mock Elizabethan frontage straddled the thoroughfare, ensuring he could go no further. Fratton Park, it announced in large blue letters and, in slightly smaller print above, 1898. Blocking his path was the home of Portsmouth Football Club! Turning the car round, he drove even more slowly back towards the main road.

Halfway down on the opposite side of the road, the number he was looking for emerged half-hidden behind an enormous pyracantha, so heavily laden with berries, a fire of gold and orange, that it seemed ready to keel over.

Jack's knock on the front door was answered in less than a

minute, almost as though the woman who stared back at him from a pair of dark eyes had been primed for his arrival.

'Good afternoon.' Jack raised his fedora. 'My apologies for disturbing you. My name is Jack Carrington. I've met your son, Tommy, and I wondered if I might speak to you. I believe you might be able to help, Mrs...'

'May,' she said, still with that unsettling stare. The German name had gone, it appeared, if in fact she'd ever married Tommy's father.

'I'm looking for a Tomas Meyerhoff. I believe you knew him?' That was one way of putting it.

'Thomas? You're a bit late if you want to find him.' For the first time, the mask slipped and the slightest of smiles lit the woman's tired face. 'He's somewhere in Germany, if he's alive.'

'To be honest, Mrs May, it was you I really wanted to speak to, but I felt awkward accosting a lady I don't know.'

'Old-fashioned, are you?' she asked. 'Well, you look respectable enough. You'd better come in.'

13

Mrs May led the way through a long narrow hall to a room at the rear of the house which overlooked an oblong of garden that hadn't been touched for years. Jack's newly aroused gardener's enthusiasm made him want to seize a spade and a pair of secateurs and get to grips with it immediately.

She saw his gaze. 'I gave that up years ago. When my boy left. Never go out there myself.'

'It was Tommy I wanted to talk to you about.'

Her sharp brown eyes widened. 'Tommy? Really?' Then, as though deciding that she, too, would like to talk about her son, she asked, 'Would you like some tea?'

'That would be good. Thank you.'

'Won't be a moment.' Delving behind a cushion for a floral pinafore, seemingly abandoned when she'd heard his knock, she retied it round her waist and whisked out of the door.

While Mrs May was busy in the kitchen, Jack examined the legions of photographs that decorated every available surface in the room. Tommy's face loomed from all of them: Tommy in his Silver Cross pram, Tommy with birthday cake smeared across his face, Tommy with what looked to be his first guitar, and one of him – professionally taken, Jack judged – on stage in front of a large audience.

He put the frame down as his hostess walked through the door with a tea tray.

'I went to that.' She pointed to the photograph Jack had been holding. 'It was a grand evening. Now, sit yourself down, Mr Carrington.'

Jack obligingly sat. 'Do you go to many of Tommy's shows?' he asked politely.

'I used to. Not now he's famous, though. Too hot and crowded, too noisy – all those girls screaming. I've a problem with my heart, you see. I need to keep myself quiet.'

That was ironic. Tommy's mother and his one-time sweetheart appeared to be fellow sufferers.

'So,' Mrs May said, pouring two cups of tea and offering him a plate of Garibaldi biscuits, 'what do you want to know about Tommy?'

Jack had always known this would be the difficult bit. He cleared his throat and made a first try. 'I met your son a few weeks ago – at the Priory hotel in Abbeymead. That's a village in Sussex. His group has been staying there. The band was booked to play at the hotel's opening day.'

'Oh, yes.' Mrs May inclined her head.

Jack took a slow breath. 'The event had to be cancelled. Unfortunately, there was a fatality on the day and the police have asked that everyone involved stay where they are until they're happy with the outcome of their investigation. Your son is more or less stuck in Abbeymead, I'm afraid, and there's a danger that the band might have to cancel valuable dates.'

This seemed to him the best way forward, appealing to a mother's wish to protect her son. 'I was in the Portsmouth area,' he lied fluently, 'and thought I'd try to find you, in case there's anything you could tell me that might speed things up.'

His hostess put down her cup. 'I can't see how there would be.'

'You might be able to throw some light on the dead woman,' he hazarded. 'I believe you knew Beverly Russo.'

'Beverly? She's the one who died?' The dark brown eyes held a perturbed expression.

'Yes, I'm afraid so. She had a heart condition.' Electrocution must remain firmly unspoken.

'Trouble with her heart? Poor child. I know how difficult that can be, but I'd no idea she was unwell. Not that I've seen the girl for a long time.'

'She was Tommy's girlfriend, though? For a while, at least?'

'More than a while. They were close, you know, for nigh on three years. I thought at one time they might get married.'

'Would you have liked that?' Jack absent-mindedly took a Garibaldi.

She pursed her mouth. 'I'm not sure, to be honest. Beverly was nice enough – to me, anyway – but I did sometimes wonder if she stirred up trouble between the boys.'

'What kind of trouble?'

'Girl stuff,' she said vaguely. 'Telling tales. Pitting one lad against the other.'

He leant slightly forward, eager to hear more. 'She sounds a bit of a troublemaker. Why do you think they continued to work with her?'

'She was a good singer. Leastways, that's what the agent said. I thought she was a bit raucous myself but he insisted Beverly was one of the best vocalists he'd ever signed. All rock 'n' roll, of course. Not really my choice, I'm afraid,' she said apologetically, 'though I did like to hear Tommy play. When it was tuneful.'

'Did she stir trouble with Tommy himself?' he asked carefully, wondering how hard he could push.

'Sometimes,' she agreed. He noticed the reluctance in her voice – it was going to be difficult to extract details.

'She made Tommy jealous perhaps?' he suggested.

'I don't rightly know, and that's a fact. He never confided much. They'd fall out on a pretty regular basis, then come back together again. But after one quarrel, she disappeared altogether. I never saw her again and never knew what the problem was.'

'How did Tommy take her disappearance?' Jack was still fishing.

Mrs May looked at him for a moment, then unbent slightly to say, 'He moped a bit when he was home, but after a while he seemed to shrug it off and never mentioned her again. I didn't know she was still in the band.'

'She was, but the rest of the group don't seem to have liked her much.'

'Girl stuff again, I expect,' Mrs May said wisely. 'Such a shame when they've worked so hard to be successful.' Without asking, she poured him another cup of tea. 'What happens now, do you think – them being without a singer?'

'I imagine their agent will find a replacement, though it will take time. Tommy has been in the music business for quite a while, by the sound of it.' He hoped the ploy might reveal more of the man's chequered history.

'He played as a child,' his hostess said, her smile wide and genuine. 'I bought him a second-hand guitar from the market and he really took to it, but then he just let it go. Like they do when they get to a certain age. It was the chaplain who got him back into music.'

'The chaplain?'

She shifted in her seat, for the first time looking uncomfortable. 'Tommy wasn't a bad lad, you have to understand, but for a while he went off the rails, just a little. Sent to what they called an approved school. Like the old reformatories. Nothing much reforming about it, in my opinion. More like a prison, though they didn't say that. The chaplain there was a nice man. Tommy liked him and when he suggested the boy take up the guitar again to pass the time, he took the advice. Thank goodness he did. Look where it's landed him!'

'Your son deserves respect – for getting himself back on his feet. He was at the school with Shane, wasn't he? Shane Carter?'

She looked troubled. 'I was never sure if it was Shane that got him into trouble in the first place. Tommy always said not but...'

'He knew Shane before they met at the school?'

'Knew each other as boys. Shane didn't have a family, you see. He was an orphan, poor lad, and in the children's home over Cosham way. He hated it there, was always absconding. They'd take him back, then he'd run away again.'

'Back to here?'

She nodded, another warm smile on her face. 'The boy more or less lived with us. He and Tommy were the fastest of friends. But they were lively lads, needed a man around and there wasn't one. It was difficult after the war. I had to work two different jobs and I wasn't at home much. I blame myself but it was the way it was. I had to keep a roof over our heads. The pair of them got involved with some local gang and before you knew it they were fighting and goodness knows what else. It wasn't nice what happened, but both Tommy and Shane paid for it while others, who were just as guilty, didn't.'

She spoke quietly, her head bent and her reddened hands wrapping and unwrapping themselves in her apron. Jack judged it best to change the subject.

'Shane evidently shared his friend's love of music.'

The woman's head bobbed up and the brown eyes came alive. 'That's right. Thanks to the chaplain, they started to play together and discovered they were good! I liked the earlier songs they did – country music, I expect that's what you'd call it – but then they heard this American stuff on the wireless and changed tack. It got a whole lot louder after that.'

'So when did Jarvis Redmond join them?'

His hostess turned an expressionless face towards him.

'The band's drummer,' Jack said. 'You haven't met him?' It seemed strange that she hadn't.

Mrs May's expression cleared. 'Oh, you mean, Johnny. Of course I've met him.'

'Jarvis isn't his real name?'

'Bless you, no. He was plain John Reeves. I expect he thought Jarvis sounded better for a rock 'n' roll drummer. Tommy and Shane met him on an outing to Oxford, of all places. Their teacher arranged a day trip to celebrate the class leaving the school for good. The boys were supposed to be looking round the colleges. I think the teacher hoped they'd be an inspiration, but Tom and Shane bunked off – not really too surprising – and sneaked into a pub instead. There was a group playing there at lunchtime and it was pretty awful, Tommy told me, but the drummer was good. Afterwards, he invited Johnny to come here for a while.'

'Jarvis, Johnny, stayed with you?'

'Only for a few weeks. The three of them played really well together. Mind, I couldn't get into my sitting room for days. I think it was Shane who did the singing then. Afterwards, they went up to London to try their luck, and it worked. Everyone knows the band now. Just fancy, you can hear them on the wireless and they've got an agent. Well, you know that.'

She didn't sound too keen on the idea and Jack decided to explore a little.

'Did you get to meet Mr Martell?'

'I did. And his business partner.' Her lips compressed. 'Can't say he's exactly my idea of a man. A bit too... smooth. But

Tommy says as how he's guided them well and it's thanks to him they've got where they are.'

Jack put his cup down on the tray and stood up. 'Thank you for the tea and the chat, Mrs May. It's been very interesting. But I mustn't take up any more of your time.'

'That's OK. It's always nice to talk about Tommy.' She escorted him to the door in silence but looking slightly bemused, as though wondering if their chat had been in any way helpful to her son.

Climbing back into the Austin, Jack wondered, too – whether he'd really learned anything. He'd had it confirmed that neither Tommy nor Shane were squeaky clean, that they had a history of violence even though it was years ago. Tommy, it seemed, had tired of Beverly's mischief and cut her out of his life without a qualm. By the sound of it, Shane had had little time for her either, and the third member of the group, Jarvis, had his own problems which he may have tried to conceal with a false name. He was most definitely a drunk, but Mrs May hadn't touched on that. And Max Martell? It was clear she didn't like the agent. Not her idea of a man, she'd said.

What did that actually mean? And what, if anything, did she know to his detriment, but wasn't saying?

14

Early the next morning, Jack took a mug of tea into the garden. This was the moment of each day that he'd learned to enjoy most. His sense of ownership was strong, of pride in what he'd helped to create: seeing his vegetables start their winter sprint, spotting new growth in recently planted shrubs, delighting in the colour of summer flowers that had lasted long into the autumn.

His smile was droll. It was hard to believe he gained such pleasure from a plot of land that for years he'd been happy to ignore. His mind went back to Mrs May's garden in Portsmouth, what a sorry place it had looked. A part of him felt sad for the woman; she seemed so lonely, so touchingly proud of her son, and he wondered how often Tommy found his way back to Frogmore Road these days. But there was uneasiness, too. He felt sure the woman had known more than she'd said, judging perhaps that she was helping her son by remaining silent.

In a couple of days it would be October, yet this morning was blessed by a cloudless sky and gentle sunshine. The

Saturday market on the village green would be popular and likely to raise a goodly amount. The church hall needed new curtains, Jack had been told, and Reverend Hopkirk was hopeful of raising enough money to refurbish St Saviour's hand-embroidered hassocks as well. Jack would do his bit: a swift swoop around the stalls, a few items purchased, and he could be home within an hour or so. First, though, he had books to collect.

Before Flora's clock had struck nine, he'd pulled up outside the All's Well. Through the shop's latticed windows, he saw her tidying paperwork at her desk, the red-brown waves tied back in a business-like knot. She seemed ready for whatever the day had in store, but when she looked up at the clang of the doorbell, he saw she was distracted.

'Charlie promised to come in early and look after the shop this morning,' were her first words. She tugged at her knot of hair. 'Do you know where he is?'

'I haven't seen him, but I don't think you should worry. He's sure to be along soon.'

'But when exactly? At this moment, I'm supposed to be on the green and helping to run the bookstall.'

'I can stay and wait for him if you like.'

She shook her head. 'Thanks, but I need to speak to Charlie myself. There's another delivery due this morning and he won't know how I want it unpacked. It's best if you take the books I've picked out for the stall and tell Dilys I'll be with her as soon as I can.'

'Dilys is selling books with you?'

Flora nodded, her expression downcast. 'You can guess how that will turn out. Her customers will never hear the last of how I let her down, leaving her completely alone to cope with the hordes.' She walked round from the back of the desk. 'Did you get to Portsmouth?'

'Yesterday,' he confirmed. '*And* I found Tommy's mother.'

'Really?' It was clear that Flora hadn't expected him to. 'How clever you are, Jack.' She gave him a swift hug.

'Don't get too enthusiastic. I'm not sure I learned anything that will be useful. We already knew that Tommy and Shane were naughty boys and Mrs May – she doesn't use Meyerhoff, understandably – confirmed it. Mr Meyerhoff is not around, by the way. He hoofed it back to Germany before he could be interned. Shane, I learned, is an orphan and lived more or less permanently with the Mays, when he wasn't being dragged back to the children's home.'

'It sounds as though they both had an unsettling childhood. Did you discover how naughty they actually were?'

'She was cautious, but it seems they were in quite deep trouble. Joining a gang. Involved in neighbourhood fights.'

'Violence? That's worth knowing. Had his mother met Beverly? Did she say anything about her?'

'She knew the girl but said only that she and Tommy quarrelled a lot of the time and, after one particular row, Beverly disappeared from Mrs M's life. She'd no idea she was still with the band. She did say Beverly was a girl who enjoyed stirring up trouble, mostly, I gathered, between the boys.'

'You know, I quite liked Beverly, but she's not coming up roses, is she? Perhaps I let my judgement slip.' She reached under her desk for a canvas bag, then brought up a double stack of books she'd tied together with string.

'Here's the bag you left. In the end, it wasn't big enough to take my books as well and I've had to pack them separately.' She handed both bundles to him. 'None of these,' she tapped the double stack, 'have sold for months and I can't return them, so they might as well do some good, though I'm doubtful anyone will find *Cave Dwelling in Transylvania* too appealing.'

He grinned. 'You'd be surprised. I'm sure Dilys will welcome them with open arms!'

'Suspicion does seem to be pointing to Tommy, doesn't it?'

she said, returning to their earlier conversation. 'He has a history of violence, he quarrelled frequently with Beverly – we were witnesses to their last awful row – and she evidently took pleasure in taunting him.'

'Much the same could apply to Shane. He shared the same childhood and it seems Beverly wasn't particular who she taunted. And don't forget Jarvis. He's pretty dodgy as well. It's not even his real name, apparently.'

Flora turned round, a flicker of surprise in her face. 'A stage name? That's intriguing.'

'I thought so, too. He was originally plain old John Reeves – it might be worth trying to discover his history as well. And, of course, we mustn't forget the unnervingly sleek Max. Tommy's mother wasn't exactly complimentary about him.'

'I can't see why Martell would be a suspect,' she protested. 'He had too much to lose from Beverly's death, surely.'

'All I'm saying is that Mrs May was tight-lipped when his name was mentioned. It might simply be that she doesn't like him, but I had the feeling it went deeper and maybe we should probe a little. On the drive back to Abbeymead, I remembered she'd talked of a business partner of Martell's, yet we've never heard mention of him.'

'Would we, though? I assumed Max was a one-man band. If he ever had a partner, it must have been ages ago, when he first started out.'

'It can't be that long ago, if Mrs May knew him,' he countered, heaving Flora's stack of books into his arms. 'By the sound of it, Tutti Frutti had been playing a while before Martell got involved.'

Flora followed him to the bookshop's white-painted door. His hand was on the polished brass door knob when he turned to say, 'It might be interesting to trace this partner, whoever he was. I should have got his name, but it didn't occur to me at the time. He's bound to know something of Max's history.'

'I think that's wasting our time. Martell can't be a suspect. He's hardly likely to have killed Beverly, is he? She was his favourite singer, someone who was going to make him a lot of money. At least, he hoped so. He crowed about how wonderful she was, how she made Tutti Frutti the band they were. He more or less said they'd be nothing without her, so why on earth would he kill her?'

'Jealousy, revenge,' Jack said vaguely. 'We know she was adept at playing one band member off against another. Why not her agent as well?'

Before Flora could answer, the door crashed open and Jack was sent staggering backwards. Charlie Teague fell into the shop, his bicycle sprawled across the pavement where he'd skidded to a halt.

'Sorry, Miss Steele, I was cleanin' out the guinea pig and forgot the time.'

Flora fixed him with a minatory look. 'I don't believe a word of it, Master Teague – unless you were being paid to do the cleaning. And you'd better move that bike before someone has an accident.'

Leaving Flora to do the scolding, Jack walked through the open doorway to his car and packed the books into the boot.

'I'll see you at the stall,' he called out, climbing into the driver's seat.

When Jack pulled up at the village green five minutes later, the market was already buzzing. Most of the activity centred on the tables selling fresh vegetables, but a queue had begun to form at the cake stall that Kate Mitchell was running – Alice or Ivy must be looking after the café. He spotted the bookstall on the far side of the green, hedged in by two large trestles filled with second-hand clothes.

They were already attracting interest. An elderly customer

was cautiously fitting a tweed skirt to her figure, a younger woman was opening and shutting a large black leather handbag, and yet another had abandoned a pair of worn brogues and was slipping her feet into one after the other of the five pairs of shoes she'd lined up on the grass. Dilys, from the nearby stall, was watching them with a mournful expression.

'Good morning, Dilys,' he greeted the postmistress cheerfully.

The expanse of electric blue cardigan swathing her ample form seemed at odds with her mood. 'Where's that Flora?' she demanded. 'She promised to be here.'

'She's coming very shortly. A slight hiccup with the help this morning.'

Dilys gave a muffled snort. 'I've had to lay out the stall all by myself and these books aren't light, you know.' Since Dilys was built very much on the model of a rugby forward, Jack took the comment with a pinch of salt.

'I'm here now,' he said. 'I'll do any fetching and carrying you need until Flora arrives. I've brought some reinforcements, too.'

He dropped the bag of books he'd brought from Overlay House onto the grass and walked back to the car for Flora's offering. When he returned, he found Dilys turning over the volumes he'd donated.

'These are good,' she said, sounding surprised. 'I reckon they'll sell.'

As if to prove her right, Flora's bloodthirsty pensioner, Elsie, bustled up to the stall at that moment. Slightly out of breath, she swooped immediately on a book that detailed the most common poisons.

'This yours?' she asked Jack.

'It is.'

'Did you use what's in here?' She tapped the book sharply on its cover. 'In one of your crime novels?'

'I did. *A Tryst with Belladonna*, if I remember rightly.'

Elsie's eyes popped. 'I'll take it, as long as it's no more than a few pence.'

'What's it worth, Mr C?' Dilys asked.

He gave a small shrug. 'Whatever the lady judges.'

Elsie beamed at him. 'Spoken like a gent.' She tipped a few coins into Dilys's open hand and tucked the book deep into her wicker basket. 'I've seen a nice little blouse next door.' She nodded to the stall alongside. 'I reckon it'll suit me fine.' She didn't wait to hear the postmistress snort.

Despite Dilys's fears of being overwhelmed, the bookstall was one of the quietest in the market, and to amuse himself Jack began to leaf through the books that had been donated, interested in what his fellow villagers read and, at the same time, looking out for anything he could take home himself. There was an unusually large pile of travel guides – Abbeymead seeming keen to visit faraway places even if only between the pages – a host of romance novels which he would expect, and a fair number of craft manuals.

'I'll have that one,' Dilys said, whisking a knitting guide from under his nose. 'Probably won't tell me anything I don't know already, but I'm always willing to learn.'

Still startled by flashes of electric blue, Jack hoped the knitting manual might have some hints on colour and wished Flora would turn up. What could she be doing with Charlie all this time? Trade had become a great deal brisker in the last half hour and he wasn't the quickest at wrapping books and taking money. Openly critical, Dilys heaved a sigh every time she sold two books to his one.

'Can I see that one?' a gentle voice asked. Miss Dunmore, the vicar's housekeeper, pointed to a volume at the back of the table. It had a picture of Jesus on the cover which seemed appropriate.

'It looks perfect for Sunday school,' she said, smiling.

He leant across for the book and was handing it to her when he saw the volume that had lain partly beneath. *A Beginner's Guide to Electrical Circuitry.* He stared at it until Dilys whisked Jesus out of his hand and made a big play of wrapping the book herself and taking Miss Dunmore's money.

The housekeeper tucked the book into her bag and looked happily around the green. 'The village is such a wonderful support,' she said, still smiling. 'Vicar will be so pleased with today. Such a shame he can't be here. His lungs, you know.' She patted her meagre chest as emphasis. 'And he works far too hard, poor man. Still,' she brightened, 'he's decided to look for help – a new curate – and that should make all the difference.'

Dilys and Jack nodded in unison. A new curate was obviously a very good thing. But when the housekeeper had trotted away to a neighbouring stall, Jack returned to the volume that had caught his eye and held it up for Dilys to see.

'I can't believe a book on electrical circuitry will sell, even a beginners' guide.'

'You never know.' Dilys looked bored. 'One of those chaps could buy it.' She waved a hand at the assorted farmers in their weekend best wandering between the stalls. 'There'll be times when they need help in mending stuff. Anyways, we should be grateful for every book. The more we have, the more money we'll take.'

There was a prize for whichever stall did best, Jack had learned, and it was clear that Dilys was gunning for it.

'Still, I'd have thought electrical repairs are best left to an expert,' he remarked mildly.

'Not if you don't have the money.'

'Who donated it, I wonder.'

'How would I know?' Dilys began belligerently, but then a flicker of recognition passed across her face. 'It was Miss Jenner, one of the books she brought down from the Priory. Though what Lord Edward ever wanted with electricals, I dunno.'

For a moment, Jack was stunned. 'It came from the Priory library?'

'Mebbe, mebbe not.' She chewed at her cheek. 'I dunno where Miss Jenner got it from, but it was good of her to find any books with all she's got goin' on at the moment.'

'Sally Jenner donated this?' He had to double-check.

Dilys frowned at him. 'What's wrong with that? Said she didn't need it any longer.'

He was digesting this surprising piece of information when Flora arrived in front of the stall.

'About time, too,' Dilys muttered.

'I'm so sorry, but I'm here now. Why don't you go over to the tea stand and treat yourself to a cup and an iced fancy?'

Slightly mollified, the postmistress buttoned the dazzling cardigan to the neck and picked up her handbag. 'I'll be back in five,' she promised.

'Make that twenty.' Flora sounded quietly amused. 'What's the matter, Jack? You look as if you've swallowed something very nasty.'

He handed her the guide he'd been nursing. 'This was donated and it's made me wonder why.'

She took the book and turned it over, reading the description on the back, then turned it again to read the title once more: *A Beginner's Guide to Electrical Circuitry*. Her hazel eyes held a thoughtful look. 'I can see why you've picked it out. But would anyone donate a book they'd used to stage a murder?'

'They might. It seems to me a pretty astute way of ridding yourself of evidence – a market stall where everyone's books are mixed together. It's only that Dilys is a smart cookie that I know where it came from.'

Flora waited and, when he said nothing, prompted. 'Well, where?'

'From Sally.'

'Sally Jenner?' A deep crease appeared between her eyes. 'What was Sally doing with a book on electrics?'

'Exactly. Unless it's one she found in the Priory library and decided it didn't fit.'

'It would never have been in Lord Edward's library.' Flora's voice was firm. 'He might have been good at administration, the signals centre in the war, but technical knowledge passed him by entirely. There was nothing more technical in his library than an atlas of the world.'

'So it's Sally's own book and we come back to the fact that she's an unlikely owner.'

Flora fidgeted with the display, standing several of the larger books upright and nudging others into line.

'If you're going to say that Sally used it to rewire the amplifier that killed Beverly, I think I'll laugh,' she said at last.

'Stranger things have happened. You like Sally, I like her, but she has to be in the frame. She seems to have been jealous of Beverly.'

'She was.' There was reluctance in Flora's voice. 'Very jealous. And she wasn't around when Beverly first jumped on the stage. She only appeared when Dominic asked her to go across to the house and sit with the body.'

'So, think opportunity. She could have had the chance to modify the amplifier during Dominic's opening speech – he didn't use the microphone, did he? – and afterwards, a few minutes to dump the rogue cable when the kerfuffle was happening on stage. She also had motive,' he said, thinking it through as he spoke. 'She's in love with Dominic, that's what you told me. She might have guessed he'd been Beverly's boyfriend at one time, even if no one mentioned it directly. Maybe suspected he still had an interest in the woman, even while he was telling *her* something very different. She'd think he was cheating and might have decided to get rid of the opposition.'

'All true, but the book is far more likely to have belonged to Dominic himself.' Flora cradled her chin in her hands. 'There's something you don't know.'

And in between customers, Flora related what she'd learned the previous day when she'd visited the Priory.

'You're saying that Dominic was actually engaged to the girl?'

'Engaged but wanted out. It explains why the ring went missing. He took it from Beverly's dead body! Can you imagine, Jack? He didn't want any questions asked, I suppose – like how Beverly came to wear the ring. Didn't want anyone to know he'd promised to marry her.'

'Did Sally know about the engagement, do you think?'

'Not unless she guessed and kept silent. Dominic more or less confessed to me that it was Sally he really cared for and begged me not to tell her.'

'That certainly puts a different light on basic electrics. If he was desperate enough to get rid of Beverly, he could have learnt how to tamper with the amplifier. Whether he'd have had time to do it is another matter.'

'We mustn't get ahead of ourselves. We don't know for certain that the book *was* his. Sally could simply have been clearing the Priory of clutter.'

Jack finished serving a customer who'd been looking for books on houseplants before he said, 'It might just be clutter. On the other hand, if Sally suspects he's the guilty one, she could be covering for him.'

Flora burrowed beneath the trestle table looking for more stock to fill the stall's empty spaces. 'We have far too many loose ends at the moment,' she grumbled.

15

The suggestion that Sally was more deeply embroiled in Beverly Russo's fate than Flora had thought, was a worry. Jack had tried to reassure her – Sally had certainly been jealous of the girl, but jealousy didn't have to lead to murder. And the book he'd found could have been left at the Priory by a host of people: workmen, waiters, one of the band even. Walking back to her cottage after sending Charlie home for his lunch and closing the bookshop for the day, Flora clutched at the idea.

It was what she wanted to believe. That, or the fact that Sally was shielding the man she loved. Jack had offered to go to the Priory and talk to Dominic, attempt to discover just what his role had been on that fateful day, but Flora felt keenly that she should be the one to go. She had a ready-made excuse. Sally had given her permission to search the stables for Beverly's medicine and return the bottle to the surgery – another visit she'd promised herself. Tomorrow was Sunday, a day of long lunches and peaceful afternoons, and it was likely she could seek out Dominic for a quiet chat without anyone being the wiser.

The secrecy, though, made her uncomfortable – it seemed as though she was going behind her friend's back – but if Sally had had any involvement with Beverly's death, even if it was simply the withholding of information, she would need help and Flora felt she should be the one to offer it.

Approaching the brick and flint cottage that had been home to her for so many years, she was surprised to see Alice waiting at the gate. Another unexpected visit! Her friend must have come straight from the Nook when Kate returned from the village green.

'Did Katie sell out early?' Flora called, as she drew near.

Alice turned. 'She did that. I could have baked double the rhubarb tarts and she'd have sold every single one.'

Taking her friend by the arm, Flora walked with her up the garden path. 'Have you had any lunch?' she asked, unlocking the old oak front door and standing back for Alice to enter.

'Not yet, and I'd lay a bet on it neither have you. Which is why...' – she delved into the basket she carried – 'I brought us a couple of meat pies. They should go down nicely with a pot of tea.'

'You're a treasure,' Flora said, walking into the kitchen and putting the kettle on to boil.

Her mind, though, was busy imagining why Alice had called again. The last few days must have been very tiring for the cook – she had baked an enormous quantity of cakes, while also serving in the café – yet she had chosen to visit rather than return home for a rest. Meat pies were not a good enough reason.

It wasn't until they were halfway through their meal that Flora learned why her friend had come.

'I'm worried about my niece,' Alice said bluntly. 'I know I've said it before, but she's got far too close to that Dominic for my likin'.'

'And you don't like him,' Flora finished for her.

'He's charmin' all right, but I don't trust him. I've tried to, the Lord knows. I'm not stupid. It means a lot to Sally, I can see.

She don't get on with her parents, well it's her stepfather really that's the problem, and I know she was keen to do a job that she really loved and be her own boss – not be at someone else's beck and call – so I tried to be happy about her buyin' the Priory. But I don't trust that Dominic,' she repeated.

'Is there anything in particular that makes you feel that way?' she asked cautiously.

'Well, for one thing I don't believe he's any relative of Lord Edward's. Do you?'

'I never did, to be honest, but I suppose we can excuse a little storytelling if he saw it as a way of establishing himself in Abbeymead. The village can be too close-knit at times – can close ranks when strangers arrive.' Flora felt herself playing devil's advocate.

'A little storytelling if you need a foolish girl to commit to loans she may never pay off,' Alice said tautly.

'Is that what Sally has done? I thought it was Dominic who had negotiated with the bank.'

'It was him all right, but she put her name to the documents. Whatever he's borrowed, she's in it, too.'

'It couldn't be that large a sum, surely. Dominic wouldn't have needed to borrow a huge amount. He sold a chain of bars, didn't he?'

'If you believe he did. What if that's a story, too?'

Flora gaped. 'You think it could be?'

'I was talking to that Jarvis. He's always moochin' round the village and yesterday he walked into the café for a bag of dough-nuts. Katie was taking an order so I came out from the kitchen to help.'

'And...'

'He was some fed up with being stuck at the Priory, mutterin' and moanin' about it, and I asked him, just out of interest, how the band came to be booked in the first place. It never seemed like a good fit to me, a rock 'n' roll group and a posh hotel.'

'Didn't Dominic know them before he came to Abbeymead? They played at one of his clubs, I think?'

'They did, in a manner of speakin'. One single club. I said to this Jarvis that it must have been a good start for them with Mr Lister owning all those bars in London and the chap looked vacant. When I pushed him and said as how knowing Dominic must have meant the band had plenty of choice where they could play, he laughed. There was only the one venue, he said. "A scrubby little dive in Bermondsey", that's how he described it.'

'Jarvis was sure of his facts?'

Alice nodded, putting down her knife and fork and taking a long sip of tea.

'He was sure all right. He didn't believe they owed Dominic anythin'. But Tommy May – he seems to be the one who says what's what in the group – insisted they did. They owed Dominic a favour, he said.'

'I did hear something like that,' Flora admitted, remembering the quarrel she and Jack had overheard at the stables.

'The thing is...' Alice leaned across and grasped Flora's hand. 'What if Sal has got herself into a mess? She's put all the money my brother left her into that hotel, every shilling she owned, and last night she confessed to me that she signed all the papers Dominic gave her, meanin' she's liable for the loan he took out. And she don't even know how much it was!'

'She didn't see the figures?' Flora couldn't believe that. Sally was far too shrewd.

'She saw one figure and signed, but then she says she signed other pieces of paper and didn't look at them properly.'

How could Sally have been so foolish? Of course, Flora knew how. The girl had stars in her eyes and trusted Dominic implicitly.

'She's stupid over that man,' Alice said, echoing Flora's thoughts. 'Goodness knows what will happen if the hotel fails.'

Her friend looked near to tears and Flora squeezed her hand. 'It's not going to fail. Sally will make it a success. Think how well she ran the All's Well while I was away in Cornwall. She actually increased sales!'

Sally's successful management of the bookshop still rankled a little, but now was not the time to remember.

'That's all very well.' Alice got up and began clearing the plates. 'But when's the hotel goin' to open again? Jarvis isn't the only one walkin' up the wall. The police are so darn slow and without that Inspector Ridley to poke them into action, the Priory could be closed for weeks, if not months.'

Flora wondered whether it would reassure her friend to know that Jack and she were doing their best to solve Beverly's murder, just as Sally had asked them. Would it brighten Alice's life to know they were following the few leads they'd uncovered and found evidence they hoped might eventually reveal the villain? But thinking how little, in fact, it amounted to, she decided to say nothing for the moment.

'The inspector will be back soon.' It was spoken with confidence, though Flora had no real idea if this was true, but it was the best she could offer. 'The police will really get going then. We'll just have to be patient.'

'It's mighty hard,' Alice said miserably.

Flora put her arms around the motherly figure. 'Leave the washing up and go home and put your feet up. You're tired out and things are bound to look their worst.'

'I s'pose,' Alice said, picking up a gaberdine raincoat that had seen better days.

Flora waved her off from the door. 'Thank you for the pie,' she called out. 'Delicious – as always!'

.   .   .

She couldn't concentrate that evening. Laying aside a new book that had arrived in this morning's delivery – *Dead Man's Folly*, she must let Elsie know it was in – she switched on the wireless. The BBC Concert Orchestra were playing and, for a while, she curled up in Aunt Violet's favourite chair and tried to lose herself in the music, but her concerns over Sally were too great.

It looked as though the girl had jumped into a sea of trouble and was beginning to drown. She had agreed loans she would be lucky to pay back, a total at which she could only guess. In addition, it was possible she was covering for Dominic. She was clearly entranced by the man and likely to do anything he asked of her. Even worse, though Flora refused to believe it, Sally herself might have been the one to plot and carry out Beverly's murder.

She must speak to her – tomorrow, if possible – after she'd tackled Dominic. Speak to Sally and ask her face to face exactly what had gone on. Things were looking decidedly black and Flora needed to know just what the young woman was up against. Only complete honesty would do.

In the event, when she dragged Betty from her shed at the cottage and cycled to the Priory the following afternoon, she saw neither Sally nor Dominic. The mansion's huge front door was unlocked but, when Flora walked into the empty foyer and called, no one answered. A wander around the ground floor, through the panelled hall, a detour into the library where Lord Edward's wonderful collection of books sat tall and proud – how could a basic guide to electrical engineering have ever found its way through the doors? – was equally unsuccessful.

She took the stairs down to the kitchen, as empty as she'd expected, with no evidence that anything had been cooked there for days. Letting herself out of the rear door, she followed the path that ran alongside the Priory's honey-coloured walls to the stables, thinking that at least she could search for Beverly's medicine, and had just rounded the corner when Jarvis Redmond came into view.

'I was looking for Sally,' she said. 'Or Dominic.'

He shook his head. 'You won't find 'em. Not today. Off on a picnic.' For once Jarvis appeared sober.

'On a picnic,' she repeated stupidly. It seemed impossibly trivial when Sally was facing such dire trouble.

'Love's sweet dream,' he said acidly.

'They're a couple? How surprising!' Flora studied his face, wondering how best to get him to talk. 'I'm obviously way behind with the news, but perhaps Dominic finds it easy to transfer his affections.' She threw out the bait in the hope that he'd bite.

When her companion looked blank, she saw her chance. 'I understood he was engaged to Miss Russo. I saw the ruby ring on her right hand.'

'Oh, that.' Jarvis seemed relieved that he'd understood her allusion. 'Conned it out of him, I'd say.'

'How would she have done that?'

'Used her feminine charms, isn't that the phrase? Though I saw precious little sign of 'em.'

'I can see they'd be wasted on you,' she flattered.

'It wasn't for trying. She tried it on all of us, just to rile Tommy.' There was a long pause while his foot traced a pattern on the gravelled pathway. 'Bev was a total bitch, you know,' he said at last. 'One of those women who cause trouble, hurt, wherever they go. I reckon whoever killed her did a good job.'

She tried not to look shocked at his blatant hostility. It was important to keep him talking. 'Was Beverly successful? Did she manage to rile Tommy?'

'For a while, till he got wise,' Jarvis said laconically. 'When he'd had enough, he offloaded her onto Dominic, glad to see her go.'

'How did Beverly feel about that? Was she glad to be "offloaded"?'

He gave an indifferent shrug. 'I guess, at the beginning. Thought Lister would be a better bet long term, I s'pose. He was a bloke who talked big, but she backed the wrong horse there. All that talk turned out to be flim-flam. She should have aimed straight for Max. He'd have been a good match. Both of them creeps.'

'Max and Beverly?'

'She had him, Max, marked for her next victim. That's why Tommy blew a fuse that afternoon. He thought she was about to two-time his mate. Couldn't see that our Dominic would have been only too pleased. Would have danced with joy to lose his chains. Tommy never was one to read a person.'

'Dominic must have been in love with her, for a while at least, or he'd never have got engaged.'

'Who knows? Maybe he just liked the idea of hanging around with a rock singer. Liked it until she got a bit too grabby. That's when he tried to run.'

'He doesn't seem to have succeeded, judging by that ring.' Had Jarvis seen what happened the afternoon Beverly died? Flora wondered. Had he seen Dominic take the ring? She looked directly at the drummer, hoping for the truth.

'Succeeded now, though, hasn't he?' Jarvis grinned. 'Got what he wanted. A bloody great hotel and a girl who'll do anything for him. Pity. She deserves better. She's a sweet kid.'

It seemed to Flora she was unlikely to get anything more, though she would have liked to ask him why, exactly, he'd changed his name. That might be pushing her luck a little too far, she realised.

'I'm sorry, I'm holding you up. You were on your way some-where. Sally said it was OK if I searched Beverly's room for the medicine she was taking.'

He looked nonplussed. 'Why?'

'The doctor's surgery wants the bottle returned. I've no idea why, but Maggie, the receptionist, was insistent and Sally couldn't find it when she looked so I said I'd try.'

'You're welcome if you can find anything in that flea pit of a room. I gotta go now. Gotta keep in training for the drums, you know. Walking three miles a day.'

'And Tommy and Shane? Will I be disturbing them?'

'Gone to Brighton. Looking for some life,' he muttered, slouching away.

16

She needed to be methodical, she told herself. The medicine was unlikely to be in any of the men's rooms, which left the sitting room, the bathroom and Beverly's own bedroom. She'd tackle the sitting room first. In the event, it took her little time, finding the few shelves almost bare and the one cupboard empty. The only items of interest – a collection of instruments and several piles of sheet music – were lumped between the chairs and two small tables.

Bumping against one of the tables laden with paper, she knocked something to the ground. A wallet. According to the initials stamped on the leather front, JR, it belonged to Jarvis. She picked it up and made for the door, meaning to run after him, but by the time she reached the courtyard, he'd disappeared from sight.

Retracing her steps to the sitting room, she walked back to the table, intending to replace the wallet where she'd found it. It fell open as she shuffled papers to make space and Flora found herself looking at a photograph of two young girls. She looked closer. One of them, she'd swear, the one on the left, was a much younger Beverly with her arm around an unknown girl.

Why did Jarvis have a photograph of Beverly at – what age would she be? – no more than sixteen, if she was that. His remark that Beverly had always been a bitch reverberated in Flora's mind. Did this confirm that Jarvis Redmond, John Reeves, had known her before she joined the band? And if so, who was the unknown girl sharing the image?

It was a mystery she wasn't going to solve, short of asking the man directly, and for the moment it was something she must put to one side. It was important to finish her search before Tommy and Shane returned. A brief detour to the bathroom where the medicine should have been but wasn't, and then she was standing outside Beverly's room.

It was plain that it had been hers and no one else's. From the open doorway, Flora gazed in horror at the disarray. No wonder neither Sally nor Maggie had been able to find the medicine. Clothes covered every inch of the floor, except for where a suitcase lay open, its contents spilling forth. Crammed with bottles, the dressing table remained undusted, its mirror liberally smeared with lotion. A powder compact had been thrown into the easy chair and an open lipstick had marked its delicate blue velvet with a streak of violent red. Walking into this room must have broken Sally's heart after she and her household staff had spent so much care making it attractive.

Where to begin? A shuffle through the clothes on the floor revealed nothing amiss, the suitcase harboured only trivia, the dressing table bottles proved innocent and the bedside table seemed not to have been used. Of the medicine, there was no trace. Moving on to the chest of drawers, Flora discovered it crammed with a ton of underwear, most of it scanty and lace-covered, and most of it needing a wash, she thought fastidiously.

The wardrobe remained the only place left to search. A row of stage clothes filled most of the space, with only a few outfits approaching any kind of normal wear. Flora flicked through the hangers, delving into any pockets she could find, then stood on tiptoe to investigate the top shelf where a variety of Beverly's exotic stage headwear had been stored. She caught a glittering tiara as it toppled to the floor and, for a moment, was tempted to try it on, then remembered why she was here. Tommy and Shane might return very soon – she couldn't imagine Brighton on a Sunday would keep them busy for long – and she'd no wish to be discovered searching.

Kneeling down, she made her way through ranks of precariously heeled shoes, and had almost given up when a bottle slid out of the toe of a crystal-embellished stiletto, the surgery label still attached. She clambered to her feet, holding the bottle up to the light. Even through the smoky brown glass she could see that the bottle was full. Completely full. Beverly had not taken a single drop.

When had she collected the medicine from the surgery and delivered it to Beverly? Flora did a swift calculation and realised that she'd handed over this same bottle nearly a week before Beverly had met her dreadful death. A week when the girl had made no use of a medicine prescribed to keep her healthy. Had that been because she'd felt better and judged it more sensible to forgo medication? But the post-mortem had showed a definite problem with her heart, and it was unlikely she would have felt any sudden improvement.

Why then? A dislike of medication generally – so why go to the doctor in the first place? Or a suspicion that this particular medicine might do her harm? And what might have prompted that fear? Flora pocketed the bottle, deciding she must call at Overlay House immediately. She would return the medicine to the surgery, but not before she'd siphoned off a sample. And that was where Jack would come in.

As soon as Flora turned the bookshop's notice to Closed and locked the All's Well's sturdy front door the following day, she set off for Overlay House. There was no possibility of telephoning Jack – he was still on the waiting list for a receiver – but, in any case, she needed to meet him face to face if her mission was to have any chance of success.

She found him in the front garden watering the last marguerites of the year.

'A surprise call!' he said, looking up as the gate hinges creaked. 'And probably an uncomfortable one.'

'Why do you say that? This gate needs oiling, by the way.'

'*That's* why I say it. Whenever you come here, it's to chivvy me into mending this, or changing that – and don't ask, I have a new chair coming for the sitting room next week.'

Since chivvying could fairly be described as what she was about to do, Flora chose diplomacy.

'I fancied a walk after work, that's all,' she said airily, 'and thought I'd make my way home the long way round. A cup of tea would be nice – when you've finished.'

'I have finished and so have these. Almost.' He looked regretfully at the marguerites, no longer as robust as their summer form.

'They've done very well,' Flora said judiciously. 'I must say you've turned out to be a heaps better gardener than I ever thought.'

'I can thank Charlie Teague for that. A diminutive mentor, but a very good one.' He led the way indoors, walking through to the kitchen with Flora following.

As soon as he'd filled the kettle, he turned to face her. 'Now, what is it you want?' There was suspicion in his voice.

Flora looked at him, wide-eyed.

'You want something or you wouldn't be here, and praising my efforts at horticulture.'

'That is so cynical,' she scolded. 'Let's have a drink first.'

He abandoned the kettle and walked towards the larder. 'How about a glass of wine instead? I've been sent a crate of this

Italian stuff. Arthur again! He says he ordered too much but more likely he thinks I need invigorating.'

Flora glanced at the curved bottle he'd brought out of the larder. 'Asti Spumante,' she read. 'Is it any good?'

'It's been described as the poor man's champagne – but that's wine snobs for you. It's decent enough, but I could do with some help to drink a whole crate.'

'Pour me a glass then. I wouldn't know how it compares. I'm far too poor to have ever drunk champagne. Can we sit in the garden, d'you think? It's just about warm enough still.'

When they'd taken their glasses onto the rear terrace that ran the width of the house, Jack fetched two chairs and a small table from the garden shed.

'I'd put these away, thinking that summer was over. But you're right, it's mild enough to sit out for a while.'

He clinked his glass with hers and took a long sip, Flora following suit. 'OK, let's have it, sleuth.'

She reached down into her handbag and pulled out a medicine bottle containing several inches of liquid and placed it carefully on the table.

'How thoughtful! You've brought me a tonic!'

'I've brought you a sample of the medicine that Dr Randall prescribed for Beverly,' she corrected.

'How on earth did you get hold of it? More to the point, why did you get hold of it?'

'How is simple. Maggie Unwin was desperate to have it returned to the surgery and Sally had given up trying to find it. Which is no wonder. You should see the room Beverly occupied – it's an absolute dog's dinner. I offered to look for the bottle, partly to help Sally but also it seemed a good opportunity to have a poke around for anything that might be helpful.'

'And was there anything, other than the medicine?'

'Actually, there was. A photograph of Beverly when she was younger, with a girl I didn't recognise. It was in Jarvis's wallet.'

When Jack looked askance, she said quickly, 'I didn't go looking – the wallet fell open by accident. But you see what it suggests. That he knew Beverly long before she joined the band and that they both have some connection to an unknown girl.'

Jack rubbed his chin. 'Did you ask him about it?'

'Not yet, but I think we should. He seems willing enough to talk. I spoke to him before he went off for a walk. He reckons Beverly was making a play for Max Martell and that was the reason for Tommy's outburst at the hotel opening. Tommy counts Dominic as a friend, apparently, and he believed Beverly was deceiving him.'

Stretching out his long legs, Jack laid back against the wicker chair. 'Which she probably was. It gives Dominic a get-out, doesn't it? If Beverly was going to dump him for Martell, he had no need to murder her.'

'Only if he knew that's what she planned,' Flora countered. 'It's interesting in another way, though – what it says about Martell. Beverly wasn't the only one sowing discord in the group. Do you remember what Tommy said about seeing him on the stairs with the girl?' She grimaced at the image the memory brought back. 'Still, we've only Jarvis Redmond's word that it went any further.'

Jack pointed to the small bottle on the table. 'You proved better at searching than Sally, unless she didn't want to find it.'

'It was more that she'd no wish to touch Beverly's possessions. I found it tucked into a pair of shoes, so it's not surprising it was overlooked. Hideously spangled shoes at that,' she finished as an afterthought.

When Jack fell silent, she decided it was time to break the real news to him. 'This isn't actually the original bottle,' she remarked casually. 'That one is back at my cottage. I'm going to take it into the surgery first thing in the morning, but I wanted a sample of the medicine.'

'Why?' His voice held deep misgiving.

'So that we can get it analysed.'

'Why do that? The medicine, whatever it contains, didn't kill her.'

'But what if it was designed to kill her and failed?'

'You think Randall moved on to electrocution at some point?' He laughed.

'At the moment, I don't think anything, but we have to consider every possibility.'

'That definitely isn't a possibility. The doctor couldn't have tampered with the amplifier. He wasn't even at the Priory.'

'He was nearby,' she pointed out. 'You saw him by the Priory gates. He certainly wasn't where he should have been, at the surgery, or where he said he was, at home.'

'If your theory of a secret liaison with his assistant is true, he was probably coming away from meeting her when I found him.'

'A meeting in the Priory grounds, perhaps?'

'Even if that were so, he couldn't have got near the stage without being seen,' Jack protested. 'There were too many people around.'

'That number of people makes it easier to disappear, and the amplifier was at the side of the stage and not in full view of the audience. Or in view of any of us, for that matter. We were on the opposite side, outside the marquee.'

He shook his head at her. 'It would be almost impossible for him to do it.'

'But not completely,' she argued. 'There's something strange about this whole Randall business. The bottle was full when I found it – Beverly hadn't taken a single drop despite having an obvious health problem, and the receptionist was almost frantic to get the medicine back. Like I say, we need to get it analysed.'

'Let's rewind a minute here. *We* need to get it analysed.' He took another long drink of his wine.

'More precisely, you.'

'Ah, we're getting to it at last. Why me? I'm a writer, not a lab worker.'

'Maybe not, but you do know someone who works in the laboratory used by the police. You could ask him.'

'Flora!' He exploded, banging down his glass so hard that a fizz of wine spilt across the wicker.

She held up her hand as if to hold back the coming onslaught. 'I'm not suggesting you get in touch with Alan Ridley, just the lab. The one that analysed the poisonous flowers we found.'

'The chap who came up with the answer to that question was a botanist, not a lab technician,' he reminded her.

'Eventually, it was. But there was someone beforehand who analysed the pollen stains on Cyril's jacket. You could ask *him* – as a favour.'

'A favour for what?'

'You'll think of something.' She put down her half-empty wine glass and stood up. 'I must go. Michael is calling tonight to replace the faulty lock on Betty's shelter. She's not happy if she feels insecure.' She paused for a moment, then said airily, 'You could always tell the lab chap that Alan Ridley said it was OK to go ahead. That would work.'

In a second, he was on his feet beside her. 'Flora Steele, you are the most impossible person I've ever met. How many times have I told you I am *not* using my contact with Ridley. I'd like to shake you very hard.'

'I can't be the most impossible. I don't like to remind you—'

'If you're going to mention my one-time fiancée, don't. Helen wasn't impossible, just deceitful.'

'Well, I'm not that.' She gave him a sunny smile and saw the grey eyes lighten, then darken again. 'No,' he agreed. 'You're not.'

'You can shake me if it makes you feel better,' she offered.

'It won't. Though something else might.'

'Tell me,' she said, laughing up at him.

'Give me the bottle and go home.' He pushed her back through the kitchen door and into the hall.

'Let me know the results as soon as you get them,' she said at the front door. 'I think they could be important.'

17

Flora was up early the next morning, dragging Betty from her newly secured home and pedalling quickly to the doctor's surgery on the corner of Greenway Lane and the high street. It would be a quick visit before she opened the bookshop for the day's business and she was hopeful of seeing Maggie at the receptionist's desk.

There were several patients already in the waiting area when Flora arrived, each one being careful to monitor who had walked in before them and who after. When Dr Randall opened his door and called for the next patient, a young mother jumped to her feet, baby in arms, ready to claim her turn. Maggie was at her desk explaining to an elderly villager in as kind a manner as she could that if the woman was well enough to walk to the surgery, a home call was unnecessary.

As soon as the uncooperative patient had huffed her way out of the building, Flora approached the desk. She was shocked to see how ill Maggie looked. The girl's face never held much colour but this morning it was as white as the surgery walls, and her eyes were swollen and red. It looked as though she had been crying, and crying a lot.

'Hello, Maggie,' she began, 'I was hoping to speak to you for a few minutes.'

The girl looked up and, to Flora's horror, tears began to dribble slowly down her face. 'Whatever's wrong?' she asked, appalled. 'Are you unwell?'

Maggie reached into her uniform pocket for a handkerchief, dabbing at her cheeks and blowing her nose.

'Sorry, it's just... it's just...' She couldn't seem to finish what she wanted to say and Flora walked round the desk and took her by the arm.

'Come outside for a minute,' she said. 'You'll feel better in the fresh air.'

'I can't.' The girl gestured at the waiting patients.

'Mrs Harris will be with the doctor a while. You've time for a short break,' Flora urged.

Maggie allowed herself to be led through a side door into a small courtyard in which Dr Randall's car took up most of the space. At least, Flora presumed it was his.

'I hate to see you so upset,' she said tentatively, once Maggie had taken several deep breaths. 'Can I be of any help?'

The girl shook her head dumbly. 'It's over,' she murmured, 'that's all. But I can't seem to believe it.'

Flora thought quickly. 'Your... friendship... with Dr Randall... is over?'

Maggie nodded. 'It was wrong, Flora, I know. I did a wicked thing but...' She trailed off hopelessly.

'More unwise than wicked,' Flora soothed. 'It sounds as if you made the right decision in the end.'

'I didn't make it,' the girl said miserably. 'Brian did.'

'Then he made the right choice for both of you.'

Why had he done it now? was the question at the back of Flora's mind. By the look of it, their so-called 'friendship' had been going on for several months, possibly since Dr Hanson left on his sabbatical, so why choose this moment to finish what must always have been a doomed relationship?

'I'm sorry,' she said gently. 'It must feel very bad for you right now, but maybe in time you'll come to see the break as a good thing.' She wondered if she should say more, then took the plunge. 'It's likely that Dr Randall would never have left his wife.'

'He wouldn't!' Maggie sounded shocked. 'He has a family to consider.'

'There was no future for either of you then, was there?'

The receptionist hung her head. 'I've known that for ever, but I did love him. I do love him.'

Flora patted her hand in what she hoped was an encouraging gesture. 'There is one small thing that might cheer you up. I've brought the medicine you were looking for.'

Maggie stared at her, her eyes those of a small, startled creature.

'Beverly Russo's medicine,' Flora reminded her. 'You went up to the Priory to get it. Miss Jenner couldn't find it at the time but I managed to dig it out – you wouldn't believe where,' she said, in an attempt to sound jolly, holding out the bottle for Maggie to take. 'Secreted in the most amazing pair of shoes—'

She broke off. The girl's face had grown paler than ever, if that were possible, and her mouth was working convulsively.

Why was she staring at the bottle as if it was about to explode? Was she worried that Beverly had taken a spoonful or two? Or did she realise it was Flora who had taken a sample? But how could she and why did it matter anyway?

The girl wrenched the bottle from her and turned tail, scuttling back into the surgery. By the time Flora reached the waiting room, the medicine had disappeared and Maggie had a firm smile pinned to her face as she welcomed another patient through the door.

~

Jack was filled with misgiving as he drove to Brighton. He was about to approach the pathology laboratory he'd visited almost a year ago and somehow persuade a technician that analysing the contents of the small glass bottle in his pocket was essential. Last year he'd managed to twist Alan Ridley's arm into agreeing to have a jacket belonging to Kate's dead father, Cyril Knight, put under the microscope. That had been difficult enough, but today the inspector wasn't around to be persuaded – it was unlikely, in any case, that persuasion would have succeeded – and Jack was faced with concocting a story that would convince the laboratory the medicine was important to a police investigation. He couldn't bill the inspector for the analysis. He'd have to pay out of his own pocket, and that in itself could arouse suspicions that the police knew nothing of his request.

Why did he allow himself to be inveigled into these situations? If the medicine proved as innocent as it looked, he'd feel a fool, and a fool short of money. When he'd called Flora impossible, he hadn't been wrong. Once she got an idea into her head, it stuck. She was like a terrier digging for a rabbit, and it was tough luck on anyone who got in the way.

Helen had never been impossible. On the contrary, she'd been amenable, ready to fit in, her opinions fluid. Did they share those characteristics, he wondered, the reason they'd ended up together? Something she'd said when he'd last seen her was fixed in his mind. That she'd never really known who he was. It was one more excuse, of course, for walking out on him three weeks before their wedding day, but still there was some truth in it. Perhaps that had been the problem. Neither of them had really known the other or, for that matter, known themselves.

Was it different with Flora? He really shouldn't compare them – one was the woman he'd been about to marry, the other just a friend. 'Just a friend' – the phrase had a dismissive ring to it, yet even after the short time he'd known Flora, he could often predict how she'd react to different people, how she'd deal with different situations. He smiled to himself. Much of the time he could guess what she was about to say. If that was being 'just a friend', it felt a lot closer than anything he'd shared with Helen.

Pulling up outside the laboratory, he realised he'd answered his earlier question. The closeness he had with Flora was precisely why he was about to accost a lab technician with a bottle containing two inches of brown liquid. Walking into the foyer, he had a piece of luck, coming face to face with the same man who had undertaken the analysis on Cyril's jacket. Luckier still, the technician recognised him.

The man bobbed his head, looking over Jack's shoulder as though searching for someone. 'Inspector Ridley with you?' he asked.

'No, but I do have something for you to look at.' Jack congratulated himself. He hadn't actually lied, had he? Simply allowed the man to assume he was working alongside Ridley.

'What have you got then?'

He pulled the bottle from his pocket and passed it over.

'Medicine? Doesn't look too interesting but it could be a nasty concoction.'

'It would be good to know how nasty. Could you take a look?'

'Sure. It shouldn't take too long. When does Ridley want it by?' The young man's open expression made Jack feel guilty. He was coming closer to lying with every minute.

'I can pick it up tomorrow or the next day if that works for you.'

'I'll knock it off in my lunch hour. Unless it's more complicated than it looks, tell the inspector there won't be a charge. He puts a lot of work our way, it's the least we can do.'

Jack crept away, feeling all of five inches tall.

18

It seemed sensible while he was in Brighton to pursue another avenue, one which Flora had dismissed as trivial but that Jack considered had possibilities. He'd been the one to speak to Mrs May after all, not Flora, and there had definitely been a hint in the woman's voice when she'd spoken of Max Martell that had alerted him to what wasn't being said. Hesitation, there'd certainly been, but also something darker, more ominous. He might be mistaken, but it would be good to find Martell's erstwhile partner, if only to check how reliable his own instincts were.

He left the Austin parked outside the laboratory and took a bus into the town centre, getting off at the Pavilion. If he'd had the time, he would like to have visited the palace. It had naturally not been on Charlie's wish list when they'd treated him to a day out in Brighton last winter, but it was an extraordinary building, its exoticism like nothing Jack had seen before. When this murder business was over, it would make a pleasant day out, except that Flora was sure to have done the guided tour already.

Brighton Museum and Library occupied what had once been George IV's royal stables and had kept much of its original eastern splendour. Two copper domes rose from the roof and every window was encrusted with Islamic ornamentation. Inside the porch were panels that wouldn't have looked out of place in the Alhambra and the staircase and walls were extensively patterned in geometric tiles of the deepest blue and green. The reference library was on the first floor, its walls furnished with antique bookcases and the entire space lit by three glass domes in the ceiling.

It was the grandest reference room Jack had ever visited, but he spent little time in admiration, instead strolling immediately to the desk where a grey-haired woman had her head bent over a sheaf of papers.

The woman looked up as he approached, adjusting a pair of cat-eye spectacles and pushing the papers she'd been working on to one side.

'Good morning,' he began. 'I'm looking for a list of booking agents. Agents who deal with musicians. Would you have such a list?'

The librarian's eyes did a rapid blink. 'Music agents? It's not something I've ever been asked for.'

'No, I'm sure it's not, but I think there must be such a list. I'm looking for the contact details of an agent who was in the music business around ten years ago.' It was a wild guess since he had no real idea how long Martell had been operating as a one-man business.

'Let me think.' The woman tapped her teeth with a pencil. 'I'm fairly certain the library has nothing that's specific to music. I'd say your best bet would be *The Stage*. The journal concentrates on theatre news and reviews, articles on current artistes, that kind of thing, but they do run an advertising section and it's possible the agent you're looking for advertised his services there.'

'You have *The Stage* – the past numbers?' Jack asked eagerly.

'We do. Let me show you where they're kept.'

She led the way to the far end of the room and bent nearly double to reach the lowest shelf, running her fingers along the assembled calf-bound volumes. 'Here we are. Bound copies from – I didn't realise *The Stage* was that old a publication – from 1900, but it looks as if the first edition was published before even then.'

'I don't think my agent is that old.' The joke fell a little flat – they always did, he thought ruefully.

The woman gave him a sheepish smile. 'I'll leave you to it then.'

Martell was aged around forty, Jack estimated, and during the last war would have been liable for military service which was likely to have put any career in agenting on hold for some years. He'd start with the 1946 volume and hope he was right.

Unfortunately, advertisements were dotted throughout the publication as well as in one specific section, and the process of scanning every column on every page was mind-numbing. In the main, the adverts were for theatrical jobs, acting roles primarily, though some were for singers, and a fair number of jobs were on offer for technical staff, with help needed in light-ing, stage management, and so on. A few agents' names appeared here and there but almost all were concerned with bookings for the theatre.

Undaunted, Jack carried on with the 1947 volume, promising himself that he'd not go beyond 1950. By then, he reckoned, Martell would have made the break and set up on his own, probably booking Tutti Frutti for the first time around five or six years ago. Possibly, it had needed that long for the band to mature into what they'd become today.

He was halfway through the 1950 volume when at last he struck lucky. The smallest advertisement he'd ever seen was wedged into the bottom left-hand corner of the page he'd just turned. *Martell and Tinsdale*, it read, *agents to the stars*. A little optimistic, if all they could afford was an advert that most people would have passed by.

There was a telephone number which Jack noted down in the pocket diary he carried. It was unlikely that any agent would still be at that number, but if the line was in operation, someone at the other end might know how to contact Mr Tinsdale.

Buoyed up by his discovery, Jack thanked the librarian and returned to the laboratory car park to rescue the Austin. Driving back to Abbeymead, he made up his mind to call at the bookshop, rather than head directly home.

'You look excited!' Seeing him walk through the All's Well's door, Flora put down the catalogue she was browsing. 'Have you the results of Beverly's medicine?'

'Go easy. I only dropped the bottle off this morning.'

'At least you were able to drop it off. It sounds as if you found a friendly lab assistant. See, I knew you would.'

'I did, but only by compromising myself hugely.'

She laughed. 'I'd love to have heard the conversation. I bet you got yourself in a frightful tangle.'

'I didn't, in fact. I must be learning to lie as convincingly as you.'

'Could be. So why *are* you looking so pumped up?'

'I found a telephone number for Max Martell's former partner.'

'Oh, that.' Flora sounded disappointed. 'You're barking up the wrong tree, Jack.'

'Let's see, shall we? If I can use your telephone...'

'Be my guest.' She picked up several discarded paperbacks from the window seat and began to reshelve them.

It was more in hope than expectation that Jack dialled the London telephone number, but there was a voice at the end of the line and, amazingly, it announced he'd reached Tinsdale's Booking Agency.

'Mr Tinsdale?' Jack stammered, taken by surprise. 'My name is Jack Carrington.'

'Nice to hear from you, Jack.' There was a slight pause, before the man at the other end murmured, 'Awfully sorry, but I can't quite place you at the moment. Are you on my books? I have to tell you that right now there's not a great deal going.'

'Actually, Mr Tinsdale, I'm not after a job. I was hoping to talk to you about your former partner.'

There was a deathly silence on the line.

'Max Martell,' Jack added.

'I know who my former partner was,' the man said sharply. 'What do you want to know about him?'

'I wondered how long you were in business together and when it was that Mr Martell left to set up his own agency.' That would do for a start, Jack thought.

'Four years,' Tinsdale said briefly. 'Four years together. And Max didn't leave, I booted him out. If he's telling you something different, he's a liar. Which, of course, he is.'

Flora's eyebrows shot up. She had shelved her books and come close to listen.

'You had a falling-out?' Jack suggested, hoping Tinsdale would be encouraged to say more.

'You could say that. If you call a sock on the jaw and a shoe up the backside a falling-out. My fist and my shoe, by the way.'

'It sounds as if there was a real problem.'

'Do you always go in for sugar coating, Mr Carrington? Martell was a sleaze. A dishonest and dangerous sleaze.'

'Ask him why,' Flora whispered, beginning to bob up and down.

'If you could tell me the details, it would be a great help. It's not idle prying, I can assure you. It matters.'

'Met him, have you, Martell? There's a strict rule in our line of work, Mr Carrington. Leave the clients alone. Max never could and he dabbled one too many times. Lovely girl, but vulnerable, you know. Alone in London, no parents. In a way, we're kinda in loco...'

'In loco parentis.'

'That's it. Look after the youngsters when they're far from home. Not Max, though. Seduced the poor kid then laughed at her when she wanted to get married.'

'I see—'

'No, you don't. That wasn't the end of it. The official line was she'd suffered a bad accident. Her friends thought different – they believed she'd done it to herself after Max walked out on her. Me, I doubted it was either. Something much worse, that's what I thought. She was getting in the way, see. Cramping his style.'

Flora's mouth had fallen open.

'That's dreadful,' Jack said, feeling slightly sick.

'That's Max for you. A little bit of advice – steer clear and make sure any ladies you know steer clear, too.'

'Doubts,' Flora mouthed. 'Ask him.'

'When you say you doubted, what did you mean exactly?'

'The girl electrocuted herself. Stuck a metal knife in a toaster that was live.'

'That does seem as though it could be an unfortunate accident,' Jack said cautiously.

'Not to me, it doesn't. She hardly worked and was as poor as dirt – what would she be doing with a toaster? Cost a fortune, they do. And the kid was obsessed with keeping thin. No potatoes, no bread was her motto. Why would she be making toast?'

'Thank you for talking to me, Mr Tinsdale, and for being so honest,' Jack said faintly and replaced the receiver. He stood looking at Flora.

'He was suggesting—' she began.

'That Martell killed the girl. Killed her because she was

pushing to get married. Not quite Mr Smooth after all. No wonder Mrs May was tight-lipped about him – she must have heard the story.'

Flora went behind her desk and plumped herself down on the stool. 'You were right, Jack. I honestly didn't think Martell should be in our sights, but now... maybe, if Beverly was pushing him to marry *her* – if she'd decided to cast Dominic adrift and make Max her new security – she signed her own death warrant.'

Flora fingered the silver charm bracelet she wore daily, a gift from Violet to mark the ending of an interminable war. 'What if Beverly had become too demanding and her beautiful voice wasn't enough to save her?' She twisted the bracelet round her wrist several times. 'Maybe in the end it was less important to Martell than getting rid of her.'

Jack walked over to the desk and studied Flora's worried face. 'It looks as though we have two men who wanted to be rid of Beverly for much the same reason. She was just too pushy. And, of course, a girl who wanted the same.'

He watched Flora closely for her reaction. She must know he meant the suspicions swirling around Sally, but she didn't answer directly.

'*Four* men,' she insisted. 'Don't forget Tommy May. *And* Dr Randall. He's up to something, I'm certain. And there's Jarvis and Shane, too.'

Jack thrust his hands in his pockets. 'No one said it was going to be easy!'

19

Flora was wheeling Betty from her shelter early the next morning, when she heard the front gate click. Today was lunchtime closing and she had a host of jobs to complete even before she opened the shop. She really didn't have the time to talk – whoever was making their way to her front door would have to come back.

But when she walked around to the front of the cottage, it was Sally who was halfway up the brick path. Flora resigned herself. Her friend was unlikely to have walked all the way from the Priory this early in the morning for a simple social call.

Sally looked round at the sound of bicycle wheels.

'You're off to work already,' she exclaimed. 'I thought I'd catch you before you left.'

'Busy day ahead,' Flora said apologetically. 'Could we have tea this afternoon?' It was at least worth a try.

Her friend looked doubtful. 'I suppose we could. It's just... I've been working myself up to speak to you,' she confessed, 'and now...'

It definitely wasn't a social call. Flora leant the bicycle

against the gate and walked back up the pathway, wriggling past Sally to open the front door.

'Come on through,' she said, and led the way into the sitting room.

'When I stayed at the cottage while you were in Cornwall, I always loved this picture of your aunt,' Sally said, picking up a photograph of Violet from the sideboard.

It was Flora's favourite, taken the summer before her aunt fell ill. Wearing a faded pair of dungarees, a battered sunhat and a broad smile, Violet stood clutching a lettuce in one hand and a beetroot in the other.

'She looks... steadfast. Honest and trustworthy...' The girl's voice faltered.

'Sit down,' Flora said gently, 'and tell me what this is all about.'

Her friend flopped into a fireside chair, as though her legs had finally failed her, and stared ahead at the whitewashed wall. 'It's Dominic,' she said at last.

'I thought it might be.' Flora sat down opposite.

'It's what that woman Russo told me – before she died.'

It wouldn't have been after, Flora thought, but then took herself to task for flippancy. Sally was evidently deeply upset.

'I didn't mention it earlier,' the girl went on, 'because I didn't want you to think badly of Dom. I know Aunt Alice doesn't like him and I thought that you probably didn't either.' She looked across at Flora, an appealing expression on her face. 'I wanted you to know the good things about him.'

'And this isn't a good thing?' Her companion was silent and Flora had to prompt her to continue. 'What did Beverly say to you?'

'She was a horrible woman.' Sally wrapped her hands deep in her cotton skirt and twisted the material into an unrecognisable shape. 'She guessed how I felt about Dominic ... she taunted me about it. She was jealous.'

'That made two of you, though, didn't it? I think *you* were equally jealous of Beverly.'

Sally dug her toes into the hooked rug and studied them intently. 'I may have been,' she admitted, 'but I didn't spill venom into her ear. Not the way she did to me. And there was no reason for her to be so unpleasant. She'd been his girlfriend for months, although I didn't know it at the time.'

'That was the reason, surely. She knew you were in love with Dominic and guessed that he'd fallen for you. She must have suspected he was trying to get out of his... his friendship... with her.'

'Do you think he really has fallen for me?' Sally asked tremulously.

'Let's stick with what Beverly told you that you didn't want to tell me earlier.'

Her friend bit her lips. 'She said that Dominic had lied about being part of the Templeton family.'

For a few seconds, Flora remained impassive, the revelation seemed so tame. She had always assumed that Dominic had lied.

'She did it out of spite.' The girl's voice was trembling again.

'You mustn't upset yourself, Sally. Very few of us believed his story. We reckoned he'd made up the Templeton connection in the hope he'd be more accepted in the village. I don't think it worked, but it wasn't that important.'

Sally looked stricken. 'But it is – important. Not because of Abbeymead, but because of the bank.'

'The bank?' Flora was mystified. 'What has that to do with anything?'

'I can't be completely certain, but I think the bank gave Dom the loan he asked for because he was a relative of Lord Edward's. At least, that's partly why they did. The Provident is where the Templeton family banked for centuries.'

Flora was unsure whether a financial institution would base

their lending on such a tenuous connection, but Sally seemed so convinced that maybe she was right.

'How well did you know Dominic before you decided to go into business with him?'

It was a crucial question and one that had never been answered, as far as Flora was aware. The man's background remained a mystery, unless he'd been a lot more forthcoming with Sally than with anyone else.

'Not that well, I suppose,' she admitted. 'I met him just before you and Jack went to Cornwall. At Carol's wedding. She was an old school friend of mine and we'd kept in touch, more or less, all the time I was working in Germany.'

'And Dominic? How did he come to be at the wedding?'

'He was someone the bridegroom knew from his work. Carol told me that Peter, that's her new husband, had done several business deals with Dominic and they'd been fine. Carol really liked him and introduced me at the reception. Dom was... mature... sophisticated... and he'd run this successful chain of bars in London.' She looked fixedly down at the rug. 'I suppose I was flattered by his attention,' she confessed, 'and we spent a lot of time at the reception together. When I told him about Abbeymead and Aunt Alice losing her job at the Priory and the place being up for sale, and how I'd always wanted to work in the hotel business, he said he'd been looking for a new investment and would I consider being a partner in it. It just seemed so perfect.' Her voice faltered again.

'You'd only known him a few hours when you accepted his offer?' It was worse than Flora had imagined.

'Yes,' Sally said in a whisper.

'Did you meet any other of his friends before you signed the agreement with him?'

Sally shook her head, her mouth drooping.

'And his family? What did Dominic actually tell you about his relationship to the Templetons?'

'He said' – Sally took a deep breath – 'that he'd travelled to Australia last year – as a break from managing his bars in London – and that he'd worked on a farm in the outback. The work was hard and, at the end of the day, the farmhands would go off for a beer or two. The boss would sometimes come with them and it was when Dom was talking to him one night and they exchanged family details that he realised he was a distant relative of the chap. Some kind of second or third cousin. And this man, the owner of the farm, was related to the Templetons. In fact, he'd inherited the estate when Lord Templeton died, but it wasn't much use to him in Australia so he sold it. The chap didn't go into much detail and it was only after we became partners and Dom came to Abbeymead for the first time that he realised the connection with the Priory. It was a huge coincidence.'

It was, Flora thought drily. Meeting a distant relative in the Australian outback sounded highly unlikely, but it was possible, she conceded, and the details of the inheritance mentioned by Sally were spot on. But still...

'The Australian man Dominic mentioned sold the Priory a few years ago for a great deal of money, but you're telling me that he's still a working farmer?'

'Dominic asked him about that and the chap said he'd tried splashing the money on a big place in the city and hated the life so much that he'd gone back to farming in the outback.'

'When Lord Edward died, the solicitors looked for relatives and could only find one distant cousin, the man that Dominic met,' Flora said thoughtfully, 'but I suppose it's possible there were others – Dominic himself, for instance.'

'You think he may be telling the truth?' Sally grasped at the straw.

'I've no idea,' Flora said frankly. 'Beverly may have lied to you out of spite or she could equally have told you the truth – still out of spite. The only way you'll know for certain is to contact this man in Australia and ask him. From memory, his name is Anderson. Reggie Anderson.'

'I can't do that!' Sally shook her head vigorously. 'Dominic might find out and he'd never trust me again.'

Flora's eyebrows twitched together. In her opinion, Dominic and trust were hardly close companions, but it would be good to have the matter settled. 'I could try to contact Mr Anderson for you,' she offered.

'Would you? Would you really, Flora?'

Almost immediately, though, the excitement vanished and Sally slumped further into the chair. 'You can't, though, can you? How would you ever find him?'

'I'll think of something,' Flora said, already thinking.

Jack had spent Thursday morning in the garden, emptying summer pots and planting a couple of evergreen shrubs, and was washing his hands at the kitchen sink prior to walking to the village when the door knocker sounded. He felt slightly aggrieved. Today was when Alice cooked cheese and potato patties for Katie's Nook and he'd been looking forward to collecting one for his lunch. If he didn't get there by midday, the café was likely to have run out.

To his surprise, it was Alan Ridley standing on the threshold.

'You're back,' he said, stupidly. It was evident the inspector was back.

'Back and wanting to talk, Jack. Fancy a beer?'

Jack gave an inner sigh and resigned himself to a very different kind of patty.

'Fine,' he said. 'I'll fetch my jacket.'

A brisk walk took them to the Cross Keys in minutes and, once they were seated in Ridley's favourite corner, drink and food on the table, he turned to his companion to ask the obvious question, 'Tell me, how was Suffolk?'

'Different.' Ridley grinned over his pint glass. 'Very rural.'

'Sussex is pretty rural, too.'

'Doesn't come close, my friend. Far more tractors in Suffolk to get pinched. And they don't have a town like Brighton on their doorstep, needing very different policing.'

'I take your point.' Jack swallowed a mouthful of glutinous pork and thought longingly of Alice's cheese and potato.

'I hear that while I've been away you've got yourself involved again, old chap. Another mystery, another crime.'

Jack attempted to scrub his face clean of expression. So this was what the meeting was about. 'Involved?' he asked innocently.

'The murder at the Priory. A singer, Miss Russo, was the victim.'

Jack could feel the trap closing in on him but, out of nowhere, Alan Ridley said, 'You did well finding that cable. You and your girlfriend.'

'She's not my girlfriend.' How many times did he have to repeat that? 'Your sergeant showed you the evidence then.'

'Did you think he wouldn't? Don't you trust him?' The inspector spoke lightly, but Jack detected a certain irritation.

'I'm sure he's extremely efficient,' he hastened to say, 'but I left the cable with him a week ago and there doesn't seem to have been much movement since.'

Ridley sighed and polished off his beer. 'I needed that,' he said, wiping froth from his lips. 'I agree with you. One hundred per cent. There hasn't been movement. As soon as I walked through the station door, I reviewed the case and, to be honest, we've got nowhere.'

'But you have the cable – that must be something.'

The inspector shook his head. 'We have it and it might have been vital, if there'd been fingerprints we could use. We'd have been galloping ahead. It was obvious from the start that the amplifier had been tampered with—most of the screws holding the back in place had disappeared—and it's pretty obvious that the piece of cable you found was the means by which it was done. Even without getting the boffins in, I can see that.'

'But the fingerprints – what happened to them?' Jack felt a heaviness weighing on him.

Ridley sighed again. 'Whatever prints there might have been have turned out indecipherable. Well and truly smudged. My men took prints from everyone involved that day – those on the stage, those standing close by. Yourself, your girl – sorry, Miss Steele – her friends. But there's not a hint of a match.'

Jack was thoroughly disheartened. In the absence of any other evidence, the cable had been his one hope. He could see now that he'd been counting on Ridley getting back from Suffolk, pouncing on their discovery, and taking charge.

'So,' the inspector continued, 'we're still at square one. Though I am intrigued by the bottle that arrived on my desk this morning. It contained two inches of liquid and had a written report attached to it.'

Jack's spirits plummeted further. The lab technician had returned the evidence directly to the police station rather than contacting him, and now he had more explaining to do. Probably more lies to tell.

'I don't know where you got the stuff from,' Ridley said, 'but the report made interesting reading.'

'I'm sorry, Alan. I should never have asked the chap to do an analysis, or at least I shouldn't have let him believe it was from you. I'm more than happy to pay the bill if there is one.'

'No, no need.' Ridley brushed aside his apology. 'Like I say, it was an interesting report.'

'Well?' Jack was on high alert. Could Flora be right about Dr Randall? She was annoyingly right about a lot of things.

Ridley gave a lazy smile, teasing him he could see, but then the inspector relented and said, 'Belladonna, that's what was in it, apart from something that looked and smelt like cough medicine. Just enough belladonna to make someone very sick, but not enough to kill them, my tame scientist said. All very fascinating, but where did it come from?'

'It was mine,' he said quickly. 'I wasn't thinking of taking the medicine. It's just an experiment I'm interested in.'

It was a poor excuse, but he'd had to think swiftly. If he told Ridley the truth, the doctor would be under arrest within an hour, his career forfeited, a prison sentence looming. And it might have been an honest mistake, though he couldn't think it. Still, he'd felt he should at least give Randall the chance to explain.

Alan Ridley was staring at him, his eyes clouded with suspicion. 'I'll let you get away with that – for now. I'm so far behind in this investigation, I haven't the time to pick up on every niggle. But if there's something I should know—'

'You'll know,' Jack promised.

The inspector chewed through the rest of his pie and it was several minutes before he could speak again. 'You know, you could set up a detective agency, you and the girl. You're pretty good at it.'

Jack pulled a face. It had been a throwaway comment he'd made to Flora months ago but neither of them had taken it seriously. It seemed, though, there might be a grain of truth in it.

'It's an idea, but not one I think I'll be pursuing! Not when I have a new novel on the horizon. Which reminds me, Alan, I'd better get back to my typewriter.' He slid out of his seat and bent to shake hands with the inspector. 'It's good to see you back – and thanks for the beer.' The pie, he felt, was best left unmentioned.

20

Jack had intended to return to Overlay House as soon as he left the pub, deciding to sketch out the first few chapters of the new book in advance of hearing from Arthur. But the Cross Keys' pork pie lay so heavily on his stomach that he couldn't in the end face sitting down at his desk. That was the story he told himself. The Remington was left waiting beneath its cover and, instead, he went for a long walk that took him past St Saviour's and up Fern Hill. Turning left at the top, he followed the lane that ran past Pelham Lodge, the palatial home of the Barneses, a couple still at loggerheads according to village gossip, and from there walked back into the village.

By the time he hit the high street, his stomach was feeling a good deal more comfortable and, looking at his watch, he realised that Flora would be closing the shop very soon. It was a good time to catch her, tell her his news and hear the inevitable 'I told you so.'

She was serving a customer when he walked through the door and shot a swift glance at him. Whatever she saw in his face had her smile broadly. As soon as the customer left, she danced towards him. 'You have news! Was I right?'

'It grieves me to say it, but yes. Dr Randall is definitely dodgy.'

She held on to his jacket sleeve and dragged him to the window seat. 'Tell me everything,' she commanded.

'As far as I can make out, belladonna had been mixed with cough medicine.'

'Ugh, that must taste and smell revolting. No wonder Beverly never took any. Or do you think she guessed it was risky?'

'I've no idea. What would have made her query its safety? The question must be why was Randall poisoning her? Alan Ridley was clear about what the analysis showed: enough belladonna to make Beverly very sick but probably not enough to kill her. Apparently, doctors can prescribe it sparingly, but for stomach cramps, not the heart.'

'Inspector Ridley? He's back?'

'Yes, he's back, but focus on the question.'

'It's obvious, isn't it? The doctor wanted to disable Beverly but not be responsible for her actual death. Isn't that part of the medical oath? Doctors promise to abstain from harming anyone.'

'Randall interpreted the oath pretty loosely then. Beverly wouldn't have died from that medicine, but she would certainly have been harmed. The question is still why would he do such a thing?'

'I don't know, but I think I may know someone who will. Now, what about the inspector?'

'There's not much to tell. He's survived the rural badlands of Suffolk and is back on the case, feeling dismal about the lack of progress.'

'And so he should. The sergeant he left to get on with it is clueless.'

'You don't know that.'

'No? Then why has nothing been done with the cable you

handed him? It's a crucial piece of evidence. It may be the *only* piece that's needed.'

'Something has been done. They've checked for fingerprints and there's not one clear print to be had. So, although the cable explains the method, it's useless as evidence.'

'Oh!' The air seemed suddenly to have been pumped out of Flora. 'That is a major blow.'

'As Ridley said, he's back to square one. He sounded fairly desperate, even hinting he'd be happy for any help we can give.'

'That is a turnaround. Except we don't have any help to give. I think I can find out what Randall was up to, but if he was poisoning Beverly Russo, he wouldn't be electrocuting her, too.'

'Unless he got fed up waiting for her to fall ill. Just because there wasn't enough belladonna to kill, doesn't mean he didn't want it to. He might have been unsure of the correct dose.'

'No,' Flora said decisively. 'If Beverly had died from poisoning, the medicine would have been the first suspect and led straight back to Randall. I've a strong feeling he wanted to make her ill, no more than that. Maybe encourage her to leave Abbeymead. We'll have to look elsewhere for our killer and there are plenty of suspects. Any member of the band will do, Tommy May in particular. And then there's Dominic.'

'And don't forget Martell.'

'I wasn't. We should talk to him, Jack, try to find out just what his relationship with Beverly was. We've an hour before it gets dark – we could go and find him now.'

'No, we couldn't,' he said, equally decisive. 'I need to eat. A pork pie from the pub is all I've had all day and it was disgusting.'

'Don't say you're getting to like decent food at last!'

'I'm getting to like decent cooking,' he said hopefully. 'You wouldn't by any chance...?'

'I suppose I could.' She stood up, holding out a hand. 'Come on, of course I could. I have some nice pork chops – just the thing after that pie.'

He groaned, but locked the All's Well's door behind them and threw her the keys.

'My potatoes?' Jack queried, digging his fork into one of the roasties Flora had just served, a hint of smugness on his face.

She managed a nod across the table. It was annoying that Jack had managed to grow a crop far superior to her own.

He took a large bite. 'How do you get them to taste so good? All crispy on the outside but fluffy in.'

'Did you never watch your mother cook?' she asked sniffily, refusing to be won over with praise.

Jack stared at her across the table, a second potato skewered on his fork and halfway to his mouth. 'My mother, cook? I doubt she'd know an oven if you stood her in front of one.'

Flora was aware of how dysfunctional Jack's family had been, but this seemed extreme. 'How did you eat, then? Surely not sandwiches all the time?' He had a passion for sandwiches which she'd never fathomed. Perhaps this was the reason.

'Nothing so common. These are *very* good, Flora.' He managed two more potatoes before he spoke again. 'We had a cook when my father was in the money, and since he was a pretty good poker player that was fairly often. But when he started losing, which could happen, the cook was dismissed and my mother ran a tally with the local restaurant. Once Dad was winning again, the restaurant got paid – thinking about it, they must have been extremely patient – and she'd hire another cook.'

'That was it? Cook, no cook, cook, no cook?'

'Just about,' he said cheerfully. 'I never actually went

hungry but I ate some odd concoctions – that's when I wasn't eating stodge at my boarding school.'

'No wonder...' she began.

'No wonder what?' he challenged.

'Never mind, eat your greens. They'll do you good! And the cabbage you're eating is mine, by the way.'

'Noted, and very good it is, too. Are we quits now?'

She couldn't prevent a smile. Jack was an easy person to like. 'Quits,' she agreed.

Once the washing up was done, they took a tray of tea to the sitting room and settled themselves into the fireside chairs. While she stirred the pot, Flora made a decision. This might be the time to broach a subject she knew would be difficult but one that had been on her mind.

'Have you heard from Arthur yet – about your proposal?'

'Not yet.' Already she could hear the defensive edge in Jack's voice and wondered whether to push further but, before she could say more, he offered an olive branch.

'Arthur has already approved the outline and I don't see why he won't like the synopsis I sent so... I've decided to go ahead with the book.'

His words came as a relief to Flora. 'It's good you've made a start.'

'Not yet. But soon.'

There was a long silence until she asked, 'You're still finding it hard?'

Whether it was the warmth in her voice or a need to talk, he seemed willing for the first time to admit to problems.

'I don't know why I'm having such trouble.' He put down his teacup and smoothed back the flop of hair from his forehead. His grey eyes, she saw, were stormy.

'I'm constantly distracted, that's the truth,' he said. 'I can't settle. I start a page, then need a drink, go back to it, and need to walk, another page and I'm out in the garden checking on plants I'd checked the day before.'

'Do you think it's this investigation that's getting to you?'

He shook his head. 'I doubt it. It started way back, before we even went to Cornwall, though being away seems to have made it worse. I can't tell you the relief I felt when Arthur told me the contract for that particular book had been cancelled. It doesn't help long term, though. He's my agent and he still needs a new book. *I* still need a new book.'

Flora was unsure how to respond. She had her own theory as to why Jack was finding it so difficult to settle back into his old groove, but she knew he wouldn't find it palatable. A solution is what he needed right now and the only one she could put forward verged on the drastic.

'Perhaps you need to rethink your career,' she suggested.

'And do what? We've talked about this before and nothing has changed since then. I could go back to journalism, though it would be hard, now I've lost most of my contacts. But the truth is, I don't want to. And I don't want to give up being an author. I love it. Loved it,' he amended.

'Then take a long break and come back when you feel ready. Arthur will wait, I'm sure.'

'There's the small matter of paying the rent – and the roast potatoes – in the meantime.'

'You could take a temporary job,' she said vaguely. 'You've got the Austin, you could travel into Brighton. There are bound to be jobs available that aren't just seasonal. Or' – she had a burst of inspiration – 'talk to Alan Ridley. There may be a niche at police headquarters that you'd fit.'

Jack folded his hands behind his head and stretched. 'Ridley actually suggested I set up as a private detective, though I'm not sure he was serious.'

'Are *you*?' she asked quizzically. 'You've mentioned it before, but I thought you were joking.'

'I was. I enjoy our dark forays into the world of real-life crime, but being a private eye would be very different. It seems to be a life of spying on other people, most often married people who want a divorce. Staging scenes of sham adultery.' He pulled a face. 'It wouldn't be a life I'd want.'

'I can see that. Have you finished?' She pointed to his empty cup, picking up the teapot to refill it. 'It's quite flattering, I suppose, that the inspector thought you'd be suitable. I've always had the feeling he considered us bumbling nuisances. But maybe it's just me that's the bumbler.'

'Oh no, you were definitely included in his praise. We're both supposed to be helping him, even though we're making a poor fist of it right now. Still, after today, we can discount one of our suspects. You could say it's progress.'

'Dr Randall?'

Jack nodded. 'Randall is guilty of a crime, but it's not the one we're pursuing.'

'Can we forget Sally, too? If she bears any guilt, I reckon it's for shielding someone she shouldn't and not giving us the information she could.'

'She should stay on our list,' Jack said firmly. 'For the moment. She had as much motive and opportunity as the rest of them. And why is she holding out if she has something that could be valuable? Sally was the one who asked us to get involved in the first place. It doesn't make sense.'

'I think she'll come clean very soon, then we *can* cross her name off. She's asked me to check on Dominic's supposed relationship to the Templetons. It's evident she's come round to thinking what everyone else has always thought – that he's lied about it.'

'And that's important?'

'It might be. At the very least he could be proved a liar and thoroughly untrustworthy but, more than that, it might be that the bank loan he obtained was given on the strength of a false relationship.'

'You think the bank would lend to him based on the Templeton connection?'

'Don't you?'

'It sounds unlikely, but then I don't know how the Old Boy network functions. If it's in play here, it's possible, I suppose. But how will you check? The only surviving Templeton we know of is in Australia.'

'That's whom I intend to contact, the chap in Australia. Dominic told Sally he met him while he was working there and discovered they were second or third cousins.'

'He was working in Australia?' Jack snorted. 'I doubt Lister has ever seen a kangaroo. But how are you planning to contact... what was his name?'

'Anderson. Reggie Anderson. I paid Constable Tring a visit yesterday afternoon. He was the one who telephoned Anderson to let him know what had happened to his nephew.'

'And you got a phone number out of Mr I'll Do It By the Book? I'm impressed.'

'Jack,' she said suddenly, leaning forward and putting a hand on his knee, 'does anything strike you as odd about this investigation? Different from what we've encountered before?'

He looked surprised. 'The number of suspects,' he hazarded, 'though we've begun to whittle them down.'

Flora shook her head. 'It's the fact that I've never felt in any danger. Never felt threatened. I realised that last night. How about you?'

'No, I haven't, but should I?'

'We've always suffered threats before. You must remember. Every time there's been at least two or three attempts to hurt us, or worse.'

'Maybe it's an unwelcome indicator that we've not made

much progress. Certainly not enough to disturb the villain we're after.'

'It could be that,' she conceded, 'but maybe something else, too.'

'Like what?' he asked, clearly mystified.

'Whoever killed Beverly seems unconcerned that anyone is on their track. He or she isn't thinking about getting caught. It doesn't seem to have entered their head that anyone, even the police, is on the hunt for them.'

'That doesn't ring true. A crime such as murder brings terrible retribution. Whoever killed Beverly Russo must have the gallows at the back of their mind.'

'You would think so, but... not if what motivated them was pure emotion. An overwhelming need to get rid of Beverly, to scrub her from their world. She's dead now, just as they planned, and they can carry on their life as usual.'

'You'd have to be a very, very, cold fish to do that; cold to the point of inanimate.'

'Not if you had tunnel vision,' she argued. 'If you had just the one goal in mind and that's all you could think of – you were going to reach that goal, come what may. Just for a moment, consider the risks this person took. It must have needed split-second timing to prise open the amplifier and attach a small piece of cable at precisely the right moment, and do it without being seen. And amazing luck, to reverse the process and dump the rogue cable out of reach, again without being seen. You'd need huge nerve to accomplish that, an utter conviction that you could carry it off and remain untouched.'

Jack eased himself from the chair and stood, hands in pockets, seemingly deep in thought. 'Do any of our remaining suspects fit the image you've painted?'

Flora pursed her lips. 'All three men in the band hated Beverly,' she said eventually. 'Or at least disliked her intensely.

None of them seems sorry she's dead, none of them are even mildly concerned at the way she died. Jarvis even wished the perpetrator good luck! And I guess you could accord every one of them tunnel vision. Tutti Frutti is all that matters to them and Beverly was wrecking the group, in their opinion.'

'Tommy has a temper,' Jack said slowly, walking towards the window and back again. 'That's plain enough, and a violent past. Shane appears a peacemaker but shares Tommy's history.'

'And Jarvis must have had some kind of relationship to Beverly before she joined the group. He might well have a grudge against her, above and beyond the way she stirred trouble between the men. Any of them could have tampered with the amplifier before walking on stage and, afterwards in the mayhem that broke out, could have hidden the evidence. They'd have had virtually no time, but they could have just about done it.'

Jack came to rest in front of her. 'The same could be said of Dominic – he didn't use the microphone, did he? Is that suspicious? And the same of Martell. Both men were close by, both trying to escape Beverly's clutches. Martell has possible form from his past, according to his ex-business partner, and we think that Sally is concealing something that could be incriminating.'

'That's one bubble I'm hoping to burst with my telephone call to Australia. If she knows definitely that Dominic has lied, I think Sally will talk.'

'We've not got far, have we?' Jack sighed, collecting the teapot and cups and taking them back to the kitchen. 'Good luck with the telephone call – and with the fallout from Sally when it comes.'

'Thanks,' she said mockingly, leaning against the kitchen door frame. 'I'll let you know. Meanwhile, I better warn Maggie Unwin that the medicine she was searching for so furiously is, in fact, poison.'

'If she doesn't already know it.' Jack retrieved his jacket from the kitchen chair and shrugged himself into it. 'I'd best be off, but a lovely meal, Flora. Thank you.'

21

It was Saturday and Flora was prompt in closing the All's Well a few minutes before midday. She was hoping to intercept Maggie Unwin as she left after morning surgery and hurried along the high street to the corner of Greenway Lane, only to find the waiting room door closed and no sign that anyone had been near the building that morning.

What was going on? Flora couldn't remember a time when the surgery hadn't opened for a few hours every Saturday. Crossing the road, she walked along to Katie's Nook and found the café buzzing. Kate was serving a full lunch to three or four tables, while Charlie Teague was behind the counter, his head barely visible.

Leaving Kate to take care of her customers, Flora walked over to speak to him – Charlie was a boy who always knew the latest Abbeymead news – but, before she had a chance to ask the question on her mind, Alice appeared from the kitchen.

'Hello, my love. Come for lunch? There's a nice hotpot today.'

'And treacle tart for pudd'n,' Charlie confirmed.

'Only when you've sorted that cutlery, Master Teague.' Alice's smile belied her severity.

'Actually, it wasn't lunch I was after, though I must say the pudding looks lovely.' Leaning over the counter, Flora caught sight of the row of treacle tarts laid out on the long, kitchen table.

'I've finished the cutlery, Mrs Jenner,' Charlie put in, 'and I've repacked the spare china. Can I have my tart now?'

'I reckon so, young man.' She tousled his hair. 'Help yourself to some custard as well, but not too much, mind.'

'Alice, there's always been a surgery on Saturday morning,' Flora said. 'Has Dr Randall stopped it, do you know?'

'Saturday mornin'? That's right. Reg'lar as clockwork, Dr Hanson was. I don't know as how this new'un has changed things.'

'He must have done. I've just called there and the building's closed.'

Flora saw her companion glance at the clock over the café doorway. 'I was there just after twelve,' she said, 'and it looked as though the surgery hadn't opened at all today.'

Alice looked concerned. 'Is somethin' wrong with you, my ducks?'

'No, I'm fine,' she reassured her. 'I don't need an appointment. It was Maggie Unwin I wanted to speak to.'

Alice pursed her lips. '*That* young lady,' she said with emphasis. Meaning, Flora assumed, that Maggie's indiscretion was well known in the village.

'It was only a small thing I wanted to check, but I was hoping to catch her.'

'She lives close by.' Alice began to lay up new trays with the cutlery Charlie had sorted. 'Almost behind the surgery – Larkspur Cottage. You know old Mrs Waterford? The girl rents a room there. You could always knock.'

'You're a fount of information.'

'I do my best. Now, how about I wrap some of that tart up for you – before Charlie eats too much and makes himself sick.'

'Thank you – that's a kind thought.'

Flora left the café, brown paper bag in hand, and smiled at Kate on the way out. It was good to see the Nook doing so well, Kate doing so well, after the months of heartache the girl had suffered. Lately, she'd been looking truly happy, glowing almost, Flora realised.

Retracing her steps, she walked back along the high street, this time past the surgery until she reached a row of cottages that led out of the village. Larkspur was the first in line.

Mrs Waterford came to the door and, after Flora explained her mission, shuffled to the bottom of the stairs and yelled for Maggie in a voice that was surprisingly lusty for an elderly lady.

She had to call twice before there was any sound from above. A door opened and closed, and Maggie's face appeared at the top of the stairs. Flora saw immediately that the girl had been crying again. Trying not to think that she was about to make her life even more painful, she smiled up at her.

'Could we have a word, Maggie?'

Maggie looked hunted, her glance flicking rapidly between Flora and her landlady, her mouth puckering. 'OK, but can we go outside?' she said hurriedly.

Once the front door shut behind them, she put a hand on Flora's arm. 'I'm sorry I had to drag you out. I'd rather Mrs Waterford not hear what you have to say. She's a bit of a gossip.'

Who isn't in this village? Flora thought, but it was clear from Maggie's words that she was expecting her to bring bad news, which perhaps told its own story. 'I tried to meet you at the surgery, but it was closed and didn't seem to have opened today.'

'It didn't,' Maggie said flatly. 'We don't have a doctor.'

Flora was startled. 'But Dr Randall?' she queried.

'Gone,' the girl said. The single word was stark.

'What do you mean, gone?'

'Just that. He's left Abbeymead and taken his family with him.' She spoke in a murmur so low that Flora could hardly hear.

'But how could he have just disappeared?'

Maggie spread her hands as though she, too, couldn't believe it. 'I was working yesterday and I saw him at evening surgery. He must have left late last night.' Her head drooped before she went on, 'When he didn't turn up this morning, I went round to his house. There was no one there. The car had gone. The blinds were drawn, and the toys that are usually on the front lawn had disappeared.'

Dr Randall had done a midnight flit. How extraordinary! But perhaps it wasn't so odd if you considered the evidence piling up against him.

'I wonder how he explained such a hasty departure to his wife?' was her first practical thought.

Maggie shook her head. 'I don't know what he told her, but he could be very persuasive.'

Flora could imagine. 'And what about you, Maggie? Where does this leave you?'

'I'll find another job, I suppose, until they get another locum or Dr Hanson gets back. You don't need to worry about me.' The girl was putting on a brave front.

'I do worry, though. And you should be worried, too. It's why I came to see you. To warn you that the police might well come calling and, if they do, you must be honest with them. No trying to protect Dr Randall at your own expense.'

Maggie's cheeks were ashen. 'Is it the medicine?' she whispered.

'Yes, the medicine. It's undergone analysis and a poison has been detected. But you know about that, don't you?' Her question was matter-of-fact.

The girl was silent for a moment, unable to meet Flora's eyes. 'I tried to stop him,' she said quietly, 'but he was desperate. He promised it would only make Miss Russo a little ill. Enough to persuade her to give up the band for a while and leave Abbeymead, but nothing that would hurt her too badly.'

'Belladonna is serious and can kill,' Flora said severely. 'Why *was* he so desperate that he'd go against everything a doctor should stand for?'

'It was Beverly Russo's fault,' the girl burst out. 'She was bleeding Brian dry.'

'Are you saying she was blackmailing him?'

Maggie nodded miserably.

'What could she possibly use...' Flora started to say, then realised exactly what Beverly had used. 'Miss Russo learned about Dr Randall's affair with you?'

Another miserable nod.

'But how did she know? I suspected it, and it's plain that much of Abbeymead thought the same, but Beverly was a stranger here and no villager would have discussed their suspicions with her.'

'She heard us. She telephoned the surgery to book an appointment – her heart was racing, apparently, and it worried her.'

'OK, but I still don't see... unless... was it a party line?'

'Brian used the private phone in the surgery to call me at home but Mrs Waterford is on a party line. That's why he rarely telephoned.'

'And the phone at the Priory – or at least the one at the stables – uses the same line?'

'It must do, though we had no idea. That Russo woman listened in to our conversation. We only knew she had when we heard the click of the receiver being put down.'

'Still, she couldn't have been sure it was you, unless he called you by your name.'

'He didn't. He was careful like that. But I have a Scots accent, you might have noticed, and there aren't too many of those in Abbeymead. When Miss Russo came to the surgery for the appointment, she recognised my voice, and knew what was going on. She threatened Brian that she'd report him. If it was known he was having an affair with his receptionist, he'd be disciplined and, worst of all, might even lose his licence. Think what it would have done to his wife and children. So he paid up.'

The more Flora learned of Beverly Russo, the more unpleasant the woman appeared. A woman who deliberately set friends and colleagues at odds, who was happy to deceive the two men who'd loved her – and probably more – and, now it appeared, happy to blackmail a foolish young doctor with a wife and small children.

'How many times did Dr Randall pay her?' she asked, interested in just how greedy Beverly had been.

'Twice, but then she asked again. After the last time, he told her there was no money, but she still came back for more and he just couldn't pay. He'd given her all the family's savings, though his wife didn't know. The only chance he had was to get rid of the woman.'

'Well, he did get rid of her. She's dead.'

'Brian wasn't responsible for that.' Maggie looked thoroughly scared. 'She was electrocuted, wasn't she? That's what the village says.'

'She was and Dr Randall is fortunate that he's unlikely to face a murder charge. Fortunate, too, that Beverly Russo didn't take any of his medicine.'

'But...' Maggie started to say.

'You thought she had? When I brought the bottle back half empty? That's why you looked so frightened, of course. It wasn't Beverly, it was me. I took a sample of the liquid, but if Beverly *had* taken that medicine, Dr Randall could be accused of exacerbating the problem she had with her heart, so that when she received the full force of electric current, she died instantly. For all I know, that could mean a charge of manslaughter.'

'Oh, no!' she stuttered, covering her eyes with her hands and shaking her head to and fro.

Flora stood quietly, allowing the girl time to absorb how bad a situation she faced. Eventually, when Maggie dropped her hands, she whispered, 'I don't understand how you know about the medicine, Flora – but what are you going to do now?'

'I have no idea,' she admitted. 'Jack Carrington has told the police that the medicine is his. The inspector believed Jack's story, or pretended to, but he may well decide to start asking more questions, and you need to be prepared. It's fairly common knowledge that Beverly had been prescribed medicine.'

'Why did Mr Carrington say it was his?'

'He wanted to protect the doctor until the man had an opportunity to explain. There was an outside chance he'd made an innocent mistake, but plainly not. And by taking flight, Brian Randall has marked himself out as guilty. Hopefully, though, Jack's intervention will protect *you*, at least.'

'Tell him, thank you,' the girl said, her voice shaking.

22

Flora had turned into Greenway Lane on her way home, treacle tart clutched in one hand, when she saw a tall figure shambling towards her, head down, feet kicking at whatever stones or twigs were in his way.

It was Tommy May. Incredibly, it seemed he was out for a walk. The group must be getting very bored for its leader, as well as its drummer, to be taking walks around the village.

'Good afternoon,' she said cheerfully.

He looked up and scowled. 'You think so?'

'Don't you? You'll be leaving Abbeymead very soon – that's what I heard.'

'You heard right. Permission has arrived! As long as we give our address to the plods. The transport's been ordered and we move out next Saturday, for what good that will do.'

Flora frowned. Tommy's disenchantment seemed strange. He should be jumping at the thought of leaving the stables behind and getting on with his life.

'Has something happened? Something bad?'

'You could say that. Just another betrayal, all in a day's work,' he said bitterly.

Her puzzlement grew. Beverly had been the one he'd accused of disloyalty and Beverly was no more. 'This betrayal—' she began.

'I thought Bev was bad enough,' he said. 'Well, she was. An evil bitch, that's for sure. The way she messed with my life, then went on to Dom and started on his. Even propositioned Shane, he told me. I should have listened to him.'

'So who...?'

But Tommy wasn't taking notice. There was an evident need in him to vent his anger at the way his life had turned out, and Flora stood back and waited.

'I was the one who gave her a break, did you know that?' His face flushed an angry red. 'Yeah, if it wasn't for me, she'd have stayed behind a shop counter.'

'She was a shop assistant? I didn't know.' Flora feigned interest. You never knew where conversations might lead, particularly those fuelled by raw emotion.

'Nobody much does. It's not something she liked to boast about. I was a judge at some rubbishy talent contest run by the local youth club. Me, a judge! I think I'd been paid for all of two gigs at the time. The prize was two pounds, enough to buy a special party dress, so Bev told me later. That's why she went in for it.' His face softened, no doubt remembering his younger self, but then the glower was back. 'I wasted precious time on that harpy. Should have seen her for what she was years ago, sent her back to a till at Woolworth's. Whoever rid the world of her, good luck to them.'

For a moment, Flora was taken aback. Was Tommy admitting to murder? Not quite but, like Jarvis before him, he'd come perilously close to it. She needed to keep him talking.

'Who betrayed you this time?' she asked, still waiting for an answer. 'I hope not Jarvis.'

To Flora, Jarvis seemed the least stable of the group and the mysterious photograph he carried in his wallet had been playing on her mind. It defied explanation and things that couldn't be explained were an irritant.

'Jarvis is solid.' Tommy drew himself up to his full height, his legs astride and firmly planted on the lane's tarmac.

'He drinks a lot,' Flora said tentatively. 'How do you cope with that?'

'As long as it doesn't mess with the performance, I'm cool. I wish he wouldn't down quite as much, but he's got troubles so I leave the bloke alone.'

'What kind of troubles?'

Tommy looked uncertain, but the quiet country surroundings or perhaps Flora's guileless face or simply the fact that he'd been held captive with the same three people for nearly a month, seemed to encourage him.

'Family troubles,' he confided. 'His sister went missing and J can't find her.'

'A younger sister?' The image of two girls in a photograph came alive.

'Yeah, I guess.' Tommy scratched behind his ear. 'Anna must be about nineteen now. J's her big brother. Loved her to bits. It was four years ago and he's looked everywhere, but it's like she's fallen off the edge of the world. He's gonna fear the worst, isn't he? But the guy's OK.'

'So if it's not Jarvis and it's not Shane, who's upset you so much?'

'Who else but the sainted Max? She made a play for him, did you know? Beverly. Couldn't resist it. He was a man going places and she was determined to go with him. Mind you, she'd have gone with anyone if it meant getting top billing and her name in bright lights.' He made a sweeping gesture with his hand. 'Martell shrugged it off when I went for him. Not me, he said. I'm far too honest to be involved in anything so mucky. Like hell he was. Not too honest to drop us in a ditch, though, now she's dead.'

'I'm sorry, I don't understand.'

'Why would you? You didn't take the call. I did – yesterday. Some minor agent, some bloke we wouldn't look twice at, phoned to say that now we had no agent, he was happy to step in. I bet he was. We've got an agent, I told him, and he's booked us to play another half a dozen dates. "That's not what I heard," he said. "I think you'll find those dates are cancelled and so is your agent. He's working with Rock Solid now and I wouldn't mind betting they're the ones who'll be playing those venues. But let me know if my offer interests you."'

Tommy stamped on a lone puddle, his feet encased in a pair of dirty leather boots, sending water flying in every direction. 'Which means, Flora Steele,' he said furiously, 'that the bastard has sold us down the river.'

'He's walking out on you.' Flora had at last grasped what Tommy was saying.

'That's about it. And this is a man who once had a scruffy little office in Soho above the restaurant where I worked, an agent, so-called, who'd be lucky to book the odd skiffle group into some equally scruffy club. Walking out on us, like you say. So when the truck rolls up next Saturday, where do we tell the driver to take our gear?'

'Have you seen Max to talk to him? The truth may be very different.'

'I don't need to talk. I know the truth, whatever Shane says. The coward's gone to ground for the moment, but he'll have to show his face eventually and, when he does, look out! It's not gonna be nice.'

'What does Shane say?' Flora fixed on what seemed most interesting.

'That Martell was bound to walk when Beverly died. We're not the same band without her and Max can't pretend to the punters that we are. The venues where we're booked won't want to know. There's no loyalty in music, Shane's right there, but Max owes us. He was a nothing until he signed us. He's piggy-backed on our success. Now he's letting us go like a sack of rubbish he doesn't want to carry any more.'

Flora was fishing for something to say that was vaguely comforting – it seemed too harsh, what was happening to Tutti Frutti – but Tommy forestalled her. 'Gotta go, girl,' he said. 'Gotta plot a course out of this.' And gave her a casual wave of the hand.

She stood looking after him. Their conversation had left her as uncertain as she'd ever been. The unfamiliarity of the world that Tutti Frutti inhabited hit her anew. How to make sense of the people in it and understand their motivations when their lives felt so alien, even outlandish? What to make of Tommy's upset? How arrive at any settled view of his guilt, or of that of his colleagues?

She spent a restless night. She'd done what she could to help Maggie and hopefully the girl would not be interviewed about what she knew. With a bit of luck, the medicine would remain an insignificant part of the inspector's enquiry. It was Tommy May who was worrying her. Despite her earlier reservations, she'd grown to quite like him. He was what Aunt Violet would have called a rough diamond, but he'd overcome a bad start and worked hard for the success he'd gained. As far as Flora could judge, he was an honest man, too ready to anger perhaps but frank where his feelings were involved. And they *were* involved in the case of Max Martell, someone Tommy disliked intensely.

It was the suggestion of trouble ahead that kept Flora tossing in her bed. When Max finally put in an appearance, Tommy had threatened, it wouldn't be nice. Not nice in the way that Beverly's end hadn't been nice? Tommy had been their main suspect from the very beginning. Had she and Jack been right the first time?

It was true that any one of the band, along with the people standing close by – Kate and Alice, Sally and Dominic, Max Martell – could have slipped around to the side of the stage and in seconds removed the cable they'd fixed earlier. All that was required was to prise free the two clips and dispose of them along with the cable. And the killer could easily have donned a pair of gloves to ensure there were no clear fingerprints.

Out of all those people, Tommy had the most obvious motive. Beverly had been disloyal to him and he was certain she was about to treat Dominic in the same fashion, casting him adrift in favour of a better offer. Tommy's love for the girl had turned to hatred – that bitter row he'd had with her only an hour before the band's big performance. He seemed a man given to impetuosity, a man of strong passions and direct action, and he'd been furious. Had he acted on his fury? And would he act on it now, appearing as he did to hate Max as much as he hated Beverly?

And then there was Jarvis Redmond and his missing sister. It might have no connection to the case, but it was plain from Flora's earlier conversation with the drummer that he disliked Beverly almost as much as Tommy did. If the unknown girl in the photograph Jarvis carried, her arms draped around a younger Beverly, was the same Anna, there was a story to be told. A reason for the girl's disappearance that was connected in some way to the group's singer. Jarvis must think so or he wouldn't keep that photograph close, unless, of course, it was the only one he possessed of his sister. But then the coincidence of Beverly being Anna's friend... Flora's mind was skittering... it couldn't be a coincidence, could it?

She longed to sit down with Jack and share her concerns, but that would involve yet another visit to Overlay House and more time spent closeted together. Increasingly, these last few months, she'd tried to meet him away from home: in the village or at the All's Well or Katie's Nook. Once or twice she'd succumbed to impulse, it was true – wine on his terrace, dinner at her cottage a few days ago – but it was a path she knew she should avoid. A path that led inevitably to hurt and unhappiness.

Their friendship had changed – she couldn't disguise the fact – their feelings running a good deal deeper these days. Maybe it had been their stay in Cornwall that had subtly altered the dynamic between them. The trip they'd made together, a gift for village rumour, had served to highlight their closeness. No matter how many times she'd insisted on it being a research trip, that she and Jack were going away on business and definitely not sharing a holiday, the gossip had endured. Two single people living alone under the same roof. How scandalous!

The village hadn't been that wrong, she reflected drily. Living under the same roof for several weeks had led to a new intimacy, a desire to be together more than simple friends would or should want. It showed in different ways, but it was there. There'd been a moment a few days ago when she'd been arguing with him, pushing him to take the medicine for analysis, and he'd been arguing back. In frustration, he'd reached out, wanting to clutch hold of her, before thinking better of it. It was a moment when she'd wanted him to, she found herself admitting.

In her younger days, Flora had taken for granted that she would meet and marry someone she loved. Richard had been the one to fill that role until he'd walked away at the very time she needed his support most. The time when she'd first learned that Violet's illness was incurable. In the end, Richard hadn't been much of a loss, but the experience had left her feeling insecure, with a humiliating sense of having been stupidly naive in believing that he was on her side and would stand by her whatever.

Jack had suffered loss, too. A far greater one than hers. He'd been weeks away from walking down the aisle when deceit had come knocking on his door. He was adamant that he no longer thought of Helen, but Flora suspected her betrayal still disturbed him. Did either of them really want to take on the complications of the past? They were tempted, it was clear, but it would be far better for them both if they found a way of continuing as friends. Very good friends – and partners in crime.

For some reason, she found the thought depressing and, when it continued to hover long after she woke the following morning, she had to try hard to shake herself out of a grey mood. A roast dinner should help, she decided, even one eaten in solitary splendour. Yesterday, she'd found time to buy beef from Mr Preece, the smallest joint you could imagine – he'd joked she would need spectacles to carve it – but small was perfect for a single meal. Choosing her sharpest knife, she walked down the garden path to the vegetable patch. It was looking reasonably healthy these days and she gave herself a thumbs up, hoping Violet, the vegetable supremo, was watching. Cutting a small cauliflower and unearthing a bunch of carrots, she was about to dig for potatoes when she remembered the handful still in her outhouse, donated by Jack. Annoyingly, they were excellent roasters.

Once lunch was under way, she unearthed the telephone number she'd wheedled out of Constable Tring several days ago. As she'd expected, the policeman had been reluctant to release any information but, by dint of stressing how urgent it was for the Priory to get in touch with Reggie Anderson and promising to destroy details of his telephone number once she'd made contact, she had managed to persuade the man.

Immediately she'd arrived home that day, she'd placed a call to Australia but, when the operator put her through to a number ringing halfway round the world, there'd been no answer. It was only later that she realised how stupid she'd been, having completely ignored the time difference. The operator hadn't seen fit to warn her and the telephone must have rung in the early hours. Better prepared now, she'd asked for a call to be placed this morning. It would be evening at the farm, just after nine o'clock, and early enough for Mr Anderson not to have climbed the stairs to bed.

She was setting the kitchen table when the telephone shrilled.

Dashing into the hall, she picked up the receiver to a burst of static, a series of clunking sounds and, finally, a voice. An Australian voice. She'd got there.

'You want to speak to me, girl?'

'Yes, Mr Anderson. I'm sorry to interrupt your evening.'

'Not my evenin',' he said grumpily. 'My bedtime.'

'In that case, I'm even more sorry. I wouldn't have rung if it wasn't absolutely necessary. Something's happened here – in Abbeymead. At the Priory?' she added, in case he'd forgotten the source of his inheritance. 'Something I need your help with.'

'I know where the Priory is. Haven't forgotten Abbeymead either. Lost my nephew there.'

'That must be very painful. I'm sorry to be reminding you.'

'Not that painful. Kevin was a fool. Bound to come to a sticky end.'

Uncle Reggie was proving as hard-hearted as Flora had guessed from what she already knew of him.

'I was hoping to check a detail with you,' she tried again. 'Information on the young man who's living at the Priory now.'

'Has that tosspot sold then?'

Anderson was evidently unaware that Vernon Elliot had come to grief, not quite as much grief as Reggie's nephew, but still an unwelcome fate.

'Yes,' she replied, 'Mr Elliot sold. The man I wanted to talk to you about is Dominic Lister.'

'Oh, yeah?'

'You haven't heard of him?'

'Should I have?'

'He visited Australia last year. He worked on a farm in the outback,' she said, telling the story as Sally had related it.

'Big place,' Reggie commented.

'I'm sure it is, but Dominic mentioned you in particular. He claims he spent time working on your farm.'

'Got the wrong farm there, luv.'

'So you've never met a Dominic Lister?' Flora needed a definite answer.

'Not on your life. Wouldn't have some Pom workin' here anyway. If he told you that, I reckon he's pullin' a fast one.'

That was one thing on which she could agree with Anderson. 'Just to be clear, he also said that you and he were related to each other through Edward Templeton.'

'The English lord?'

'Yes, the one you inherited from.'

'Nah, not on your life. I was the only relation the poor bloke had left. It's why I won the jackpot. This Lister bloke – I should steer clear of him, girly.'

Flora would like to have given Sally that advice, too, and had her take it, but she merely said, 'Thank you, Mr Anderson. You've been most helpful.'

'I can go to bed now?'

'Please do,' she said, relieved the conversation was at an end and she could put the telephone down.

Not relieved, though, that tomorrow she would have to tell Sally that her fears had been realised. For whatever reason, Dominic had lied. The lie itself was trivial; it was the likely result that was critical, the possibility that Lister had obtained the loan only because of his supposed relationship to the Templetons.

Returning to the kitchen to check her roast – the beef was sizzling and the potatoes crisping nicely – Flora's mind was unsettled. Pieces of the puzzle were slowly coming together, but so much still remained unknown. Would she and Jack ever have the full picture?

23

The next evening, as soon as she'd locked the All's Well's door, Flora walked to the Priory. If the police were allowing Tutti Frutti to leave the area, it surely wouldn't be long before Sally was told she could reopen the hotel. It seemed Inspector Ridley was at a loss on how to proceed, so what point would there be in keeping the Priory closed? Witnesses had been interviewed, statements taken, and what little evidence there'd been at the crime scene, gathered days ago.

She had no idea how Sally filled her days without a hotel to run, nor Dominic for that matter, but hoped that whatever the girl was doing, she would be doing it alone. It was going to be a difficult conversation. At the Priory gates she paused for a moment, hit by a sudden thought that perhaps she should have taken Alice aside and confided what she'd learned from Australia – the news was distressing and might better come from a loved aunt. But that would simply be shirking her own responsibility and burdening Alice with an uncomfortable task. She'd been the one to promise Sally she would discover the truth or otherwise of Dominic's claim. And she had discovered it. Flora could only hope that it would make Sally think twice before definitely committing herself to the man. If Dominic had to remain her business partner, so be it, but in Flora's view that was as far as it should go.

She was in luck. Walking past the stone pillars and through the great oak door into the magnificent hall, she narrowly avoided a ladder leaning against the wood panelling. Sally was at the top, waving a feather duster at a row of Templeton portraits.

The sound of footsteps had her turn, her spare hand clinging to the ladder. 'Flora! It's good to see you.'

'Have you taken on the cleaning now? Is that wise?'

There was a streak of dust on one of Sally's cheeks and her short blonde hair was home to what appeared to Flora, several feet below, very much like a spider's web.

'I must admit it's not looking too wise from up here,' she said cheerfully, 'but I'm being careful. The thing is we can't afford cleaners when we've no paying guests, yet the Priory still insists on getting dusty.'

'This place is far too big for one person to clean,' Flora said, feeling frustrated that Sally was beset by so many problems. Almost instantly, though, another feeling wriggled into being and what Jack called her sleuth mode took over. 'The library, for instance, must be a nightmare.'

She had never tackled her friend on how exactly the guide to electrics had appeared on the fair's bookstall. Whenever she'd met Sally recently, the girl had been too upset for her to probe further and it was Jack, in any case, who'd pushed the notion that Sally could, in some way, be involved in the murder. Flora herself had always been hugely sceptical, though both of them agreed the girl was hiding something. Today, she sensed a possibility – that she might finally be able to cross Sally from their list of suspects.

'Dottie does the library, thank goodness.' Sally ran her

feather duster across the top of the nearest oil painting. 'She's one of the few maids I've been able to keep on.'

'A brave woman! At least she won't have quite so many books to dust this week.'

Sally looked blank.

'Have you forgotten? You took a pile of them to the market.'

'The market on the village green? Yes, that's right. I think I've done enough up here.' She tucked the duster under her arm and clambered down the ladder.

'I was on the bookstall that day. I didn't see you but Dilys said you called by earlier.'

'I did, but the books weren't from the library. Just odds and sods that were left lying around. I reckoned they might as well go for sale as give us even more to dust.'

It sounded plausible, but a book on electronic circuits? Would anyone leave that lying around? The image of Sally's jealous face when she'd talked of Beverly was still vivid.

Flora grasped the nettle, knowing it might sting. 'Who on earth would have left behind a book on basic electronics?'

'Was there one?' her friend asked innocently. 'I didn't read the titles, just went round collecting them from here, there, everywhere, and bundled them together. I don't suppose anyone would have bought that particular one.'

'Dilys thought a farmer might – in case their machinery broke down.'

'Good idea,' Sally said briskly. 'I need some tea. How about you?'

Flora nodded and her friend walked over to the reception desk to ring the bell. 'Dottie will be here soon,' she said, smiling. 'Did the market do well?'

If she was acting, she was doing it brilliantly. 'It did. I met Miss Dunmore at the baker's the other day – the vicar's housekeeper – and she told me that enough had been raised to order new curtains for the hall and send at least half of the hassocks to professional repairers. Dilys didn't win the prize for the most lucrative stall but the books did very well.'

'That's wonderful.' Sally's voice had become lacklustre. 'Dottie,' she said to the girl walking towards them, 'would you take a tray of tea to my sitting room please?'

'Yes, Miss Jenner.' The maid adjusted her white pinafore and gave a small bob.

'You look tired out.' Now her friend was standing beside her, Flora was conscious of Sally's sagging shoulders. 'I hope Dominic is doing his bit, too.'

Sally gave a grin, a reminder of her usual liveliness. 'I can't see Dominic with a feather duster, can you? He's trying to keep the grass trimmed, at least around the house. We've had to lay off the gardeners as well.'

'Better news is on the way, I'm sure. Inspector Ridley is back from Suffolk and I'm certain you'll be allowed to reopen very soon.'

'I don't see his being back will make any difference,' the girl said a trifle crossly. 'The police haven't found the murderer and, as long as that's the case, they'll want the Priory shut.'

'I understand the team are nowhere near solving the case,' Flora confided, 'and keeping you closed won't help them. Tutti Frutti has been given the go-ahead, so why not you?'

'Dom told me about the band. I'll be delighted when they go. The atmosphere at the stables has become quite toxic. There was an awful row – did you know? Apparently Max Martell is ditching them. I won't be sorry to see *him* go either. He's a slip-pery customer.'

Walking up the sweeping staircase, Flora had been trying to find a way of broaching the difficult news she'd brought, when Sally suddenly stopped and fixed her with a stare. 'I don't suppose you've discovered anything – you know – what we were talking about?'

'I did—' She hadn't finished the sentence before Sally had

grabbed her by the hand and dragged her up the remaining stairs to the first floor and into the pretty room she used as a retreat. The tray of tea sat waiting for them on the occasional table.

Sally shut the door firmly behind her. 'Tell me,' she commanded, her face screwed into a grimace, as though she were expecting a hammer blow from above.

Which, Flora thought, just about summed it up. 'I telephoned Australia and spoke to Reggie Anderson,' she began. 'He's the man who inherited the Priory. Mr Anderson told me that he doesn't know a Dominic Lister. He's never met anyone of that name. And he never had a Dominic working on his farm, so there was no discussion either about the Templeton family. Reggie is certain that he's Lord Edward's only living relative.'

Sally slumped down into the Windsor tub chair. 'So it was a lie.'

'Yes.' There was no way to soften the blow.

'And Dom told the bank a lie to get the loan.'

'It would seem so. But we don't know if the loan was granted because of his supposed relationship to Lord Edward. In fact, I doubt it. I would try not to worry too much, Sally.'

The girl sat staring down at the oriental woollen rug, until she lifted her head and Flora saw a tiny trickle of tears making its way down one cheek.

'Even if the loan wasn't granted in that way, what other lies has he told me, Flora?'

'I don't know, but I'm going to find out.' Flora came to a swift decision. 'I'm going to speak to Dominic.'

Her friend leapt up from her chair. 'You can't do that. He'll know I've been talking about him.'

'Sally, he's told you lies. Very serious lies.' And not told you what he should have, she thought to herself, that he was actually engaged to Beverly all the time he was making up to you.

Sally hung her head. 'I don't know what to do.'

'It seems simple enough to me. Do you want to continue running the hotel?'

'Of course I do.'

'And do you want Dominic to be more than a business partner?'

'I love him.' The expression on Sally's face was so tender that Flora had to look away.

'OK, but if you're to have any kind of future together,' she said determinedly, picking up her bag and marching to the door, her tea forgotten, 'you need to clear the air.'

24

She found Dominic in the small, square office beside the library, a room that still made her shiver. He looked around at her knock.

'Hello, there. Looking for Sally? The last time I saw her she was off to clean the foyer – maybe you missed her.'

'No, I saw Sally and talked to her. It's you I want to speak to, Dominic.'

'Oh yes,' he said uneasily.

'But it's Sally I want to talk to you about. If you care anything for her, you'll start being honest.'

He pushed back his chair and walked towards her, a scowl on his face. 'If you mean that business with the ring...'

'I do mean the ring, but a whole lot more as well.'

'Like what?' His question was aggressive.

'Like lying about the Templetons.' Flora refused to be daunted. 'You're no relative of Lord Edward's and you've never worked on Reggie Anderson's farm. He's the chap who inherited the Priory, by the way. I doubt if you've even been to Australia.'

Dominic had come very close, seeming to want to push

Flora out of the room but, at these words, he fell back, leaning against the desk.

'Well?' she demanded.

'OK, maybe I stretched it a bit.'

'Stretched it! *Have* you ever been to Australia?'

'Well, no, but I was intending to. And I had to think of something to persuade the bank to lend.'

He pushed himself away from the desk and began pacing the carpet, unsure, it seemed, of just how much he should say. When the words began to spill out, it was evident to Flora he was telling the truth – at last.

'I found out about Edward Templeton's death when I came to Abbeymead and how the Priory had gone to some long-lost relative in Australia who sold it on. Sally was putting in a stack of money and I needed to match it. I was stumped for a while but, when I learned the Provident had been the Templetons' bank for centuries, I came up with the idea of being one of the family. Tapping into what seemed to be an Old Boys' network and using it to get the loan.' Dominic gave a sad shake of his head. 'It was the only thing I could think of.'

'Why didn't you tell all of this to Sally?'

'It's obvious, isn't it? She would have dropped me instantly and the project would have fallen off a cliff edge.'

'It didn't stop you telling Beverly,' she pointed out.

'That's precisely why I kept quiet.' He gave a resentful grunt. 'That wretched woman used it as ammunition against me.'

'And you think Sally would have done the same?'

'No, but... it was difficult. The bank was on the brink of saying no and I'd promised Sal I'd get the money.'

Flora frowned. 'I don't understand the difficulty. Why was the bank so uncertain? You had considerable assets – you'd sold a chain of London bars. You couldn't have been asking for too much of a loan.'

He refused to look Flora in the eyes, and she knew that this was yet another lie to be uncovered. 'It wasn't a small loan, was it?' The deep anger she felt reverberated in her voice.

'It was a big loan,' he agreed, his eyes still refusing to meet hers.

'And why was that?'

He didn't answer.

'How many bars did you actually own?' Alice's conversation with Jarvis was in Flora's mind, but she wanted to hear the truth from the man himself.

There was a long silence until Dominic burst out, 'One, if you really want to know. A flea-bitten dump in Bermondsey which I sold for peanuts.'

Her heart did an unpleasant jump. What on earth had her friend signed up to?

'So you allowed Sally to risk her entire inheritance, the only money she possessed, when you were putting in virtually nothing?'

'I put in all the money I had.' A hint of his old belligerence resurfaced.

'While lying to her,' Flora continued remorselessly.

'I'm not proud of what I did, but I wanted to escape the life I was leading. And Sally made the Priory sound wonderful. She was so enthusiastic about Abbeymead, how she loved the village and how she'd love to be able to buy the hotel herself. I wanted to help her.'

'You wanted to help yourself.'

'If you like. But I really care about Sally. I've cared about her from the moment I met her.'

'But not enough to protect her, it seems.'

His hands shot out in a gesture of pleading. 'Look, we're going to pull through this. Together. I'll make it right for her.'

'Will you?' It was Sally's voice, her figure silhouetted in the doorway. 'You are utterly shameless, Dominic. You've lied. You've deceived. And you've broken my heart.'

'Don't say that, Sal.' He swivelled towards her, his hands still pleading. 'I want this to work.' He swallowed hard. 'I've never said this before – but I do love you.'

'Like you loved Beverly?'

He shook his head violently. 'I never loved her. I might have thought I did, one time, but it was an illusion. She fascinated me – for a while – that's all.'

'All?' Flora asked, determined that Sally should hear the full truth.

Dominic looked daggers at her.

'It's best to get it over with,' she advised him.

Sally cast a bewildered look from one to the other. 'What are you two talking about?'

In the quietest voice Flora had ever heard him use, Dominic said, 'We were engaged, Sal, sort of.'

'You and Beverly?'

His pinched face answered her question.

'Engaged! You mean you were actually going to marry the woman?'

'Yes... no.' Dominic was struggling. 'She wanted a ring, kept pressing me for one. I'd told her about the loan and lying about the Templetons and she said she'd keep quiet but the price was a wedding. I wasn't sure if she meant it, but I couldn't risk her blabbing. I thought if I agreed, I'd buy time and eventually she'd forget about the marriage and move on. I bought the ring to shut her up. A ruby – and it cost,' he finished sulkily.

'The ruby in your desk.' Flora nodded towards the small middle drawer.

He gave the desk's carved supports a fierce kick. 'I bought that ring, knowing I didn't feel a thing for her. By then, I'd met you, Sal. I knew how I felt about you. I asked Bev to forget the engagement. She could keep the ruby if she wanted, but the two of us would go our own ways. She wouldn't agree.'

Flora's interest was caught. According to Tommy May, Beverly had transferred her affections, such as they were, to Max Martell, so why had she refused to walk away from Dominic, given the chance to do so with a very expensive ring she could sell?

Dominic's face had hardened. 'Beverly was a first-class bitch. She wanted to hurt me and hurt Sally because she knew I cared for her. When I confronted her, begged, pleaded with her, to forget the promise I'd made, do you know what she said? "A girl can never have enough security."'

Sally had been standing motionless, her face pale and set. She gave a final shake of her head as though she were dispensing with Dominic for good and walked towards the door.

He rushed after her, clutching hold of her arm. 'Don't go, Sal. I know I can do better.'

Wriggling free of his grasp, she turned, her face a mask of sorrow. 'Can you? You lied about your relationship to the Templetons, lied about the clubs you owned, lied about how much of your own money you'd invested. You tricked me into risking every penny I own, and now I learn that every day you spent sweet talking me, you were engaged to Beverly Russo. You do better? How could you do worse?'

'It doesn't look good,' he agreed, 'but I won't mess up again, I promise.'

'Your promises are empty, but in any case' – a sudden thought seemed to strike her as she spoke – 'you won't have the chance to mess up.'

'If you could only—'

'I'm not talking about the lies you've told,' Sally said calmly. 'This is something far, far worse. You killed Beverly and the police are bound to find you out. At first, I couldn't believe you would do such a thing, it seemed so pointless. But now I know what was going on behind my back, everything makes sense. I know why you did it. You killed her to get free.'

'What are you talking about?' he spluttered.

'That book on electrics. The one I got rid of at the village market. It was yours. I found it here in this office. It was you who tampered with the amplifier. You learned how to do it from the guide. I donated it to the stall, thinking it would be lost among all those other books. I tried to cover for you.' She gulped back a sob. 'But I can't any more. I still love you, Dominic, but you're past saving.'

Flora gave the shattered man a long look and followed her friend out of the room. She must tell Alice, alert her to this latest disastrous turn of events. Sally was going to need her aunt's comfort for days to come.

When Jack put his head round the All's Well door the next morning, Flora pulled him to one side, out of earshot of several browsing customers. In a few words she told him as succinctly as she could what had happened at the Priory the previous day, only omitting Sally's accusation of murder. The girl had been in a highly emotional state and, though they'd speculated days ago on Dominic's ownership of the electronics guide, Flora was unsure how much credence to give to Sally's claim.

Jack gave a slow disbelieving shake of the head as she finished her recital. 'That is one whole catalogue of lies. Does Alice know?'

'I called in at the Nook before I opened this morning and told her. Kate rushed off to fetch her hat and coat, telling her to go to Sally immediately and never mind the Victoria sponges she was going to cook.'

Jack sat down on the window seat, glancing through the latticed panes, his expression grave. 'Poor Sally,' he murmured.

'The awful thing, Jack, is that the girl still loves him.'

'You shouldn't be surprised. Loving someone defies explanation,' he said quietly. 'Maybe they'll find a way through it together. Let's hope so. Whatever the personal stuff going on, Sally is locked into a business contract with the man.'

Flora took a seat beside him. 'Dominic tried to defend himself by saying that Beverly blackmailed him into buying her that ring. She threatened to tell everyone he wasn't as well off as he'd claimed and that he'd lied to get the bank loan. I can believe she did, too. Blackmail was obviously something she was good at.'

She turned her head to look at him. 'She was doing it to Dr Randall, you know.'

Jack started back. 'Really? When did you find that out?'

'Saturday. I was going to come and tell you but...' Her voice trailed off, and she took to fiddling with her hair that today fell in loose waves around her face. She couldn't say what was really in her mind, that it was important they keep to neutral ground. 'He's gone anyway, Randall. Up and disappeared over night. Let's hope, for Maggie's sake, Alan Ridley doesn't start asking more questions about the medicine.'

Jack gave a small puff of resignation. 'If he does, it will be me doubling down on the lies.'

'At least you lied to help someone, not to dupe them.'

'This Russo woman seems something of a force of nature, so maybe Lister deserves a little sympathy.'

Jumping to her feet, Flora looked crossly down at him. 'How do you make that out?'

'She seems to have been intent on safeguarding her future, no matter what the cost. Chewing her way through men, even as she was climbing the show-business ladder. First, it was Tommy, then Dominic and, if she hadn't departed this world, she would have moved on to Martell, no doubt.'

'That's certainly what Tommy May believed.' Flora's face

lost its crossness. 'I saw him in Greenway Lane the same day that I spoke to Maggie. He was actually taking a walk!'

'What did he have to say?'

'Mainly, a furious tirade against Martell. Apparently, the agent has dumped Tutti Frutti now that Beverly is no longer their singer and, as far as I can make out, he's taken on another group in their stead. Tommy sounded sickened, as bitter about Martell as he is about Beverly.'

She stared ahead and the shelves of books stared back at her. 'It started me wondering if, maybe, you were right about him. If Mr Tinsdale's accusation was true.'

'That he killed a young girl because she clung too fiercely?'

'Beverly would be fierce, too. Something that Dominic said about her stuck in my mind. "A girl can never have too much security," that's what she told him. What if Tommy is right and Beverly decided she needed to enmesh Max in a personal relationship as well as a business one? She would be super pushy.'

Jack shook his head. 'Even if she were, I doubt Martell would take such dramatic action. He has his own agenda, that's clear, but I've come round to your original thinking that killing Beverly would be killing the golden goose. The band was pretty mediocre until she came along. She was his star asset, the money-maker. No matter how much she was pressurising him, I reckon Max is a canny enough operator to slink free.'

'I can't be that sure. Anyone capable of betraying trust in the way Max has done is capable of doing just about anything to get what they want. I don't think we can write Martell off just yet.'

'We have a problem, don't we?' Jack said regretfully. 'Too many suspects. All of them disliking Beverly intensely, if not hating her, and all of them capable of killing.'

'My story about Jarvis... is there any point in following up that photograph?'

'We should try to find a missing person?' He shook his head.

'There'll be far too many names for us to check. The police must have tried to trace her when she disappeared and evidently failed.'

'The family come from Oxford and it's not that big a town.' She was unwilling to relinquish the idea. 'There might be a report in the local paper on her disappearance. Maybe an article or two written at the time that could hold clues to her whereabouts.'

'It's a long shot, but I suppose we could try. I could telephone the *Oxford Mail*, pose as a journalist—'

'It wouldn't even be a pose,' Flora interrupted.

'—pose as a journalist interested in resurrecting the story of a missing girl. Maybe pretend I've uncovered new information. The family name?' Jack searched his memory. 'Reeves, that was it. But the girl's?'

'Anna,' Flora pronounced. 'Tommy told me.'

'Anna Reeves. It's a start and if there's nothing to it, we can cross Jarvis off the list. Personally, I don't see him as a killer. I know he disliked Beverly, they all did, but I can't see him ever being sober enough to plan such an intricate murder where split-second timing was essential.'

'Unless, of course, he had a reason to kill that we know nothing about,' she warned. 'A reason strong enough for him to stay deliberately sober that afternoon.'

25

Jack had meant to telephone the Oxford paper later that morning. He'd need to return home for a notebook and pen, but then wrap up the enquiry over Jarvis and get down once more to turning his synopsis into an actual book. He still hadn't heard from Arthur on the notes he'd sent, but at the back of his mind was the dread that the longer he delayed settling to write, the more likely it was that he'd not go back to his typewriter at all.

He had reached the front door of Overlay House when he saw Charlie Teague running at full speed along the lane towards him.

Glancing at his watch, he walked back to the garden gate. 'Shouldn't you be at school?'

It was close to lunchtime but he knew for a fact that Tommy stayed to eat school dinners.

'I came to tell you, Mr C,' Charlie panted. 'There's a right goin' on at school this morning. Another body.'

Jack was startled. 'Is this a joke, Charlie?'

'No, honest. It's true. In the wood behind school. That chap in the suit. Had his head bashed in. The police are all over and school's been shut. We were told to go home, but I thought I'd tell you first seein' as you write them crime books.'

'That's thoughtful of you,' Jack said faintly. 'The man in the suit, do you know his name?'

Charlie shook his head. 'He was at the Priory, at the big do. I think he's a kind of man'ger.'

'Mr Martell?'

'Prob'ly. I gotta go. I haven't had my lunch. They're not serving dinners.'

'That is a problem,' Jack commiserated.

'S'all right. Mum will have somethin',' the boy said confidently, turning to run back towards Swallow Lane.

He wouldn't disturb Flora again to bring her the news, Jack decided. She had a shop to run while he... he should be working but wasn't. He'd walk along to Church Spinney – the school backed onto the spinney and must be the place Charlie had meant – find out what was happening and then get back to his study. The telephone call would have to wait.

His young informant hadn't been wrong about the police presence. A rope barrier had cordoned off a large square between the thickly clustered trees, their leaves now thinning but still forming an attractive canopy. Or helpful shelter for an assassin, Jack thought. Blue uniforms appeared to populate the entire wood, but he spotted Alan Ridley almost immediately in urgent conversation with one of his men. As soon as the inspector dismissed his sergeant, Jack crunched his way through a carpet of crimson leaves to speak to him.

'This is a bad business, Jack,' the inspector said, as he approached.

He had never seen Ridley look so worried. There were two people dead and still not an inkling as to who the perpetrator might be.

'Is it Max Martell?'

'News travels round this village like wildfire.' Ridley's expression was peevish.

'I have a small spy. He told me the victim had been hit over the head.'

The inspector sighed. 'In a manner of speaking. The wound is pretty horrible but it could have been worse, I guess.'

Jack was intrigued. 'How's that? What kind of weapon was used?'

'A cymbal,' Ridley said baldly.

'A cymbal? You mean—'

'A musical instrument, yes. Thrown like a frisbee, I'd say, though we'll have to wait for the pathologist's report. Darn thing could have decapitated him, but luckily it didn't. Severe head wound, though – I reckon he bled to death.'

Jack flinched.

'Died quickly, old chap,' the inspector said, a wary eye on Jack's face. 'With an injury like that, it wouldn't have taken long.'

'Someone threw a cymbal as though it were a frisbee?' It sounded an absurd death and Jack was having difficulty absorbing it. 'That's insane.'

'It is, but I'm pretty sure it's what you'd have to do, to slice into a head that deeply. The killer must have concealed themselves in the trees and thrown. The victim wouldn't have known what hit him. Literally.'

'The cymbal was left behind, I presume?' It must have been for Ridley to know exactly what weapon had been used. Jack was trying to think objectively, but feeling slightly nauseous.

'Oh yes, bold as brass, if you'll forgive the pun.'

'So, fingerprints?'

'What do you think? This murderer doesn't leave much to chance.'

'Except,' Jack said thoughtfully, 'he or she does take chances, don't they? This wood' – he glanced around him –

'people walk through it all the time. It's broad daylight, there's sun filtering through the trees, the killer could have been spotted by anyone taking a short cut to the high street.'

The killer had taken a massive risk with the amplifier, too, he thought. Secreting themselves around the side of the stage to tamper with cables, while all the time looking over their shoulder. There had been dozens of people around – guests who had come early, others like himself helping with the catering, members of the band getting ready to play.

'No one spotted anything,' Ridley said, bringing Jack back to the present. 'We're putting out an appeal, but so far it appears these blasted woods were empty this morning. What's puzzling me most was why the chap was here in the first place. His shoes – fancy black patent numbers – are hardly fit for walking more than a few yards. Certainly not a traipse through woodland.'

Another man who had taken a surprising walk. It seemed to have become a habit for the Priory's unwelcome guests. According to Flora, she'd met both Jarvis and Tommy intent on taking a constitutional. And now Max Martell was dead after walking in the wood, the last place you'd have expected to find him.

'He must have been lured here,' he said aloud.

The inspector nodded. 'Looks like it, though what could have encouraged him to plod through a wood wearing a wool suit and patent pumps is beyond me.' Another loud sigh followed. Clapping Jack on the arm, he said, 'I'd better be off. At least, look as if things are on the move. Don't forget, get in touch if anything useful turns up.'

Jack nodded absent-mindedly and began the walk back to Overlay House. Martell's death sounded horrible – he was glad not to have seen the body, glad that this time Flora hadn't seen it either – but this second murder left them in as much a muddle as ever. Trudging homewards, he felt drained of energy. The only small success they could claim was that, with Max's death, another name could be crossed from their infamous list. But Jack yearned for real progress, hating the feeling of being stuck, of drowning in the stodge of a puzzle that became more unfathomable by the day.

Abruptly, he came to a stop and stared into the ditch. They needed to eliminate more suspects, that was the only way forward, and perhaps he could help inch ahead by jettisoning one more. He'd forget the book, he decided, forget the notepad, and get on to the *Oxford Mail*. Turning on his heel, he headed back to the village and the telephone box.

When Flora first suggested they search the newspapers, he'd considered it a long shot but, thinking it over, he'd begun to change his mind. If Jarvis – or Johnny, as he'd once been – had been so upset by his sister's disappearance that he'd become a serious drinker, Jack guessed the chap would have raised a storm at the time. Which meant that the incident was likely to have been covered by the local paper.

It was their news desk he spoke to first.

'My name is Jack Carrington,' he introduced himself. 'I'm a freelance journalist, hoping to revisit a local story from about four years ago. I think the *Mail* may have reported on it. I wonder – do you remember a local girl who went missing? She would have been in her mid-teens at the time. Her name was Anna Reeves.'

'I've only worked here a year,' the girl on the news desk said, 'but I can take a look at our records if you like and get back to you.'

'That's kind, except I do have a slight problem. I'm calling from a telephone box.'

'I shouldn't be long. Give me your number and I'll call back as soon as I can.'

Jack did as he was asked and, finding a convenient stone on the nearby grass verge, he propped open the kiosk's heavy metal door and crossed his fingers that no one in the village would be desperate to ring out.

For what seemed an age, he paced back and forth in front of the open door, feeling uncomfortably conspicuous – the village gossips would be enjoying the spectacle hugely, he was sure – but his senses on the alert, the first ring had him leap into the box and snatch up the receiver.

'I found it,' the girl said, sounding pleased with herself. 'The *Mail* covered the story, though fairly briefly. Just a small article well into the paper – on page six, I think it was. Anna Reeves was expelled – from St Catherine's. I don't know if you know it, but it's a Roman Catholic secondary school in north Oxford. Apparently, she got a hiding from her dad when he found out and as a result, it seems, she disappeared. There was a police search but they didn't find her.'

'Does the article say why she was expelled?'

'It doesn't go into details. I can see that it was Phil Marsden who filed the story. He still works for the paper and I think he's in today. Would you like to talk to him?'

'I would – if it's possible. Don't forget I'm in a public phone box and I may have to disappear.' More crossed fingers.

'He works just down the corridor. I'll fetch him.'

There was the clunk of the receiver as it hit the desk, then a shuffle to the door, some muted sounds in the distance, more shuffling, and a few minutes later, a voice rattled into Jack's ear. 'Phil Marsden here. You're a journalist, I believe, Jack?'

'That's right. Working temporarily for the *Daily Mercury*.' Really, he was getting adept at this lying business, but he *had* been on their staff, he told himself, for a good five years. 'I've been asked to see what I can dig up on Anna Reeves' disappearance. I believe you followed the story.'

'I tried to, but the headmistress of St Catherine's was a right... martinet. Military discipline and all. I went along to the

school to talk to the girls, but was shown the door before I managed
to get two words from any of them. Luckily, on my way out, I met
the kid who'd actually accused Anna. Well, not lucky. I reckon the
girl was waiting for me. Wanted to broadcast her side of the story
to the world. In the end, I didn't use what I got from her. I'd only
her word for it, after all, though the headmistress seemed to have
swallowed it. These two, Anna and this girl, had been bosom pals,
apparently, and the kid sounded shocked that her best friend
could have done something like that. Said she was desperately sad
she'd had to report her. I took that with a pinch of salt.'

'What was the story?'

'That there'd been thieving from the girls' lockers and this
kid had seen Anna Reeves taking stuff.'

'Who was the girl? Did you get a name?'

'Let's see. I unearthed my notebook for that year before I
left my office.' There was a sound of flicking pages and Jack felt
his heart thump more loudly than it should.

'Here it is. Unusual name for an English kid. Russo. Beverly
Russo.'

'Thank   you,   Phil,'   Jack   managed   to   say.
'That's... interesting.'

'Oh, that *is* interesting,' Flora said, when he called at the All's
Well on his way home and recounted his conversation with the
Oxford Mail. 'It gives us a completely different motive for
Beverly's death. If Anna Reeves disappeared as a result of a
false accusation – and now we know Beverly so much better, I'd
wager anything that it was false – then Jarvis had a very good
reason to kill her.'

'It stunned me for a minute when Phil Marsden told me
what he'd discovered,' Jack admitted. 'I had it stuck in my mind
that Beverly died as a femme fatale, not as a mean schoolgirl.
But Jarvis as a murderer is still problematic. If he *was* respon-

sible for the tampering, he must have sobered up for days beforehand.'

'Perhaps he did. I can see why he'd be angry enough to stop drinking, if it meant a satisfying revenge. Jarvis has spent the last four years searching for his sister, Tommy May said, with no idea if she's alive or dead. He would blame Beverly fair and square. That's what the photograph is all about.'

Jack fidgeted with Flora's most recent display of books, thinking hard. 'When did Beverly join Tutti Frutti, do you think?'

'Martell said she'd been with them for two years.' Flora pushed back the book spines he'd dislodged.

'Anna Reeves has been missing for four years, which means that Beverly joined the band two years after Anna was accused – falsely, we think – of the school theft. Did Jarvis recognise the new singer from the photograph he carries? He must have done. Or did he know her already? If she was once best friends with his sister, that must be the case. So wouldn't they have spoken of Anna's disappearance? I can imagine Beverly saying how devastated she was that his sister had gone missing! Yet the subject never seems to have been broached or I'm sure we'd have heard of it.'

'It's possible Jarvis didn't know her before she came into the band,' Flora said, her forehead wrinkled. 'How old is he, do you reckon? Knocking thirty?'

'Late twenties, at least.'

'Four years ago he would already be well into his twenties while, at a guess, his sister would be around fifteen. Jarvis must have left home by then and maybe he never went back, particularly if he had a father prone to handing out beatings. It's possible that he never met Beverly.'

'And possible that he never knew of their friendship?'

'That's a different matter. The photograph I saw in his wallet suggests he did.' Flora plumped herself down at her desk, waving her hand at the spare stool she kept nearby. 'Sit down, Jack. This really is interesting. Anna could have given her brother the photograph, I suppose, or he may have found it in his sister's room after she vanished. It wouldn't take much to find out from one of Anna's school friends who the girl in the photograph was. Or to find out that the girl with her arm around his sister was the very one who'd accused her.'

'OK.' He wriggled to get comfortable on the stool. 'Let's say the girl in the photograph is unknown to Jarvis, but he's been given her name and told that she was the one who lied about Anna. Then Max Martell proudly introduces the group's new singer and Jarvis knows her immediately. She's the one he holds responsible for his sister's disappearance and possible death. But that was two years ago. Why wait until the Priory's opening day to exact his revenge?'

'Perhaps it took him that long to find the right opportunity. To find the courage to do it. To sober up enough.'

Flora might be right, Jack mused. Jarvis was a mess. It would have taken an almighty effort to put the whisky bottle away, gain sufficient knowledge of electrical circuits, and have the dexterity to switch those cables in the few seconds he'd have. It was possible he'd taken the best chance he'd been given.

'So where do we go from here?'

'We tackle Jarvis,' she said firmly.

26

'Martell,' Jack said, suddenly jumping to his feet and sending the stool flying.

How could he have forgotten there'd been another murder? It had been his interest in tracking down Anna Reeves, his journalistic nose for a story, that had pushed the earlier news from his mind.

'What about Martell?' Flora picked up the stool and set it to rights. 'What do you know that I don't?'

'He's dead.'

A laugh started in her throat but then stuttered to a halt. 'You're serious! Max Martell is dead?'

'Murdered,' he said briefly.

'But where? How?' She rushed over to him, grabbing him by the wrists. 'Tell me everything.'

Jack disentangled himself from her clutch. 'His body was found in Church Spinney. I had it from Charlie. The school was closed – it backs on to the spinney – and the children sent home. Charlie rushed to Overlay to tell me.'

'Did you go to the spinney?'

He smiled. 'I did. I knew you'd want me to, but there was

nothing to see. A police cordon had been thrown up which made it impossible to get close to the crime scene. Though after what Ridley told me, I'm not sure I'd want to,' he added as an afterthought.

'What do you mean?'

'Alan is in charge of operations, of course, and I spoke to him for a few minutes. Apparently, Max Martell, our Mr Smooth, had his head cut open and bled to death.'

Flora shuddered. 'How horrible.' She thought for a moment. 'How was it done? Did they find the murder weapon?'

'It would have been difficult to miss,' he said drily. 'A four-teen-inch cymbal.'

'A cymbal? As in—'

'As in a drum kit.'

'You have to be joking.'

Jack held up his hands. 'Honestly, I'm not. According to Ridley, it was thrown at the man as you'd throw a frisbee. It caught Martell on the temple and the wound was so deep, he probably died in minutes. Even if someone had found him – and there doesn't seem to have been a single walker in the woods, so no witnesses – they couldn't have saved him.'

'But the police have the weapon. That's crucial. That's evidence. They'll nab the villain,' she said excitedly. 'Who-ever did it must have killed Beverly, too. There can't be that many people in Abbeymead murdering with musical instruments.'

Jack hated to disappoint her but he had bad news. 'Ridley hasn't yet had the cymbal examined, but he's almost certain there'll be no fingerprints. Or why leave it lying around?'

'Perhaps because it was just too difficult to carry away?' she suggested brightly, though almost immediately her shoulders drooped. She was remembering the cable, wiped clean of finger-prints, he thought.

'This person, whoever they are, is pretty smart and Ridley

seems all at sea. I don't think I've ever seen him quite so stumped.'

'Then we need to step up a gear, Jack. Decide who best to pursue first. We may have lost Martell from our list, but Jarvis Redmond is still there, and now he has an exclamation mark by his name.' Exasperated, she swept a hand through her hair, securing the long waves into a topknot. 'It becomes more and more complicated every day.'

An idea slid into his mind. It was one he should avoid, but it was proving too enticing. 'You're right about needing to do better,' he agreed. 'Sally, whatever her sins, is facing bankruptcy if this business isn't soon cleared up.' He waited a beat, then launched into the question he knew he shouldn't ask. 'Why don't you come for supper? A review of what evidence we do have might just trigger a brainwave in one of us.'

He saw the surprised look on her face. There was a few seconds' pause before she said, 'OK.'

It wasn't exactly a heartfelt agreement and he understood why. Since they'd returned from Cornwall, he'd become aware of a distance between them. An invisible barrier, a kind of holding off. He'd thought at first it was simply an adjustment they were both making to living alone again after sharing a small cottage for well over a month. Gradually, though, it had been borne in on him that Flora was being deliberate in keeping her distance, making sure, for instance, that they always met in a public space, preferably with others close by. And if he was truthful, he'd been doing much the same himself.

It hadn't always worked – she'd cooked dinner for him last week and earlier shared a glass of wine on his terrace – but other than these rare events, a coolness had developed in their friendship, one he found himself hating. But he owed her a meal, didn't he, so what could be more appropriate than using it to further the case they were working on? He'd ask Kate to cook for him, he couldn't expose Flora to his uselessness in the kitchen. They could treat it as a business meeting and, setting the tone in that way, would help lessen any tension.

'Tomorrow evening?'

'Fine.' She was smiling, but he knew that smile. It masked uncertain feelings.

Walking back to Overlay House, he felt pleased with himself. He'd been a coward for too long, scared of confronting feelings he'd rather not acknowledge. During the summer, he'd kept himself busy, spending days in London on novel-based research, or pretending to. It had been a useful distraction from the writing he should have been doing, and a distraction, too, from Flora. He'd gone up to town at weekends when he knew she was free to meet, even started investigating her family history to prolong his time away. The search had proved oddly fascinating. One day, he'd visited Highgate Cemetery where Flora had said her parents had been buried, but been unable to find their graves and the trail had gone cold.

It had all been an excuse, an escape, nothing more and, at the same time, she'd been set on escape, too. It was stupid, this circling round each other. They were a team investigating a murder – murders now – and there was a lot to discuss. Forget the feelings bubbling beneath the surface, feelings neither of them seemed able to resolve, and get on with something they could do.

Flora dressed carefully for the supper at Jack's. She'd been too surprised by his invitation to refuse and now she was glad she hadn't. It would be as he said, a review of what small progress they'd made, more necessary than ever in the light of what they'd learned in the last day or so.

Nevertheless, she was pleased to have a new dress in her wardrobe, ordered several weeks ago from the Marshall Ward catalogue: pale blue linen, long-sleeved and boat-necked, with a cinched-in waist and fitted skirt. It had been delivered to the post office, Dilys poking the parcel suspiciously as she handed it over. When Flora confessed to it being a new dress, the postmistress's response had been characteristic. *Don't say, you've got a beau at last!* she'd said loudly, then roared with laughter.

Flora had felt unusually ruffled. Was she that spinsterish that Abbeymead had decided she would never find an admirer? Then realised with a shock that it wasn't the village that had decided, but herself. Now the exigencies of war were over, the path she'd chosen was very different from one most women followed – marriage in their early twenties, two or three children in quick succession, and the rest of their days spent tucked away at home. That wasn't for Flora, it never had been, but it didn't mean her social life was dead, she thought indignantly, or that she couldn't look stylish when she wanted.

As long as she didn't have to take over the cooking tonight! The skirt was just a little too tight for bending over an oven. A dab of crème puff and a lick of pink lipstick and she was ready. Thank goodness the days of beetroot juice were over – she pulled a face in the mirror – it was what the older girls at school had experimented with when make-up was scarce. It had been incredibly messy.

When she arrived at Overlay House, a delightful smell was drifting from the kitchen and Jack met her in the hall looking remarkably relaxed. She raised an eyebrow.

'I asked Kate for help,' he confessed.

Flora couldn't subdue a giggle. 'How very sensible.'

'Sorry if you were expecting poached eggs.' He took her jacket and hung it carefully on the lopsided coat stand.

'I'm deprived of your speciality? Never mind, you can cook them for me another time. What am I expecting tonight?'

'Kate has been brilliant. She's done a magnificent supper, I'm almost embarrassed to tell you. Devilled eggs, followed by roast chicken and all the trimmings.'

'A chicken! Is it Christmas already?'

Flora walked past him into the kitchen. The bare wood table had been covered with a newly laundered floral tablecloth and set with what she recognised as the Nook's best china. Jack's mismatched cutlery rather spoilt the effect, but a bottle was cooling in a plastic bucket on the Formica counter.

'And wine?' She began to wonder how much of a business meeting this was going to be.

'It will help us concentrate. We can talk while we eat. According to Kate' – he glanced at the large round wall clock – 'we should be eating the eggs right now.'

'It's an age since I've eaten devilled eggs and Katie's are absolutely delicious!'

Flora sat down and straight away began helping herself from the brightly patterned dish. She took a mouthful before saying, 'You never said much about Alan Ridley. How was he when you saw him?'

'Essentially, fed up. He's still getting nowhere. There are no witnesses to either murder, no evidence except two weapons that lack fingerprints, and no rock-solid motive.'

'I've been thinking about the motive.'

He poured her a large glass of wine. 'Drink up before you reveal all!'

'Don't mock, Jolyon. I may not always think in a straight line, but I usually get there.'

'You do,' he said mournfully, 'much to my shame.'

'The thing is...' She took another mouthful. 'Mmm, this so good! If we're adding Jarvis to our list of suspects, the second murder doesn't make sense. If he thinks his sister is dead, which he probably does after all this time looking for her, I can see him murdering Beverly because, in effect, he believed her guilty of killing Anna. But why would he also have killed Max? The man was his agent, finding the band work, and probably didn't even know Jarvis had a sister.'

Jack took a long sip of his wine. 'I've been thinking along those lines, too, and the only thing I came up with was that Max somehow rumbled him.'

She tilted her head. 'I can't somehow see Max as the rumbling sort. He was so bound up with himself, I reckon he had little or no curiosity about other people. I don't think he'd have the energy to worry over who killed Beverly. He'd be too busy worrying about himself.'

'He was self-absorbed, I agree, but wouldn't he have been miffed at losing his best asset? Surely, he'd want to find out who murdered her. She was about to make his fortune, at least I imagine that's what he believed.'

Jack got to his feet, stacking their empty plates to one side and, opening the oven, brought out a beautifully bronzed chicken. 'Martell revealed his true thoughts,' he went on, 'when he let slip that he considered the band was nothing much without Beverly.'

'Let me bring those.' Flora jumped up, ready to carry the vegetables to the table – peas, carrots and some tasty late runner beans – but he forestalled her.

'I'm host tonight. Which means I serve and you sit.'

She subsided meekly into her chair and watched as he carved her slices of chicken breast.

'This is truly delicious,' she said with the first mouthful. 'Kate has surpassed herself.'

'She has.' Jack settled himself to enjoy the treat. 'And delivered to my door, too! That chap, the one Alice calls her under cook, turned up.'

'Tony Farraday?'

'That's him. He drove Kate over and helped her unload the food, course by course.'

'Katie seems a bit starry-eyed over him.'

'Don't you approve?' he teased.

'It feels a little soon, I suppose. It's barely a year since that wretched husband of hers went missing and only nine or ten months since his funeral.'

'If Kate really likes the chap... I think it's great. She's simply seizing the moment.' When Flora rolled her eyes, he went on quickly, 'Martell and Beverly – we should focus on them, what was going on between them. I'm sure there was more than the obvious. Beverly was making a play for the agent, that seems generally agreed, but what if it was business as well as pleasure? What if they'd made a pact together – to forget Tutti Frutti and make a fortune for themselves?'

'I see what you're saying.' Flora chased a potato around the plate. 'Beverly's murder could have made Max feel he'd had fame and fortune snatched from under his nose, and he'd want to know who'd done that to him. Particularly if he could see the police were getting nowhere.'

'And particularly if he suspected it was one of the band who'd robbed him of the money he'd been looking forward to. Have you finished – no more veg?'

She shook her head. The fitted skirt was feeling just a little more fitted.

'Stay where you are,' he instructed, as she got up to help, 'we have more to come. There's an equally brilliant dessert waiting in the larder.'

He delved into the cupboard and, like a magician with his rabbit, brought out a pineapple upside-down cake and a jug of cream.

Flora eyed it appreciatively. 'I really didn't think I could eat more, but maybe I can manage a small slice. I must make sure I thank Kate.'

'Don't do that. I told her I was going to pretend it was all my own work.'

'But you didn't.'

'Honestly, Flora, would I ever have convinced you?'

'Not a hope, but this is yummy. Try some.'

'Right,' he said, spooning cream over a large slice of pudding. 'Back to Max. We have him suspecting the band.'

'Or suspecting Dominic maybe. Just because it was a cymbal that killed Max, it isn't necessarily the drummer who's the guilty one.'

Jack paused, spoon in the air. 'That's true. We mustn't forget Dominic. OK, Max watches them all like a hawk and then spots something or other that gives one of them away. Let's make it Jarvis for the moment. Perhaps he tackles him with it, hoping it's not the way he thinks it is. After that, Jarvis knows he's in trouble and has to take action.'

'It's a bit weak, isn't it? Spotting something or other.'

Jack sighed and inwardly she joined him. No matter how much they talked the matter over, the fact remained they had virtually nothing to point them in the right direction.

'At least we've reduced our number of suspects,' she said consolingly. 'If it's not Jarvis, it's Tommy or Shane, and Shane is just Tommy's shadow.'

'Or Dominic. We're forgetting him again. What's happening on that front, by the way?'

'I don't know except there's trouble. Alice called at the shop this morning before you arrived. She seemed harassed and unhappy, bemoaning how things were going from bad to worse at the Priory and how she'd always been certain the project would lead to disaster.'

'What do you think? Is disaster in the offing?' Jack leaned back in his chair, finishing the last of his wine.

'I'm expecting more trouble,' Flora said wearily. 'You should have seen Sally's face after Dominic confessed all. It was as bleak as midwinter. But it was also desperately sad. It didn't bode well, whichever way you looked at it. She rang this evening, just as I was leaving the cottage – apparently, the police have said the hotel can open again.'

'That should make her happier.'

'Mmm,' Flora murmured. 'It didn't seem to, but perhaps I'll know more later. She didn't say much on the phone, just that she wanted to see me.'

'When are you going?'

'After work tomorrow, I thought. I'll cycle to the Priory once I've closed the shop.'

'I can give you a lift if you'd like.'

'That's kind of you, Jack, but Betty needs the exercise. It doesn't do her joints any good just sitting in the shed. Otherwise, all she has is a five-minute ride from the cottage to the shop.'

This evening had been special: the food, the wine, the way they'd talked across the table as they'd used to do in Cornwall. She would remember it with pleasure, but there was a line, one they both recognised, and she wasn't going to overstep it.

27

There was a decided chill in the air when, the next evening, Flora locked the All's Well's door and collected Betty from the courtyard behind her shop. It was mid-October and the subtle aroma of oakwood fires accompanied her ride along the high street. Labouring up Fern Hill towards the Priory, she found herself cycling through drifts of leaves feet thick, the result of a fierce night-time wind. Winter was very much on its way.

In the hotel grounds, much of the grass had lain uncut for several weeks and twigs and broken branches were scattered across what had once been smooth lawns. Without regular gardeners, it was clear the Priory would soon return to its earlier shabbiness. No wonder Sally was so unhappy. She lacked the money to keep the estate neat and attractive, yet potential guests were unlikely to knock on the door of a hotel that looked so bedraggled. It was a circle that would be difficult to escape.

Finding the front entrance open and the foyer empty, Flora skipped up the magnificent oak stairway to the first floor and knocked on the door to Sally's sitting room.

'Flora, hello.' Her friend jumped up to greet her. 'I'm sorry to drag you out after work, but thank you so much for coming. Let me get you a drink.'

Sally was embarrassingly grateful and Flora felt a twinge of guilt that really she'd done so little to help her. 'Nothing for me, thanks.' She sank down into squashy chintz, her eyes searching Sally's face. 'Now, tell me how things are with you. Truthfully.'

Sally picked up a cushion and plumped it nervously, then seemed to steady herself. 'I'm going to sell,' she announced.

'Sell the Priory?' What else would she be selling? Flora thought stupidly. But it seemed a very sudden decision. A wild decision, even.

'I've told Auntie and I wanted to tell you before the rest of the world gets to know.'

'And Dominic?'

'He's agreed. Well, the truth is he's been forced to agree.' Sally took a seat opposite, her hands clasped together in a fearsome knot and her expression stricken. 'It's not just the lies, Flora. They're bad enough. It's not even that he deceived me so completely over Beverly. It's... it's... I can't work with him any longer, not thinking he's a... a murderer.'

Flora was taken aback. Dominic was certainly on their list of likely villains, but nothing had been proved against him and her friend's decision appeared premature. A few days ago, it was true, Sally had flung the same accusation at him, but Flora had attributed that to the intensity of the moment. Now, as she looked across at her friend, it was plain the well of emotion had retained its hold, but this time chastened and controlled. Sally was serious.

'What if Dominic is entirely innocent?' she asked. 'There's no definite proof against him, at least none that I know.'

The fact that he was still at the Priory and had made no attempt to escape, suggested to Flora that he might well be innocent. On the other hand, he might simply be hoping to brazen it out. Sally had evidently plumped for the latter.

Her friend's hands had unknotted but were now frantically twisting in her lap. 'Who else could it be?' she asked, anguish in her voice. 'It has to have been someone near or on the stage just before Beverly began to sing. I've worked that out. It wasn't one of us – you, Jack, Kate, Auntie – and it wasn't one of the band.'

'Why do you think that? It could easily have been one of those men. They could have tampered with the amplifier seconds before they took their place on stage.'

'But why would they? Beverly was the reason they were doing so well.'

'That may be true, but every one of them had a grudge against her. Tommy was furious for what he saw as her two-timing, Shane was furious over the way his friend had been treated, and Jarvis... let's just say that Jarvis had as much of a motive as the other two.'

Sally shook her head. 'I hated the girl, Flora, you guessed my feelings, but did you hear her voice? It was like nothing I've ever heard before. Pure and powerful. It's obvious she was the band's greatest asset. They would never have got rid of her.'

'One of them might, in a temper,' Flora argued. 'Anger is irrational. It can make people do terrible things. And you've not even considered how Max Martell fits into your version of events. You know that he's met a sticky end?'

Sally looked down at her toes, encased in knitted slippers. 'It's ghastly, isn't it? And yet another reason for me to sell. It means the Priory becomes even more notorious. And I did think of Max. The same person had to have killed him as well as Beverly, and for a few hours I felt so much better. I thought it couldn't be Dominic after all.'

'Because Dominic had no reason to kill him?'

'That's what I thought – but not for long. After I'd talked to Tommy May, I knew he had a reason. A strong reason.'

Flora frowned. 'What on earth did Tommy tell you?'

'He said that Martell knew all about Dom's engagement to

Beverly. They all did, apparently, even though Dominic thought he'd kept it secret. According to Tommy, the agent was delighted when he found out. Said how brilliant the wedding photographs would look in *Queen* magazine and what a great story it would make. Dominic, a distant relative of an ancient family, marrying a girl from the wrong side of town. One who'd struggled through a miserable childhood, alcoholic parents and all, but who possessed this divine voice.'

Flora's frown deepened. 'I still don't see how that gives Dominic a reason.'

'It's obvious, isn't it? Martell was pushing for Beverly to marry him. The publicity would be wonderful and, maybe at the same time, he saw it as a way of ridding himself of her advances. She was after Max, everyone seems to think it, and I agree. Dominic would never have been enough for her.'

'And Dominic's motive?' Flora asked, still struggling to understand where Sally was leading.

'Dom was desperate to be free of Beverly. He felt himself being forced into a marriage he didn't want. So he killed her first, and then him.'

'But when Max Martell was killed, Beverly was already dead,' Flora pointed out, feeling her friend's mind must have buckled beneath the pressure. 'There would be no marriage. Dominic *was* free.'

'It was too late by then. Dom only killed because he wanted rid of Beverly. He wanted to be with me.' Her voice faltered and Flora saw her swallow so hard that she could hardly whisper her next words. 'It didn't work out that way. We had this terrible row – after you left the other day. He tried to find excuses for his behaviour but I pushed him away. I told him there was no chance for us, ever. That's when he blamed the agent for splitting us up. He said it was all Martell's fault that Beverly was dead and still causing mayhem. If Martell hadn't encouraged her to push for a ring, Dom said, he and I would be together. He believed all his troubles were down to Max and I think he wanted revenge. Dominic can be like that,' she finished limply.

It was limp, Flora thought. Dominic was a contender in the murder stakes, she agreed, but no more than any of the band members.

'You mustn't be hasty, Sally. Take the time to think about your future,' she advised. 'You've sunk every penny of your savings into this business, and you'll never recoup all the money when you sell.' *If* she managed to sell. It would be a struggle in the Priory's present condition, and with the kind of rumours that must already be circulating.

When Sally made no response, she intensified her appeal. 'Do think carefully,' she implored. 'By the time you've paid the bank back, you'll be left with nothing.'

'I don't care.' The girl jumped up from her chair, her knuckles bunched. 'I just can't cope with this worry any more.'

She seemed to have aged twenty years. The bubbly girl she'd once been looked strained and utterly weary.

'Will you hold off for a few days at least?' Flora urged. 'Until we get the chance to talk again. I may have better news by then.'

Truthfully, she was unsure what difference a few days would make since their investigation – it hardly passed for an investigation at the moment – appeared to be going nowhere. But it had to, she told herself, it simply had to, and she and Jack must make sure it did.

Sally nodded slowly but her face, as Flora said goodbye, was bereft of hope.

The smell of burning was strong as she walked out of the Priory's front entrance. Someone burning leaves. Dominic, perhaps? At least he was doing something useful, though on second thoughts it didn't smell like a bonfire of leaves. Flora wrinkled her nose. What did it smell like? It was coming from the enclosure where Cyril Knight, Kate's father and one-time head gardener at the Priory, had had his workshop.

She walked around the side of the mansion, past the stables, eerily quiet – what were the band members doing this evening? – and came to the kitchen door at the rear of the building. Cyril's enclosure was to one side and the gate to it, usually padlocked, was wide open.

There was a small fire, almost burnt out, in the middle of the gravelled space, reminiscent of that other fire she and Jack had found almost a year ago. That had led them to an accidental poisoning, and a deliberate one, too. But this time, it wasn't plants that had been burnt. It was paper.

Flora bent down and picked up a charred remnant. The paper felt thick to the touch, not any old piece of notepaper, then, but something more expensive, more official. She brought the fragment close to her eyes. It was dusk and growing darker with every minute, but she could just make out what looked like a capital 'C' then a small 'o' and next to it an 'n'. Tucking the slip of paper into her handbag, she walked up to the door of what she still thought of as Mr Knight's shed. The door was unlocked and, for a moment, she stood on the threshold, taking in the general untidiness. Cyril would have hated it. His tools were still there, though many of them now rusting. The bench he'd worked at was dusty and uncared for, and most of the space was taken up with cardboard boxes, emptied of their contents and left to clutter what had become an unloved workshop.

She was turning to go when her foot crunched against something lying on the floor, invisible in the half light. Peering down, she could see nothing other than bare boards, but there had definitely been a noise, a crackling she thought that shouldn't be there, and she was keen to know what it was. She took several paces towards the open door, testing her footsteps. Nothing. But as soon as she walked back to where she'd started, the crunching began again. Intrigued, she bent down and touched the boards. Her fingers felt something sharp. Puzzled, she pinched whatever it was very carefully between two fingers and took it to what light still existed. A copper sheen met her eyes. She walked back again to where she'd found it and, taking a handkerchief from her pocket, scooped up a small pile of what seemed to be brass or copper threads and tucked them into her bag along with the singed paper.

A low thrum of excitement had begun deep within, though she counselled herself not to listen to it – realistically there was little to be excited about. But was it at all possible that this discovery was connected to the murders? Anything, she thought, was worth pursuing if it helped Sally. There was definitely a mystery to unravel here, though one best solved at home along with a cup of tea and a plate of toast.

That night Flora dreamt of music – of guitars, of drums, of cymbals – unsurprising when they had featured so heavily in her life in recent days. But when she woke, it was only the one instrument that stayed in her mind. It was a cymbal that had killed Max Martell. She went to her handbag and unwrapped the handkerchief. She'd been too tired last night to think much about her discovery, slipping into bed an hour or so after her scant supper.

But now, looking at what lay in the square of white linen, she made the connection. They were threads of metal, as she'd guessed, copper-coloured and very sharp. They'd come from a cymbal, she was almost sure, which meant that someone had used Cyril's workshop to sharpen the large, round disc –

sharpen it sufficiently to cut deep into flesh and cause terminal bleeding. The cable she and Jack had found had proved useless as evidence, but would this be the best clue they'd discovered so far?

It was still early, but Flora knew what she had to do. After a hasty bowl of cornflakes, she pulled Betty from her shed and made for Jack's house. Betty did not like being used as a racing bike, and certainly not this early in the morning and, as her owner pounded along Greenway Lane, the bicycle's nuts and bolts creaked angrily at the affront. Flora left her leaning against the front gate and ran up the path, banging loudly at the door.

It was minutes before Jack appeared, blinking drowsily on the threshold. 'How did I know it was you?' he asked in a voice that was wearily resigned.

'Because I have news. Well, not news, but something important. Something you must do.'

He groaned. 'No, Flora, not until I've had a shave and something to eat.'

She dismissed this with a wave of her hand. 'Trivialities. This is what's important. You need to telephone Alan Ridley and ask him about the cymbal he found at the crime scene.'

'I don't have a telephone,' he protested, 'and he'll think I've gone mad. Madder than usual.'

'Then use the phone box. Or come to the All's Well and use mine. It doesn't matter how you do it, but call him.'

'Why me? Why can't you telephone him if it's so important?'

'Because you're his friend, his pub comrade,' she said, slipping past his outstretched arm into the hall. 'And he doesn't like me.'

'I wonder why.'

'Stop wasting time. Call him and ask him if the cymbal he found in Church Spinney has a sharp edge.'

'What?' He screwed up his face – in puzzlement? Annoyance probably, she thought, but ploughed on.

'Just do it, Jack,' she urged.

An hour later, he walked into the bookshop as Flora was emptying new cash into the till. His fedora had made a return, now the weather had turned colder, and its brim was pulled low over his forehead. Even so, Flora could see that he wasn't best pleased.

'Well?' she asked, determined not to let his bad mood spoil what she was sure was a breakthrough.

'I telephoned the inspector, Madam Sleuth, and it seems the cymbal has a sharp enough edge but no more than Ridley would expect from a musical instrument. Let me tell you, I felt a complete fool. I hope it was worth my embarrassment.'

She slammed the till drawer shut. 'It was,' she said firmly. 'It confirms that the cymbal the inspector picked up in the spinney and took back for analysis wasn't the one that killed Max.'

Jack took off his hat and smoothed down his hair. 'It has to be. It had blood on it.'

'That's easy enough to fake. When Ridley gets the fingerprint report, it will be as he suspected. There won't be any prints and he won't be able to use that cymbal as evidence.'

'But if that isn't the murder weapon, where is the one that killed Martell?'

'I don't know.' She grimaced slightly. 'All I know is that there is another one. There has to be. Look at this.' She unfolded the handkerchief sitting on her desk and showed him the collection of copper fibres. 'These were shaved off the real weapon, to make certain it would kill. And this' – she reached into her handbag and pulled out the charred fragment of paper – 'may help us find whoever did it.'

Jack fumbled in his pocket for his glasses and walked to the latticed window with the slip of paper. 'C - o - n?'

'I thought it looked official.'

'Maybe. The paper feels weighty. Originally cream-coloured, I reckon. Posh stuff. C - o - n. Contract?'

'That's it!' She rushed over to him, hugging him round the waist and dancing him back towards her desk. 'It's a contract, that's just what it is. Tutti Frutti are still at the stables – and the workshop is close by. One of them has burnt it.'

'Because they didn't like cream paper?' he joked, freeing himself with difficulty.

'Because they didn't like Beverly Russo. And they didn't like Max Martell,' Flora returned.

Jack had left unconvinced that the burnt document had once been a contract, though Flora was certain it had. An agreement that someone hadn't wanted to keep, or hadn't wanted known about. But as evidence, she had to admit, it was tenuous and, in between cleaning bookshelves, serving customers, and bringing her accounts up to date, she tussled all day with the problem of how it might help them to move on with the case.

If the burnt document *had* been a contract involving Tutti Frutti – and who else could it have involved? – and if it was connected to the missing cymbal – that was far less certain – it was pointing to what had always been her main hunch. That it had been one of the rock 'n' roll group who had killed Beverly first and then Martell. Forget Dr Randall, forget Dominic and, most of all, forget Sally. Whatever the motive turned out to be, the murderer was a member of the band.

She could ask Jack to call on Alan Ridley, offer him the fragment of paper and the copper shavings, tell him their suspicions, but the inspector wouldn't and couldn't arrest anyone based on such flimsy evidence. And, at the moment, that was all it was, plus a strong hunch. How frustrating to know, or almost know, the identity of the villain but be unable to do anything about it. Tomorrow, the band was leaving the Priory and, though the inspector would be careful not to lose sight of its members, it seemed to Flora that the chance to unmask the killer would dissolve along with the miles they travelled from Abbeymead. There was so little time left and she could think of nothing that would make it count.

28

The band was due to depart today and, before she'd left the Priory on Thursday evening, Flora had promised that she'd help Sally return the stables to their former immaculate condition, once the group was on the road. It meant closing the All's Well on a busy Saturday morning, but it was the least she could offer to a good friend in deep trouble. Jack had also agreed to join the work party and suggested he collect her in the Austin early that morning, despite her protests that she could easily cycle. *It's going to be a hard day*, he'd said, *so why not make it easier on yourself?*

There was certainly a good deal of work ahead. Tutti Frutti had left a trail of mess and spoilation in their wake, not only at their base in the stables but throughout the hotel. If Sally were to go ahead with the promised sale, she would need the Priory looking its best, and the skeleton staff, which was all she could afford at present, would be far too stretched to finish the job.

Jack was outside the cottage in Greenway Lane before nine o'clock, dressed in what Flora could only describe as army surplus.

'Left over from the Italian campaign,' he said cheerfully,

seeing her expression. 'Just the thing for shifting beds and moving wardrobes. Tough but light.'

He'd been sensible. Rather than an over-warm corduroy skirt, she wished she'd had the nerve to wear the new pair of jeans that Kate had given her. What had possessed Katie to buy them in the first place, Flora had no idea. Maybe it was the starry-eyed stuff, the seizing the moment stuff. Whatever it was, Kate's legs had turned out to be too long, the denim finishing way above her ankles. *They look ridiculous*, she'd told Flora, *but they'd fit you*. Flora had rather liked the way she'd looked in the mirror when she'd tried them on that day, but still felt too self-conscious to wear them in public. Particularly on a day like today when she'd be among a crowd of people.

How much of a crowd, she hadn't realised, until Jack brought the red Austin to a halt outside the Priory's front entrance. As they pulled to a stop, she spied Inspector Ridley walking towards them and behind him at least three other policemen.

'What are you two doing here?' the inspector asked, as Flora climbed out of the car. His voice was tinged with suspicion. 'Brought me more evidence I can't use?'

She had a strong desire to point out that, unlike the police, they had at least come up with evidence, but Jack intervened before she could speak. 'We're on a mission, our good deed for the day, helping Sally Jenner,' he said easily. 'How about you, Alan? I didn't expect to see you and your men here.'

'Thought we'd have a last poke around,' the inspector said. 'Before these chaps leave. Make sure we know exactly where they're heading. There's been some confusion over that, some dispute about their bookings, and I don't want to lose sight of them.'

It was good news at least that Ridley would be keeping tracks on the band, but for how long? Flora wondered. If no further evidence came to light, Tutti Frutti would walk clear, shaking off murder as a dog shakes off water. Yet one of them was a killer.

Leaving the inspector with Jack, she walked over to the lorry parked in the semicircle of gravel that fronted the house. It was already half full of the group's equipment and, at that moment, Tommy May appeared around the side of the building, carrying two full suitcases with Shane dragging a third.

'You look well organised,' she greeted him, hoping her smile would disarm any suspicion. Even at this late stage, there could be evidence waiting to be discovered.

'Gotta be,' Tommy said. 'No one to nanny us now.'

'And your bookings? I heard there might be problems.'

He thumped the cases down on the gravel and took a breath. 'We get to play the first venue on Max's programme, but only because it's too late for them to cancel and find a band more to their liking. So, off to Manchester we go. After that, who knows?' The bitterness was still there, mixed this morning with a tired resignation.

'You've nothing else fixed?'

'The rest of the rubbish have ignored our calls. Back to playing lousy clubs again, I guess.'

'We've had one offer that looked hopeful, haven't we, Tom?' Shane put in. 'A brand new place up north. We're working on the fee before we definitely agree.'

'Working on the fee means they're haggling to get us at the lowest possible price.' Tommy's expression was grim. 'But hey, it's a gig. I'll sling these on board and go back for the rest of the clutter. Not much more now.'

'Let me know when you're through,' she called after him, 'and we'll make a start on the stables.'

'The clean-up squad, eh?' Tommy turned and gave her a grin. It seemed he wasn't wholly defeated.

Flora watched as he threw the suitcases, one at a time, into the back of the lorry, avoiding crashing into Jarvis's drum kit by a whisker.

Jarvis himself shambled into view carrying a single holdall. 'He travels light,' Shane said laconically, and got into the passenger seat of the cab.

'You'll have to lump it with the baggage, J,' Tommy said. 'Only two seats upfront. But we can swap places at Warwick.'

'You're driving yourself?' Jack had finished his conversation with the inspector and walked up to them.

'Hiring this lorry took every bit of cash we had. That bastard, Martell, has tied up our money so tightly it will take months to get a penny of what's left. So no chance of booking a driver, but that's OK. I drove delivery vans once. Got a licence.'

'A man of many talents,' Jack remarked, as together they watched Jarvis clamber into the back of the lorry and settle himself as comfortably as he could between the drums and the rest of his percussion kit. Flora's eyes fixed on the collection of cymbals. As Tommy pulled the shutter down and Jarvis was lost to view, her gaze became more fixed and there was a fidget in her limbs.

'What is it?' Jack asked. As always, he'd known immediately that something was wrong. And there was something, except she couldn't put her finger on what exactly it was.

'I'm not sure.' She frowned. 'It's Jarvis and the drums.' She was annoyed with herself at being so vague.

Tommy May was in the driving seat and had switched on the ignition, but a buzz had begun in Flora's mind, becoming louder and louder. Those drums, those cymbals. Her mouth dropped open. Was it at all possible?

'You need to stop,' she yelled at the driver. 'And Jack, call the inspector!'

Behind the wheel, Tommy's face was pressed against the windscreen, his expression a mix of bewilderment and irritation. Then, out of nowhere, it seemed, Shane flew into life, pushing Tommy May hard against the cab's side window and usurping the driving seat for himself. The lorry's engine roared into life and, looking up, Flora saw the white blur of a face and a pair of eyes, Shane's eyes, cold and calculating, staring down at her through the windscreen. So this was their villain.

'We have to stop him. He mustn't get away,' she yelled at Jack.

In an instant he had darted forward, placing himself in front of the lorry, his arms outstretched. Flora ran to stand beside him, her figure slender against the frightening bulk of the vehicle. Shane had worn a mask: the loyal friend, the peacemaker, Tommy's constant shadow, while all the time he'd plotted to kill, and kill violently. They couldn't let him escape.

'Move!' Shane screamed at her, his voice a tinny echo through the glass.

'What the hell are we doing?' Jack shouted over the noise of the engine, his breath coming in spurts. 'Is there a reason we've decided to die this morning?' But still he stood his ground, refusing to yield, playing for time.

Flora's throat was choking with fear and her heart pounding so hard it felt as though her chest were being torn apart. Out of the corner of her eye she'd glimpsed the inspector running towards them, waving his arms at someone out of sight.

'A few more seconds,' she gasped, sensing Jack's grip on her arm stiffen.

Then, at the last moment, she felt herself yanked roughly to his side and jumped clear of the lorry, the vehicle missing them by an inch. Flora closed her eyes and sank to the ground, feeling certain they had failed. The inspector hadn't reached them in time. Shane had gone free. Free to drive through the gates, abandon the lorry and go to ground before the police could arrest him.

'He didn't get far.' Jack bent down to speak in her ear.

'He didn't?'

She opened her eyes. One of the constables had driven the police van at full speed and swung his vehicle sideways across the drive, blocking the way. In seconds, Alan Ridley had arrived at the scene and his sergeant was wrenching open the lorry door and pulling Shane Carter to the ground.

'Cuff him,' she heard Ridley say to the sergeant, pointing to the prone man.

Tommy, pale and shocked, had fallen out of the cab and stumbled round to the back of the lorry.

'What the hell was that, Shane?' he asked hopelessly. His friend, dragged to his feet, his hands yanked behind his back, made no response. 'And what the hell are you doing to him?' Tommy demanded, turning to the inspector. 'Handcuffs? What's your problem?'

'Let's see if there is one.' Ridley smiled benignly. 'And someone let that other chap out,' he muttered, as thumps from the back of the lorry grew increasingly loud.

'Well?' The inspector turned to Flora who, with Jack beside her, had hurried to catch up. 'What *is* the problem, Miss Steele?'

Flora was struggling to regain her calm along with her breath, but said as confidently as she could, 'I know how Shane did it. Not how he messed with the amplifier but how he got rid of the weapon that killed Martell. Look at Jarvis's cymbals, the hi-hats, I think. I'm sure that one of them – probably the lower one as it's more likely to escape detection – has been sharpened. Honed to a lethal edge.'

'Check your kit,' Ridley ordered Jarvis Redmond, who had jumped down from the lorry and was idly scratching his beard.

The drummer sighed heavily but climbed back into the vehicle and began throwing bags and suitcases onto the gravel. The sound of drums being pulled to one side reached them, then Jarvis's muffled voice.

'What the...! What joker's done this?' He came to the opening. 'One of the hi-hats. It's not mine. Someone's switched it. I didn't notice – haven't practised for a few days.'

'More like a week,' Tommy growled. 'Too drunk.'

'It's as sharp as hell,' Jarvis exclaimed. 'I'd have cut my hands to shreds.'

'And if you look in Mr Knight's old workshop' – Flora turned to the inspector – 'the enclosure near the kitchen door, I think you'll find the lathe that sharpened it. It might even sport those elusive fingerprints.'

Alan Ridley glared at her, but then turned to speak to his men. 'Take him away,' he directed. 'And you two' – he swivelled round, fixing on what was left of Tutti Frutti – 'no leaving for Manchester until I get in touch.'

A nod to Flora and Jack and he was on his way back to the waiting police car, a new energy boosting his stride.

29

Three days later, Jack looked out of his study window and saw a car that was vaguely familiar pull up outside. He could have done without visitors. After the recent excitement, it was only this morning that he'd uncovered his Remington, promising himself that today would at last see him make a start on the new book. Yesterday's post had brought a letter from his agent announcing, to Jack's relief, that Arthur approved the synopsis he'd sent but – a warning note had been struck – it was getting a bit late in the day to meet the proposed publication date, so Jack should be sure to start on the novel immediately. Rummaging through the haphazard pile of papers gathered on his desk top, he pulled out the contract Arthur had mentioned and realised, with a churning stomach, that the date he'd agreed to submit the manuscript was early in the new year and here they were already in mid-October.

The knock he'd been expecting echoed its way through the hall. Swivelling his office chair to one side, he jogged reluctantly down the stairs and wasn't entirely surprised to see the inspector standing on his doorstep, his back turned and surveying Jack's front garden. He'd guessed that sooner or later Ridley would want to talk to him about events at the Priory.

'Nice job you've done there.' The inspector nodded towards the cut lawn and neat flowerbeds.

'Thank you, Alan. It's good to see you.' He tried to sound as though it was.

Ridley removed his trilby, tucking it beneath his arm, and did his best to simulate a smile. He looked like a man with a lot of work ahead of him.

'I won't keep you long, old chap. Just need a few words.'

'Of course, come in to the sitting room. Can I get you some tea?'

'A cuppa would go down well,' the inspector said, as he followed his host into the house.

Tea hardly suggested a few words, but Jack swallowed his irritation.

'Bit of a lumpy sofa, this one,' Ridley pronounced, when he walked back into the sitting room with a tray of tea a few minutes later.

'You could try another seat.' Jack ignored a compulsion to grind his teeth very hard. Wasn't it enough he suffered Flora's constant complaints? He gestured to a brightly patterned armchair sitting proudly beneath the sill. 'The one by the window is brand new.'

'No, no, I'll stay here, old chap. But maybe consider buying a new sofa, too?'

'For that, I'd have to be earning a great deal more than I do. But you've come with news, I imagine?' he asked a trifle sharply.

'I have. Your little girl was right, though it's annoying to say so.'

Jack wished that Ridley would stop speaking of Flora as if she belonged to him, and 'little girl' would have had Flora herself clenching her fists ready for a fight.

'The Zildjian hi-hat in Redmond's kit...' the inspector went on. 'Sharpened to an edge that would have split a hair. And there was blood. Under examination in the lab, the smallest traces were visible. It was definitely the weapon that murdered Martell.'

'What about the cymbal you found in Church Spinney?'

He poured his visitor a cup of tea and the inspector took several thirsty slurps before he answered.

'That one was Redmond's original cymbal – I got him to identify it. It had been wiped of any fingerprints, even Redmond's, but I was expecting that. It was left for us to find. A kind of decoy.'

'While Shane Carter hid the real weapon in plain sight?'

'Exactly.'

There was a crease in Jack's forehead. 'There's something odd about that, isn't there? Carter was very careful to wipe the cable clean – I'm presuming he was Beverly's killer, too – and very careful, as you say, to get rid of any fingerprints on Redmond's own cymbal, so why didn't he wipe clean the one he hid? You couldn't then use it as evidence.'

'You're right about Miss Russo. He was the one who killed her. No doubt about it.' Ridley finished his tea in a few gulps. 'My, that was good! Just the job for a cold morning. In fact, Carter wiped that second cymbal clean. But it wasn't going to save him, and he knew it. The Russo murder didn't involve blood, that was the difference, and once Carter had got rid of the fingerprints – if there were any on the cable, though at a guess I'd say he wore gloves – he had no worries. He couldn't be implicated. But a killing where blood is involved is something else, and he must have worked that out. I reckon he was worried that the blood had left a trail – on his clothes, on the weapon. And he was right to worry. Luminol can detect the smallest flecks, even after cleaning. The fingerprints had gone from the cymbal, but the blood hadn't. It's why he came up with the clever idea of hiding it in Redmond's kit. He'd have dumped it later, once he was clear of the Priory.'

'Will the evidence be enough to convict him?'

'I'm pretty sure it will. We've also got the fact that Shane bought his killer cymbal some time in the last few weeks. There are relatively few music shops in the area and my men are going from shop to shop right now with Carter's photograph. We'll soon discover where he bought it and he'll have to explain why a guitarist had suddenly to purchase a hi-hat cymbal. Then there's the shed in the gardeners' enclosure. Never seen so many cardboard boxes in my life, but right behind that stack was a lathe – little Miss Steele is a sharp one, we could do with her in the police – and our friend Shane had done a fairly sloppy job of wiping his prints from that. He was getting careless by then, I guess.'

'And the amplifier? How did he work out how to reroute the electrics?'

'Now, that was interesting. My sergeant did some digging into Shane's past. A bit of a naughty boy, our Shane, apparently. At an approved school for some years. The school did its best to redirect pupils into lives that were more socially acceptable, let's say. Took them on trips, introduced them to role models, that kind of thing.'

Jack nodded. It was what Mrs May had told him. Tommy's and Shane's visit to Oxford had been designed to inspire them to greater things.

'Apart from the fluff,' Ridley went on, 'the school tried to get the boys working at a trade, not exactly a formal apprenticeship but sessions to get them interested in learning a craft, so that when they reached fifteen, they could find work – as plasterers, maybe, or bricklayers. Or electricians.'

'Ah!'

'Yes, ah. I don't think Shane got much from his electrical education, but he did learn how to redirect a current.'

The inspector shifted in his seat and looked longingly down at his empty cup and, seeing it, Jack reached for the teapot and poured him another.

'And the timing for the Russo murder?' he asked. 'It seemed to us he'd have only seconds to tamper with the amplifier.'

'It's guesswork at the moment – Carter isn't talking, but give him time and he will. We reckon he must have walked down to the stage from the stables a few minutes before the rest of the band and messed with the cables just before they arrived, then appeared from around the side of the stage and joined them in tuning up, as though he'd only just arrived. The stage had been built the previous day, and it's possible he took a look at the casing once the set-up crew had left, worked out in advance how to remove the back of the amplifier quickly. Still, he took a massive risk of being detected. And a massive risk of killing the wrong person. Any one of the band could have unhooked that microphone, even his best mate.'

'He took another gamble when he got rid of the evidence.'

Ridley nodded. 'That was probably a bit easier. But not that easy. After the singer came to grief, he must have had a few precious minutes when he could disappear from view, remove the extra cable, and fit the casing back again. When my team examined the amplifier, it was clear the cover hadn't been properly secured. A hasty job.'

'He was the one who switched the microphone off,' Jack said slowly. 'I yelled for someone to do it, and it was Shane who leapt down from the stage.'

'There you are. He didn't just disconnect the mic, did he? As for the piece of cable you found, I reckon he must have dumped that when his mates were lifting the poor girl off the stage and carrying her into the house.'

'It sounds as though you have a strong case, but what about motive? Presumably Carter hasn't explained why he turned killer?'

'Not yet. He's refusing to admit guilt, let alone motive, but we'll keep him talking. From the questions we've asked and from what he *has* said, we've a fairly good idea of what's behind these murders. It appears Miss Russo was about to leave the band for better prospects. I don't think Shane likes disloyalty. He's kind of fixated on his friend and kept ranting on about how people were always letting Tommy down.'

'Beverly had a new contract?' Jack asked, thinking of the burnt slip of paper Flora had retrieved.

'That's been one of our lines of enquiry. One of my chaps managed to trace a man who'd been Martell's business partner some years ago.'

'Tinsdale.'

Alan Ridley looked at him sadly. 'You didn't mention him to me, Jack.'

'I didn't think it important, not after Max was killed. At that point, he stopped being a suspect.'

The inspector tutted. 'Withholding evidence, I could get you on that.' He seemed to enjoy his joke. 'More seriously, this Tinsdale gave us the name of an entertainment group he thought Martell might have dealt with. It's owned by some big impresario. Norris, my sergeant, contacted them and lo and behold they turned up a contract, signed and countersigned a few weeks ago by Beverly Russo and Martell himself. There was no mention of Tutti Frutti.'

Jack thought for a moment. 'It must have been Beverly's copy that Shane burned.'

'He admitted as much. Really lost his temper when he told us about the contract. Fury wasn't in it. He says he found it in Russo's room at the stables. What he was doing there, I can only guess. She was quite a girl, by all accounts.'

'I don't think there was any... romantic connection. Carter was evidently suspicious of what was going on behind the band's back and went searching for proof.'

Ridley nodded agreement. 'I went through a copy of that contract and it's clear she was billed to be a solo artist. About to hit the big time, as it were. Sad for the girl.'

'It's a document that sealed her fate. She was double-dealing, dumping the group and secretly moving on, but if Tommy's band wasn't going to benefit from Beverly's voice, no one else would – including her. But what about the agent? He'd signed the contract, too, and Carter must have known that, but Martell wasn't killed until a few weeks later.'

'That produced another rant when we questioned Carter about him. Martell might have escaped retribution, if he'd not made another mistake. After Miss Russo died, Tutti Frutti lost their selling power and Martell definitely wanted out. He was always going to dump them, but after losing his star singer, he decided to bet on a different band. The chap my sergeant spoke to at the entertainment group came up with a name – and the group's lead singer confirmed to Norris, when he got in touch, that they'd been in talks with Martell. Agreed terms with him to act as their agent. Once Tutti Frutti found out, Carter decided Max had lived too long and issued his invitation to the woods.'

'Martell was a horribly devious man. Tommy May only learned his group had been abandoned when another agent, some lesser character, telephoned him with an offer to represent them.'

'That would be the chap Carter called "some lowlife chancer".'

'So Martell had to go?'

Ridley nodded, a slight smile crinkling his tired face. 'Disloyalty to Tommy was a capital offence.'

'It would be, I imagine, after the past they shared.'

Jack recalled what Mrs May had told him, how close the two had been as boys, dragged into the same gang, locked up in the same offenders' institution, and then finding a mutual love of music together. But he said nothing of this to the inspector. It would mean confessing that he'd gone to Portsmouth specifically to search for Tommy's mother and check on the boy's early life. Alan Ridley might have invited Flora and himself to give any help they could, but he wouldn't take kindly to their having jumped the gun while he'd been detained in Suffolk.

The inspector drained the last dregs of tea from his second cup and stood up. 'I'd best get going. This Carter chap won't go on trial for months, but there's a helluva lot to do before we get to court. Perhaps you'll tell your...' Ridley must have caught sight of his expression, Jack thought, and stopped himself. 'Tell Miss Steele what's been happening, will you?'

That evening Jack walked to the cottage in Greenway Lane. He wanted to speak to Flora alone – there was a great deal to tell her – and the All's Well was rarely empty. Timing his visit to arrive after supper, he was surprised when Flora led him through to the kitchen to find both Sally and her aunt sitting at the table.

'You must have smelled the rabbit pie.' Flora gave him a mischievous smile. 'Sorry, Jack, we've finished eating, but I can make you tea. Sit down and I'll warm the pot.'

Before he had the chance to take up the offer, Sally jumped up from her seat and hurried to his side.

'I want to thank you, Jack.' She clasped both his hands in hers, squeezing them so tightly he felt the opal ring she wore dig into his flesh. 'You unmasked the villain and cleared the Priory of all blame! Already I've new bookings trickling in.'

'Good to hear, but really you should be thanking Flora. She was the one who realised where Carter had hidden the murder weapon. And it's the rogue cymbal that will convict him.'

Sally sashayed back to the table. 'I have thanked her, effusively. And so has Auntie.'

Alice nodded from her seat. 'I'm that relieved this whole

horrible business is over. And relieved you're both safe, though I did hear as it was a close-run thing. Tryin' to stop a lorry like that. It's bad enough when you're facin' wicked people miles from home, but to think of it happenin' at the Priory!'

'I bet you've written to Jessie to tell her every detail,' Flora teased.

'We've talked about you, miss – written long letters – and we both agree, you two need watchin',' Alice said severely. 'You attract trouble, the pair of you.'

Jack was forced to bite his tongue. This time, they'd had no choice but to confront trouble – it had been Sally who'd dragged them into this latest adventure, a friend they'd wanted to protect, and it was Alice herself who'd encouraged it.

Changing the subject, he asked tentatively, 'How is Dominic these days?'

'Still at the Priory.' Sally looked round the circle of faces and gave a weak smile.

'He's stopped hidin' in his bedroom, at least,' Alice said trenchantly. 'I s'pose that's progress.'

'Don't be so hard on him, Auntie,' Sally remonstrated. 'It's been a dreadful start for both of us and nothing we could ever have expected.' She ran her teaspoon along the ridge of the saucer. 'I haven't been kind to him either,' she murmured. 'I jumped to conclusions that were unfair.'

'He can't hold that against you, Sal,' her aunt said. 'He'd told you all those lies and you didn't know which way to turn.'

'*And* you tried to protect him,' Flora added. 'I imagine the book you donated must have belonged to Shane Carter.'

'One he'd kept from his sessions at school,' Jack said. 'Foolish of him to leave it lying around.'

'Just think, I did him a favour by losing it on the bookstall!' Sally held up her hands in mock despair. 'I really couldn't have got more wrong. But things are improving, thank goodness. As for Dom and me, it's work in progress, I suppose.'

Alice gave a disparaging sniff. 'Mebbe, but I can't forget how he left you to shoulder all the worry, and you desperately tryin' to make a go of it.'

'I'm not so desperate now. We've had a long talk, worked out responsibilities and Dom has put together a new publicity campaign.' Her cheeks flushed pink as she said his name. 'It's fairly low key and not too expensive,' she rushed on, 'but it should help get the ball rolling.'

'No one else has cancelled, have they?' The anxious lines on Alice's face fell into deeper creases.

'No, thank the Lord. We've guests arriving this very weekend. Either they know no fear or they don't read the papers! Hopefully, from now on numbers will keep building.'

'Which'll mean plenty of cookin' for me,' Alice said, sounding much happier. 'I'm back in my kitchen tomorrow, along with the rest of the team. It will be good to see what Tony Farraday can do at last, other than cosying up to Kate, that is!'

'It's wonderful the restaurant will be back in business again.' Flora began to clear their empty plates. 'It seems an age since it was properly open.'

There was a pause in the conversation as she clattered china and cutlery into the sink, the silence suddenly broken by Sally. 'That's it!' she exclaimed. 'You must come to the Priory for a meal.' She looked between Flora and Jack. 'Why didn't I think of it before?'

'Possibly because I haven't won the football pools recently.' Flora laughed, beginning to run water for the washing up. 'I've never yet eaten at the Priory and never likely to. Far too expensive for me.'

'Not this time, though. Not as a big thank you. A slap-up meal with wine – my treat to you both.'

Flora turned from the sink and Jack saw her look uncertainly towards him. She was as reluctant as he, but neither of them seemed able to refuse. Having dinner together in the Priory restaurant felt a little too much like an occasion.

'Haven't you got a birthday soon, Jack?' Alice asked. 'I'm sure you told me once that you were an autumn baby.'

'This week.' He knew he sounded grudging.

'There you are then.' Sally was triumphant. 'What could be better? You must come and celebrate it together. I'll make sure you have the best table in the room.'

She looked across at her aunt and Jack didn't miss the conspiratorial exchange of glances. He was fairly sure that Flora hadn't either.

'That's very kind,' he mumbled, feeling his resistance crumble.

'Yes, very,' Flora echoed faintly.

30

Flora had changed outfits three times before she heard Jack's Austin rumble to a stop outside the cottage. She was being ridiculous. She possessed few clothes and her choice should have been easy but, in her mind, this evening had become something special, something for which she needed to look her best. The dinner had assumed an importance beyond a simple thank you for uncovering a killer and helping to rescue the Priory.

Ridiculous or not, in the last hour she'd tried dressing in her best woollen frock, then discarded it – the dark green dress had been worn at Bernie Mitchell's wake and, before that, at her aunt's funeral and, looking at herself in the mirror, she'd felt the weight of too many unhappy associations. The pleated skirt and jumper she'd put on next had seemed too ordinary, even though the jumper was knitted in especially soft wool and a beautiful blue. It was too much like the outfits she wore every day at the bookshop. In desperation, hearing the car's engine grumble to a halt, she pulled from the wardrobe the dress she'd been saving for Christmas, a buttery cream crêpe, tugged it over her head and ran a brush through a now disordered tangle of waves, tugging them into some kind of order. Her best pair of shoes, ankle-strapped with red block heels, completed the ensemble. They would pinch her toes, she knew, but for the only meal she was ever likely to eat at the Priory, she had to look elegant.

When Jack appeared at her front door looking so smart it made her blink, she was glad she had tried hard. The fedora was nowhere to be seen, but a dark grey suit, brilliant white shirt and a red silk tie, must be echoes of his more glamorous past, she thought. The ever-present flop of hair had been watered flat and the scent of cedar and lime was in the air.

'Ready for our treat?' he asked awkwardly, as she stood in the doorway.

She grabbed an overcoat from the bentwood stand and her handbag from the hall chair. 'Yes,' she said, equally uncomfortable, though making sure she wore a bright smile.

Their drive to the Priory was completed in strained silence. Thankfully, the hotel was no more than a ten minute journey but how, she wondered, were they to get through a whole meal when they were feeling so desperately uneasy with each other?

Walking through the door of the restaurant, however, rescue was at hand. Neither had visited this part of the Priory for many months and both were overwhelmed at its transformation from the dingy space they'd last seen. So much so that their earlier awkwardness simply slid away. There were loud congratulations to Sally, murmurs of admiration for the crystal wall lights and minutes spent gazing at the artwork that decorated pale grey walls.

'It's so beautiful,' Flora said for at least the third time, gazing over a sea of starched white linen and sparkling glassware. 'So polished. Lord Edward would have loved it.'

Sally, buoyed by the shower of praise, smiled broadly and led them across thick blue carpet to a table tucked snugly away in one of the restaurant's alcoves. 'We've taken a few bookings for dinner tonight, which is brilliant, but our very best table is for you.'

To Flora's surprise, Dominic was already there and waiting to seat them.

'I've chosen your wine and I hope that's OK.' He sounded more humble than Flora expected. 'But if not, just say. Alice has cooked up a feast and I thought a Dom Perignon might be just the thing.' He pointed to the round curve of a bottle cooling in the silver ice bucket.

Flora found herself smiling back. 'Everything is... amazing,' she said. It had been so long since she'd known any kind of luxury that she was finding the fuss being made of her very agreeable.

'You can never go wrong with champagne,' Jack agreed.

'Tony will be your server tonight. Alice has unchained him from the kitchen.' Dominic tried a joke.

Tony Farraday, Kate's special friend, as Flora had begun to think of him, appeared at Dominic's shoulder at that moment, bread basket in one hand and a plate of delicate nibbles in the other.

'*Amuse bouche*,' Tony said.

Flora's eyes widened.

'*Amuse bouche?*' she asked, once she and Jack were alone.

'We're living high tonight. Alice has evidently gone to town.'

The thought could have made her uncomfortable again, but by the time they had polished off the nibbles and were halfway through a salmon mousse they were so deep in conversation that all she was aware of was a good friend sitting across the table from her. On his visit to the cottage, Jack had mentioned briefly that Ridley had visited Overlay House but hadn't had time to go into details, and she was keen to hear his account of the inspector's progress. His most satisfying news was that Shane Carter would very soon be charged – with double murder.

'I've no idea what will happen to the rest of Tutti Frutti now,' Jack finished. 'I don't even know if they got to Manchester as they planned, but in any case a band isn't a band with just two musicians.'

'Actually' – Flora took a last mouthful of mousse – 'that's something I can tell you. Tommy May came into the shop yesterday to say goodbye – fancy! He and Jarvis have been putting up at the Cross Keys. Apparently, the rest of their bookings have disappeared but they got some kind of pay-out for the cancelled performance in Manchester and decided they deserved a decent bed. In time, they'll need to look for another guitarist and singer, but interestingly they're putting it on hold.'

'Are they going back to Portsmouth? At least Tommy has a home there.'

'I don't think so, unless their search takes them to the city. They've decided to look for Jarvis's sister.'

'Really? That's certainly a change of plan.'

'Jarvis is hopeful she may still be alive but, even if she isn't, he wants to know for sure, and they think they have a clue to Anna's whereabouts. She loved art, she was a good water-colourist apparently, and Tommy reckons she may have found shelter in some artists' colony not far from Oxford. Oxford was her home town, of course.'

Jack laid his knife and fork to one side. 'How on earth would Tommy May know that?'

'It was Martell who mentioned the colony! Only casually, of course, and not because he thought of Jarvis's sister. It was a friend of his – can you imagine he actually had friends? – who'd joined this artists' group, a kind of alternative community, and Martell was being his usual sneering self about it. But Tommy thinks it's worth investigating.'

'Their trip to Oxfordshire is more important than making music?'

'It sounds strange, but Tommy seems utterly shaken by what Shane did. I got the impression that half his world had collapsed. In a way, I suppose, Shane Carter was half his world.

It seems to have made him determined to hang on to Jarvis, get him to stay sober and, if finding what's happened to Anna is the way to do it, then he'll forget the band for a while and go along with it.'

Tony Farraday, gliding silently over the thick carpet, a uniformed waiter by his side, appeared at their table. Empty plates were whisked away, and Tony was left to expertly serve the main course and refill their glasses.

'Lobster. What a treat!' Flora said.

'With all the trimmings,' Tony added. 'I couldn't stop Alice, she was having such fun.'

'I'm sure you had something to do with it.' Flora smiled up at him, thinking what a pleasant face he had. Nothing remarkable, but kind and attentive, his eyes holding an honesty that couldn't be mistaken. She was pleased for Kate.

'How's the champagne going?' Jack asked, when Tony had disappeared, offering her the side dishes of vegetables: buttered green beans, mashed caulifower and glazed baby carrots.

'The bubbles were a bit disconcerting at first, but I'm beginning to like it. A lot. Before it makes me forget completely, I've something for you.' She delved into her handbag and brought out a wrapped package.

'Happy birthday, Jack.'

She saw a flush tinge his cheeks. 'A present?'

'You're celebrating, remember?'

'I haven't marked my birthday for years.'

'Then it's more than time you did. I hope you like it.'

Jack carefully untied the length of blue ribbon and unwrapped an oblong of crackling brown paper. Drawing out a leather-bound copy of *Lost Stories of Sussex*, its illustrations by Wilfrid Ball, a master, he stroked the cover in appreciation.

'It's beautiful, Flora.' He turned the pages gently, taking in the fine paper, the elegant typeface, and the exquisite hand-painted pictures. 'Quite beautiful.'

Flora leaned forward. 'I'm so glad you like it. It was one of Aunt Violet's favourites.'

'The book was hers?' Jack's worry lines deepened.

She nodded.

'It's stunning but I can't take it.' He went to give her back the volume. 'It's too precious, it's a keepsake.'

'Of course you can take it.' She pressed the book into his hand. 'Violet would have wanted you to have it. She would have liked you a lot.'

'If you're sure...'

'I am. Now eat up.'

He was gazing at the book again when, their lobster finished, Alice appeared, hovering at the edge of the restaurant.

'I've brought your afters,' Alice said, while Tony skimmed past her plump figure and swiftly cleared the table.

Flora jumped up and hugged her. 'Afters? I won't eat for the next week! But what a magnificent meal, Alice. You've done us more than proud.'

Her friend glowed. 'It was fun,' she said, echoing the souschef's words. 'I haven't had the chance to go to town for I don't know how long.'

'And go to town you have.' Jack was on his feet and gave her a second hug.

'Happy birthday,' she said. 'It's baked Alaska to finish and mind you do it justice.'

'And don't forget what's left of the champagne,' Tony joined in, nodding towards the depleted bottle.

Alice wore a wide smile. 'Make sure you enjoy the rest of the evenin', both of you.'

~

'I don't know where Alice thought we were going for what's left of the evening,' Jack remarked on their way back to Greenway Lane. 'It's already past ten.'

'And I'm sleepy.' Flora stretched out her arms. 'All that champagne. But no shop to open at nine in the morning. What bliss!'

'Sunday or not, I'll need to be back at my desk and writing.' With his deadline creeping ever closer, there could be no more excuses.

'I haven't dared ask, but how's it going?'

'I *think* it will be OK. I'm feeling my way back – slowly.'

'That's a relief. But if it doesn't work out, remember, we always have a wild card – our detective agency!'

He turned his head slightly and saw the curve of her cheek as she smiled to herself.

'It's fun, isn't it?' he said, bringing the car to a halt outside Flora's cottage. 'The sleuthing?'

'Do you know, that's the first time ever I've heard you admit to liking our adventures.'

'Maybe this is a night for truth-telling.' He climbed out of the car and walked round to open her door.

Truthful or not, the evening was certainly bewitching. A frost had begun to form, the air still and crystal clear. Above them, an almost full moon filled the sky, flooding the scene with silver. Walking beside her towards the front door, he saw the bare branches of the rowan tree – Flora's favourite – brilliantly silhouetted in the moonlight.

'You should have stayed in the car and kept warm,' she said. 'Or don't you trust me to find my key?'

'I like to be sure you're safe. And it's a beautiful night.'

She stood still and gazed around. 'Almost perfect,' she said.

He watched her walk to the door, fit the key in the lock but then, as she went to open it, he reached out and took hold of her arm. Why *not* make it perfect, a small voice was saying.

'Flora!'

As she turned, he saw her surprised expression and, before he could talk himself out of it, he'd wrapped his arms around her and pulled her close. Then, forgetting past troubles, past betrayal, he kissed her full on the lips. Sensing her move closer, he kissed her again, this time, if anything, more thoroughly.

'Are we seizing the moment?' she asked. Her face against his felt warm and right.

'I think we could be,' he said, and kissed her for a third time.

A LETTER FROM MERRYN

Dear Reader,

I want to say a huge thank you for choosing to read *Murder at the Priory Hotel*. If you enjoyed the book and want to keep up to date with all my latest releases, just sign up at the following link. Your email address will never be shared and you can unsubscribe at any time.

www.bookouture.com/merryn-allingham

The 1950s is a fascinating period to write about, outwardly conformist but beneath the surface, there's rebellion brewing, even in the very south of England! It's a beautiful part of the world and I hope Flora's and Jack's exploits have entertained you. If so, you can follow their fortunes in the next Flora Steele mystery or discover their earlier adventures, beginning with *The Bookshop Murder*.

If you enjoyed *Murder at the Priory Hotel*, I would love a short review. Getting feedback from readers is amazing and it helps new readers to discover one of my books for the first time. And do get in touch on my Facebook page, through Twitter, Goodreads or my website – it makes an author's day!

Thank you for reading,

Merryn x

KEEP IN TOUCH WITH MERRYN

www.merrynallingham.com

 facebook.com/MerrynWrites
twitter.com/merrynwrites